TRIUMPH THROUGH MAGIC

TRIUMPH THROUGH MAGIC

THE SARIAH CHRONICLES™ BOOK FOUR

PETER GLENN

MICHAEL ANDERLE

DISRUPTIVE IMAGINATION®

Copyright © 2020 LMBPN Publishing
Cover by Mihaela Voicu http://www.mihaelavoicu.com/
Cover copyright © LMBPN Publishing
A Michael Anderle Production

LMBPN Publishing
PMB 196, 2540 South Maryland Pkwy
Las Vegas, NV 89109

First US Edition, August 2020
ebook ISBN: 978-1-64971-124-3
Print ISBN: 978-1-64971-125-0

THE TRIUMPH THROUGH MAGIC TEAM

Thanks to our Beta Readers
Larry Omans, Kelly O'Donnell, Allan Collins

Thanks to our JIT Readers

Diane L. Smith
Angel LaVey
Dorothy Lloyd
Veronica Stephan-Miller
Deb Mader
Jeff Goode

Editor

SkyHunter Editing Team

CHAPTER ONE

Will gave the key a firm turn in the lock of the old iron door. The mechanism squeaked in response. It took a little bit of elbow grease to make it happen, but after a moment he was greeted with a satisfying click, letting him know the lock was secure.

"Are you sure that's wise?" a chill voice asked from behind him.

Startled, he spun on his heels, almost dropping the key in the process. "Ilene," he replied in a surprised tone. "How nice to see you down here." He glanced over her shoulder to see if there was anyone else, but the two of them appeared to be alone. "Out for a stroll?"

She gave him a weak smile. "I wanted to see what all the fuss was about for myself."

Will nodded. "I can understand that."

"You sure you know what you're doing?" Ilene inquired. She inclined her head toward the door. "Letting her down there alone with that...filth?"

"What choice do I have?" He sighed and pulled on his

face. "It's not like she gave us one. She was going to do it, whether we agreed or not. At least this way, we have some measure of control."

Ilene shot him an icy glare. Her cool eyes seemed to pierce right through him. "We always have a choice, or do I need to remind you of that?"

He hung his head low and averted his gaze. "Yes, my lady."

She walked over to the old iron door and ran her fingers across it. "You sure are placing a lot of trust in our newest recruit, my dear William." Her gaze trailed back to him. "It's not like you."

Will shrugged. "I locked the door, didn't I? If she does something crazy and releases him, we still have that advantage. It's not like I gave her carte blanche."

"Yet you let her bring him back here."

His jaw dropped, and he gave her a blank stare. "What else was I supposed to do? Sariah demanded it! After that display, I was in no position to deny her request."

A small exhalation escaped Ilene's lips, then she regained her icy composure. "You shouldn't have gone off by yourself in the first place. Not after I forbade it."

Will's stomach churned. She was right. He had disobeyed a direct order, and for what? The whim of a near child?

No, he thought firmly. It was more than that. They'd scored a great victory over the Dusk Ravens on the battlefield. An entire army laid to waste, and their general captured. Surely the victory was worth a little disobedience.

"Just how much did that little jaunt of yours cost us,

anyway?" Ilene demanded. Her voice sounded almost distant. She was staring at the door again and not at him. He couldn't blame her for not wanting to look him in the face.

Will hung his head dejectedly, and he spoke in a whisper. "Eight soldiers, my lady. Including Misty, the illusionist." He had known this question was going to come, but he still wasn't prepared for it.

"I see," came Ilene's response. She went back to fingering the iron door frame and staring off into the distance.

For a moment, neither of them spoke or looked at each other. Finally, Will broke the awkward silence. "We sent far more Dusk Ravens to their graves. At least ten of them fell for every one of our own. That should count for something!" There was a grim determination in his voice.

Ilene shook her head and let out another sigh. "Yet there are still more of them than there are of us, are there not?"

"Yes, but—"

"But nothing. Do you think their master is going to sit idly by and let this latest defeat slide past?" She looked up to the sky. "The loss of an army is no small thing. He's got to be fuming. I'm sure he'll redouble his efforts to snuff us out, and we're in a worse position to defend ourselves now, thanks to you!"

Her words cut at him like a knife to the heart. He let them churn around in his head for a moment. She was right, of course, he thought at last.

She was always right. Ilene was the level-headed one of the two. He'd always been a bit brash, demanding action where she would defer. This time had been different. The need had been real, and the outcome astounding on balance.

"Come now, Ilene. It wasn't all for naught. We dealt them a mighty blow! That's got to count for something." He rubbed his face. "We can't sit by, forever letting the Dusk Ravens have their way with the world at large. At some point, we have to fight back!"

Ilene returned her gaze to him. There was a hint of warmth in her eyes. She reached forward with one hand and gently caressed his cheek, then let the hand fall. Her hand was cool to the touch, and the cold stuck with him for a few moments.

"I suppose you may be right, my dear William. It's a messy business, and we're still not ready."

Will's heart soared. He hoped she was finally coming around to his point of view.

He took her hand in his and squeezed it. "We'll never be ready, my lady. Not really," he grinned on the last words.

The corner of Ilene's lips curled into the briefest hint of a smile for a half-second, then it was gone. "Rest assured, we will talk more about this little act of yours, and there will be consequences."

Will hung his head low. "Of course, my lady." He knew better than to argue further.

She turned. "Now, if you'll excuse me, I have a memorial service to prepare for." She started walking away. "Do not leave that door unattended," she said over her shoulder.

"Heh. It's locked! What's the worst that could happen?"

Ilene scoffed. "You really think a door of mere iron could keep him at bay?"

Will winced. She was right. Again. "Got it!" he called after her.

A moment later, she was gone and he was alone. He looked at the wrought-iron door that stood between him and the Dusk Raven general who currently sat brooding in his cell thirty feet below him.

If this won't hold you, then what hope do any of us have? he wondered.

His stomach churned again. He hoped Sariah would be okay.

———

Sariah took a furtive step forward into the darkness. With each step, it felt like she left the world further away.

It was an odd feeling for her. As a miner, she had gone far deeper into the bowels of the Irth than she was going today. Yet this time felt so different and so much worse. Of course, she knew why. There was only one reason for her current malaise.

A knot of fear mixed with guilt formed in the pit of her stomach. For a moment, she worried she would lose her breakfast right there on the stone steps, but she managed to hang onto it.

She sighed, and the sound echoed along the small stairway. Am I doing the right thing? she wondered for perhaps the hundredth time that morning. She couldn't be certain, but she'd already committed to her course.

A loud clinking noise came from behind her as she heard the door to the dungeon lock. She stole a glance behind her, wondering briefly why Will had done that. The answer was obvious—he didn't trust her with their prisoner. Not completely, at least.

She couldn't blame him, she thought, shaking her head. If she were in the same situation, she might have done the same thing.

As she walked, she bit her lip to try and ward away the dark thoughts that came to her. She thought about leaving again, about going up to the door and begging to be let out, but she couldn't. This confrontation needed to happen, whether she liked it or not. Hundreds of lives depended on it.

Soon enough, she reached the bottom of the stairwell. She was so lost in thought that she tripped on the last stair and stumbled a bit at the bottom to regain her footing.

"*Scheisse!*" she swore in a half-whisper, not ready to divulge her presence just yet.

Her efforts were wasted as she heard a slight moan from the room just ahead of her. "Is that you, Sariah?" a suave, practiced voice asked.

She sighed. She knew that voice all too well. "What makes you think it is, Captain Dungbag?" she fired back, then she chided herself. She should know better than to attack him, and yet she couldn't seem to help herself.

Gabriel winced audibly. "Captain Dungbag?" he repeated. "I suppose I deserve that moniker, don't I?"

"Pfft. And a thousand more like it." There she was, taking his bait again, Matriarch help her.

"Come into the light, Sariah. Let's talk like civilized people." His voice beckoned to her in measured tones. He sounded entirely too inviting, too genuine—something she knew quite well by now he was not.

The offer was simple enough. She had come down here to try and goad information out of him. That would certainly be a lot easier face to face.

Sariah shrugged and took a few steps forward, hesitant at first and then more determined. After the first few, it got easier and she was at the entrance to the dungeon proper. She could hear Gabe's voice urging her to enter.

Despite herself, she paused a moment to consider her appearance. Her clothes were clean —she'd changed out of the bloody rags she'd fought in at Stratton—plus she'd had a bath, so the rest of her wasn't too bad, either.

Stupid girl! she admonished herself. Why should I care what I look like in front of him anymore? It didn't matter anyway. She was about to talk to one of the most dangerous people on the planet, who broke her heart no less, and she was worried about whether she combed her hair that morning. What was wrong with her?

She had no reply. She ran a quick hand through her hair, all the while silently cursing herself, then smoothed out her tunic once and stepped forward.

The room beyond was dimly lit by a small torch on one wall that had given up about half its life. There were several open cells lining the hallway, and sitting at the end was the locked cage with Gabriel in it.

As she walked forward, Gabe's eyes brightened, and he flashed her a broad grin. A small part of her melted at his knowing smile. She pushed that part of her down as best she could and kept going, saying nothing.

"Sariah, how good to see you," he said in his gilded tone. He reached his arms through the bars and made beckoning motions with his hands. "It's been so long. Come close, let me have a good look at you."

She rolled her eyes. "It's been like two weeks, you dolt. Don't act like it's been an eternity." She found herself wanting to do as he bade, so she took a few more steps and cursed under her breath a few more times.

Eventually, she came to a stop just out of arm's reach. She wasn't about to let him touch her again. The thought of his arms around her made her skin crawl.

At least not all of my body is against me.

Sariah gave Gabriel a weak, half-smile. "It's...nice to see you, too," she managed through clenched teeth. This was going to be a lot harder than she thought. Why had she decided to do it again?

Gabe seemed to warm a little at her smile. "Oh Sariah, I've missed you these past weeks," he offered. There was a dreamy look in his eye.

That was it. She'd had enough of his overbearing pleasantries. She put her hands on her hips and glared at him.

"Enough with the bullshit. We both know I didn't come down here to exchange pleasantries."

Gabe looked at her sheepishly. "Why did you come down here, then, Sariah? Come to rub your victory in further?" he sneered.

Typical Gabriel, she thought. All smiles until he didn't get his way. Looking at him in the cell, wounded and half-starved, she found her mood toward him softening.

She let out a big sigh. "Look, I'd be lying if I told you that I didn't still feel something for you on some level, Gabe," she admitted. It felt good to have it out in the open, even if she was talking to the enemy. "But let's not pretend that option is there anymore. We're on different sides of this war now."

Gabe looked straight at her and smiled. "We don't have to be, you know." His gaze looked soft and inviting again, and for a moment she wanted to wilt. "We could run off, just the two of us. Leave this whole squabble behind." He held out a hand to her. "What do you say?"

Sariah glanced down at his offered hand for a second, then back up into Gabe's big, soft eyes. For a moment, she let herself think about his offer. Talking to him without adrenaline rushing through her veins, his offer sounded tempting. It would be all too easy to give everything up and go off with him.

Then she remembered the lying, and his attempt to kill Harvey, and her expression soured. She spat on his outstretched hand, and he retracted it, nursing it like she'd just spilled poison on it. "Like that's ever going to happen."

Gabe shrugged. "It was worth a shot." He got up and started pacing around his small cell. "So why did you come down here, Sariah? What's the grand scheme this time? You've already put a stop to all of my plans. Even if I ever got out of here, the Master would have my head for losing to you."

She cocked her head to the side. Was that true? she wondered. The few things she'd heard of the Master made him out to be a pretty awful guy.

"If that's true, then help me out. Help me end him. With your help, I'm sure we could accomplish anything. Even that."

Gabe laughed, and the laugh sounded cold and bitter to

her ears. "Sure thing. Let me out of here, and we'll go right up to his door."

"Oh come on," she replied, rolling her eyes. "Nice try, but you know that's not going to happen."

He shrugged again. "I had to try."

She pressed her advantage. "You can still help me. The Master is out there, yes, but I can stop him. I'm sure of it. All I need is some information to help me on the way."

Gabe scoffed. He shook his head. "No one can stop the Master, Sariah. You don't know him like I do. His power is...incredible."

Sariah rubbed her chin. "I beat you, didn't I? I bet you thought no one could do that, either."

Gabe was silent for a moment, then nodded. "That you did. I'd still like to learn one day just how you did it. That's still nothing compared to what the Master can do. You haven't seen his power up close." His voice trailed off, and his eyes took on a glassy look.

Sariah waved a hand in front of Gabe's face to regain his attention. "Come on—just a little information. Let's start with the basics. You've been inside his fortress several times. Where's the entrance? How do I get in?"

Her prisoner shook his head and let out a long sigh. "No," he said at last. "I'm not going to give you that. I'm not going to help hasten your doom."

"Oh, come on!" Sariah pushed. She got right up next to the bars and reached into the cell, trying to grab Gabe's arm, but he'd moved away. "You said you wanted to help me once. Now's your chance! Give me the information I need, and I can end the Master's terrible reign. Then I'll come back here and…" She bit her lip to keep from saying anything further.

"What, Sariah?" Gabe demanded. He came closer until their faces were inches apart. "You'll what? Free me? You really think your friends are going to let you do that? I've killed several of them, you know. I'm surprised they let me live, but then I'm sure you had a hand in that, too, didn't you?"

Sariah looked away and let her gaze fall to the floor. Everything he was saying was true. What game was she playing at, anyway? she wondered. There was no way the Eagle's Claw Clan would let him live. Not after his usefulness waned. Surely, she had to know that deep down.

Yet, a small part of her still yearned for a future where everything worked out. She supposed she always would.

"I don't know, okay?" she admitted at last. "I don't know what would happen. At least with the Master out of the picture, we would both have a chance!"

Gabe sat on the bed and put his hands behind his head. "I'm sorry, Sariah. I can't. I made a promise a long time ago that I'd never let the Master get to you, and that's a promise I intend to keep. Even if it kills me. The answer is no."

Sariah looked at him. "Gabe. Please?" There was a hint of longing in her voice.

At that moment, Gabe rushed the bars and shook them violently. Sariah gasped and took a few steps back, suddenly afraid.

"Boo!" Gabe sneered at her. Then he went back to his bed and turned away from her.

Sariah took one last furtive look at Gabriel, then she

turned away as well. Slowly, she made her way up the stairs, wondering if there was anything she could have said or done to have made the conversation go differently. To make everything go differently. Sadly, she knew that path was dead to her now.

She couldn't help but hope just a little bit that somehow, despite all odds being against her, things would work out.

As she made her way back up to the giant iron door that blocked off the dungeon, a small tear streamed down her cheek. Hastily, she wiped it away.

Will stared at the old iron door, practically willing it to do something other than sit there. He was suddenly very worried about Sariah's safety alone with Gabriel. Had he been right to let her go down? He wasn't sure anymore.

Bear was next to him, staring at the door as well with longing in his eyes. He let out a low whine.

"Easy, Bear," he said. "She'll be okay, I promise."

The animal gave him a look that said, "she better be or else," and he winced a little. Bear was a dog, yes, but somehow so much more. Sariah had a real friend in that animal.

His thoughts returned to the door and the dungeon's inhabitant. How long had she been down there, anyway? He shook his head and blinked a few times to clear his thoughts. One thing was for sure—it had been long enough for him.

The big man kept staring at the door while tapping his foot. That's it, I'm going in there, he decided.

He ran his fingers through his hair, then reached for his keychain.

In that same instant, he heard the sound of someone knocking on the other side of the door. There was a series of five hard knocks, then silence.

Will held his breath and clenched the keys in his hand even harder. That was the first part of the sign they'd agreed upon to let him know Sariah was both safe and alone. He waited for the finishing knocks to come, beads of nervous sweat forming on his brow.

At long last, another three short raps reverberated through the metal. Will let his breath out slowly and wiped his forehead. Sariah was safe.

Hastily, he fumbled with the keys and finally finding the right one, jammed it into the lock and turned it. Seconds later, the door opened, and Sariah came stumbling out. As soon as she was free, he shut the door and re-locked it, unwilling to take any chances.

He looked over Sariah. Her eyes were a little red and puffy, and her cheeks looked grey, but otherwise, she looked no worse for wear.

Bear leaped at her, and she looked a little startled and almost tumbled.

"Good to see you, too," she said, patting him on the head. He simmered down, seemingly mollified.

"Ahem," Will started, clearing his throat., "How'd it go down there?" He was fairly certain of the answer he'd get based on how she looked, but he had to be sure.

Sariah averted her gaze and stared down at the floor

instead of looking at him. When her voice came, it was barely over a whisper. "Not well."

Will tsked. "Well, don't let it bother you much, okay?" he insisted. He reached forward and grabbed her gently by the chin and lifted it up until they were looking at each other. "Hey, you did pretty great even facing him like that. Don't let that victory go to waste."

She gave him a weak smile and pushed his hand away. "You're right," she told him. "I guess I was hoping for something more."

"I understand, dearie, but don't beat yourself up. He's not a dangerous criminal for nothing. If you could have trusted him to begin with, he never would have ended up down there."

Another slight smile formed on her lips. He could just make it out from where he was, and it brought a fresh smile to his own face.

Sariah let out a slight chuckle. "I suppose you have a point, there." She turned back around to face him more fully and started playing with her hands in front of her while she spoke. "I gotta say though, I sure can pick them."

His ears perked up. "Hmm?"

"Men," she clarified.

"Ah."

"I mean, my taste in guys must be pretty awful if Gabe's the guy I fell for, right?" She winked at him, and there was a hint of cheer in her eyes.

Will clapped her on the back. "Now, don't get too down on yourself over that, either. You're young, still, and quite new to all this."

She smiled again, and it made his lips curl upward even tighter than before. "Yeah, well, you would know, right?"

He cocked his head to the side and started to ask her another question, but never got the chance. In the same instant, the sound of someone running toward them assaulted his ears, breaking the spell. He turned to look at who was making the noise only to find Valerie of all people running toward him, looking harried.

"Will! Sariah!" she exclaimed. "I'm glad I found you both!" The older woman stopped a few feet away and took a second to catch her breath. "Please, come quick!"

CHAPTER TWO

The Master took a hesitant step forward, then another. He moved his cane with each step, being careful not to stick it into the remains of a dead body.

He was wearing one of his old man disguises, complete with a small hunch in his back and thin, knobby fingers. He hadn't done the withered old man bit in a while, so it felt like a nice change of pace. He knew no one would think the wiser of him in this costume, and since he was out in public, it seemed like a good idea to go full incognito.

As if an old man and his servant surveying the aftermath of a gruesome battle could be incognito.

The Master let out a slight chuckle, and it hurt his back. He moved his free hand and rubbed the soreness. He'd tweaked it during the last experiment, and it was still bothering him.

No matter, he thought, shaking his head. It'll fade soon enough.

He surveyed the carnage in front of him. He was

outside the walls of Stratton, where a recent battle had been fought. One that had not gone well for his side at all, if the evidence were to be believed.

"Tsk, tsk," he said aloud.

"It's a pity, my lord?" a voice from behind him chimed. It was Daniel, his faithful servant.

The Master turned to face him and gave a curt nod. "Yes, my dear Daniel. It's a pity." He felt like he'd had a similar exchange with the man not that long ago. Perhaps he had.

"Not because they're dead," he added after a moment's pause.

Daniel cocked his head to the side. "Explain, please, Master."

"Must I put it that plainly, even to you?" He let out a long sigh, and it ached, so he put his hand on his back and rubbed again.

Daniel lurched forward as if to help him, but the Master put out a hand to keep him at bay.

"I'm quite well, I assure you," he insisted. "I certainly don't need help just to breathe."

His servant backed up a half step.

"That's better," the Master continued. "Now I know what you're thinking. It's a pity that we lost so many of our number in a senseless battle to a worthless general."

He gave his servant an icy glare. He waited another moment before saying anything else. "You'd be right about that," he said at last. "But that's not all of it."

Daniel rubbed his chin and tilted his head to the side. "Then what else is it, master?"

The Master's lips curled into a wicked smile. He picked

up his cane and placed the end forcefully into the eye socket of one of the fallen Dusk Ravens. He heard a satisfying squishing noise that made his smile broaden. "The true crime is that I didn't get to kill them all myself."

Now his servant seemed really confused. He stared back at the Master with a cloudy look in his eyes. "Master?"

The Master waved him off dismissively. "It's not like that, my dear Daniel. With my new powers, think of all the good I could have accomplished if I'd used them as batteries instead of worthless cannon fodder. Think of the glory, the true cruelty that could have transpired had these soldier's lives been used to further my agenda instead of dying senselessly on a battlefield."

He paused again for a moment and took in a deep breath through his nose. All sorts of awful scents assaulted him, but he seemed to enjoy them. He lifted both arms and waved them around in a wide arc. "Why, it would have been beautiful to behold."

Whether Daniel didn't fully agree or didn't quite understand, the Master couldn't be certain, but it was likely one of the two.

Oh well, he thought. I don't keep him around for his ability to think. Who cares if he can't grasp my true ambitions?

The Master shrugged and looked over the battlefield once again. He was scanning for something specific. Some sign the stupid general he'd placed over the troops was out there somewhere, rotting with the rest of the dead.

He spent another few minutes looking and walking the field, but there was no sign of Gabriel. It appeared the man had escaped the battle unscathed. Disgusted, the Master spat on a nearby corpse and scowled.

I just can't win, can I?

"Do we know who was responsible?" the Master asked over his shoulder, changing the subject.

"No, my lord." He could sense Daniel shaking his head behind him, so he turned to face him properly. "Just rumors is all."

"Humph." The Master tsked again. "Well, let's hear it, then. What are the rumors saying about the carnage?"

"Not much, my lord," Daniel admitted. "There were few survivors, and their stories mostly didn't make sense— something about a well-armed force of several hundred storming the gates. It doesn't make sense."

Another jolt of pain shot up his back, making him wince and he rubbed at it, holding out his other hand to keep Daniel from trying to play hero again. "No, I can see why that wouldn't be the case." He huffed. "Worthless guards. We should put down the lot of them for being cowards."

Daniel simply nodded. "Of course, Master."

He let out a long sigh. "Did anyone's story make sense, my dear Daniel?"

The young servant thought for a moment, then he nodded again. "There was one story, Master. It was a bit of an odd one. One soldier, Ty Genrose, said he saw the massive army, but then it disappeared into the ether right before his eyes, leaving a motley crew of maybe twenty behind."

"Grr," the Master replied. "I thought you said this story was better than the bullshit the others fed you."

Daniel lifted a finger in defense. "Hold on, my lord. There's more to it. The people behind it—the motley crew as it were—there was a girl among them. A very specific girl."

The Master's ears perked up at this tidbit. He side-eyed Daniel, guessing what might come next. "Go on," he pressed.

Daniel nodded again. "Her description matched that of the girl who has caused us so much trouble. Sir, the girl was Sariah."

His expression soured, and he gripped his cane so tightly his knuckles turned white. In a fit of rage, he took his cane in both hands and snapped it clean in half. Then he hurled the pieces to the ground.

The action left him feeling winded, and he looked around for a place to sit and recuperate but couldn't find any.

At long last, his gaze returned to Daniel and his features softened. "How does that little bitch stay ahead of us, Daniel?" he demanded.

Daniel shook his head and lowered his gaze to the ground. "I don't know, Master."

The Master let out another long breath. "Why it's enough to make a man want to kill, I tell you."

"Shall I summon forth the generals for another council?"

"Hmm," the Master replied. He tapped his chin thoughtfully. "Not yet, my dear Daniel. I need to think a bit and plan what to do next. That little girl has always gotten the better of us. I must figure out why."

"Of course, Master."

"First, I must throw off this illusion and relax a bit." He looked at his servant critically. "I trust the last round of prisoners from Stratton are waiting back home?"

His servant bobbed his head in agreement.

"Good. I could use a distraction right about now. Come, Daniel. Let's return to my laboratory."

Daniel smiled at him. He thought he spotted a hint of greed in the man's eyes. His servant gave him a humble bow. "At once, Master."

The merchant known as Darla woke with a start. She pried open her eyes, but her surroundings were pitch black. Darker even than a night with no stars. She was in a room somewhere, though where was anyone's guess.

She felt pain in her left arm and saw it was hanging above her. Hesitantly, she tried to move it, only to find out that it was stuck in place. She tried to move her other arm, only to find that it too was stuck, though it hung loosely at her side instead of above her. A thick metallic-feeling clasp held both of her wrists fast.

Darla shook her head to clear it and regain focus, only to feel a similar abrasive clasp rubbing against her neck. It seemed she was tied down in several spots. Someone definitely didn't want her to move.

She had figured the "relocation program" she'd been involuntarily signed up for in Stratton a few days ago had been little more than an excuse to round up dissenters and send them off to prison. So she wasn't entirely shocked by this turn of events. The bonds that held her in place seemed a little severe for a mere prisoner, though.

Surely not every guest of honor was tied down this thoroughly. Do they know about my true allegiances? she wondered.

Darla shook her head again, wincing at the pain of the metal biting into her neck as she did so. It was unlikely. She never made a show of her Eagle's Claw affiliation to anyone. She always toed the line with the rest of the Dusk Raven scum when given a chance, exactly to avoid the type of mess she currently found herself in.

Yet, here she was.

She let out a long sigh and inhaled sharply. Even that seemed to hurt as the clasp around her neck dug in. She thought she felt something warm and wet bead up where the metal edges of the clasp met the tender flesh of her neck and wondered if she'd managed to cut herself. It would be just her luck to do so.

She tried to think about what happened rationally. She had been taken with a dozen other people at the same time, most of whom were Dusk Raven loyalists. There's no way they could have singled her out. This had to be some kind of misunderstanding.

She would just have to find the person in charge and appeal to their good side. Until then, she'd wait patiently.

The bound merchant woman didn't have to wait long. A moment later, she heard the sound of metal grating on metal and a door scraping open. A small shaft of light sifted into the room from the open doorway.

A large, hunched figure appeared, his features hidden by the light behind him. He made a weird motion with his hands and clapped once, then the room flooded with a harsh, white light.

Darla shut her eyes tight against the glare. After being alone in the dark for so long, the suddenness of it hurt her eyes and left her seeing spots even with her eyelids glued shut.

The sound of a rough, hacking cough broke through the stillness—undoubtedly coming from the hunched man that she could hear ambling through the room. After another moment and a little more shuffling of feet, she heard the door close.

She tried to make out how many people may have entered based on the sound of their feet against the floor and was fairly sure it was just the one—the hunched figure.

Her mind raced, trying to take in this new information and put it in its place. Who was the hunched figure? It had to be a servant and not someone in charge. She took in another deep breath. She knew how to handle servants.

Darla let her eyes flutter open softly and slowly, then focused on the hunched figure still near the door.

"Hello?" she said in a hesitant tone. "Who's there?"

The man looked in her direction and shot her a soft, heartwarming smile. "'Tis Edgar, milady, come to check on the Master's favored guests."

Darla didn't know who this "Master" person was but figured she'd find out soon enough. She just had to get through to this Edgar person first. "Well met, Edgar," she said slowly. Then she coughed a little and realized her throat was quite dry and cracked.

"I don't suppose you have some water or something, Edgar?" she asked him. Each word hurt to get out as it made her throat rub up against the clasp, but she managed the full sentence with some effort.

Edgar looked a little surprised. He took a few steps forward. "Of course, anything for the lady fair," he offered with another flash of a smile. He raised something up off the ground, and Darla tried to get a look at it. It looked like a bucket of some sort. Undoubtedly full of the water she'd asked for.

The hunched figure produced a ladle from within his outfit and dipped it into the bucked, then raised it to her lips. She drank freely of the liquid that spilled out. Each gulp hurt a little, but she wasn't about to let this gift go to waste. The fluid didn't taste quite like water, but it didn't taste bad, either. She had no idea what it was, but it made her feel better. She was so thirsty she would have drunken almost anything.

After she was done, another cough crossed her lips, though it was softer this time and didn't hurt as much. "Thank you," she mumbled to Edgar.

He smiled at her again. "Did you like it? It's the Master's favorite elixir. Good for the bones," he told her.

Darla tried to nod but couldn't quite manage it—the clasp was too tight. "Yes, very much," she replied instead. She tried to motion toward her throat. "Do you think you...could, you know, loosen this thing?" she managed. Each word was still a strain.

Edgar nodded once. He reached up with both hands and started playing with her throat clasp. After a few moments, she heard a click, and it came loose.

This is going fantastic, she thought. I'll be out of here in no time.

"Thank you," she said again. This time, it didn't hurt to talk.

Edgar waved at her dismissively with one hand. "It's all well and good. The Master likes it when his toys can talk during their little sessions," he replied cryptically.

A chill ran down Darla's spine. She was starting to hate the thought of this "Master" person quite a lot, and she no longer felt quite as safe as she once had.

She looked over at Edgar and tried to hold his gaze. "Look, Edgar, I'm sure your 'Master' is a very nice person, but I'm afraid he brought me here by mistake." She spoke quickly and with a hint of unease in her voice. "I'm sure you wouldn't want him to get all the way here only to realize the error, would you? Come, help me out of here, and I'll put in a good word for you, too."

It was a long shot, but she had very few options, and this Edgar person seemed like a nice chap.

"You can...you can come with me when we leave," she offered. She wasn't sure if it would work, but it was all she had to bargain with.

A dark, haughty laugh came from Edgar's direction. It seemed to come both from him and from behind him at the same time. The sound chilled Darla's ears and made her want to scream, but she kept her lips shut.

"How quaint of you to offer me help, when you're the one so desperately in need of it," a voice told her. The voice came from Edgar, but it didn't sound anything like him. It was a deep, smooth voice, and it was far more sinister.

Darla's blood froze, and a knot formed in her chest. What have I gotten myself into?

A second later, Edgar's form began to blur and haze,

then it realigned itself into someone else entirely. Before long, a tall, thin figure stood before her where Edgar had once been. This gentleman had a medium frame and dark, brooding eyes. She thought she recognized him for a moment, then lost the thought just as quickly. Her eyes were still a little blurry in the harsh light.

Besides, she thought, there was no way he could be here.

"Oh, my little Charles," the Master said to her. "You have no idea just how delighted I am that you still have some fight left in you, do you?"

Darla's eyes went wide, and she cocked her head to the side. "Charles? I...I'm not Charles."

The Master waved a hand at her dismissively. "You misunderstand. I don't care what your name used to be. Here, your name is Charles. It makes it easier for me to keep all my guests straight, you see." He paused for a second. "There are so many of you. Besides, it's not like you are going to stay long."

He leveled his gaze at her, and she saw terrible things reflected in those dark eyes—thoughts of torture and who knew what else. It sent another shiver down her spine.

"You...you don't mean..." she started.

"Yes." He nodded. "That's exactly what I mean." He brought one of his hands up, and it inched toward her. She thought she saw a hint of a claw at the edges of his fingers. "Now, trust me, this is going to hurt you far more than it is going to hurt me."

There was a sinister gleam in the Master's eyes as he closed the gap and placed his cold, clawed hand upon her chest.

It was only in that moment that Darla realized she was completely naked, and also completely screwed. She knew with certainty that she was never going to get out of this room alive.

The Master gave off another of his cruel laughs and started making weird motions with his hands, clawing at her bare chest. Then the pain started. It was the worst pain Darla had ever experienced.

She remained firm and didn't make any noise. The pain lasted for a few minutes, then it was gone, and she was left convulsing and gasping for breath.

"There, there, my dear Charles," the Master told her. He ran a hand over her forehead in a loving gesture that sent a wave of revulsion through her. "That wasn't so bad, was it?"

Darla looked into the Master's eyes. They were cold and uncaring and empty in a way, as though he wasn't even enjoying the torture. The thought only scared her more.

"Now tell me your secrets, dearie," he insisted.

With all the resolve she could muster, Darla shook her head. It was barely noticeable, but it was there.

The Master's cruel smile grew broader. "Now, now, my dear Darla. Don't be like that. I'll find out everything you know anyway."

Darla's blood froze. How does he know my name?

She didn't have long to ponder the question, as a moment later, another massive wave of pain rocked her to the core as the Master started his torture up once again.

In spite of her resolve, Darla screamed this time. It was a long time until the screaming stopped.

Several hours later, the Master stepped out of his laboratory and into the hallway. He was somewhat distracted and almost walked right into his assistant.

"Daniel, I didn't see you there," he said slowly.

His assistant backed up a step and bowed deeply in response.

The Master eyed his servant. "Quiet as always," he said. "One of my favorite traits about you. I really need to think up another reward for you later."

"Can I do anything for you, Master?" Daniel asked.

"Hmm..." The Master shook his head. "I'm not sure, really." He took another couple of steps, then stopped in his tracks and turned like he'd forgotten something.

"Yes, Master?"

"Maybe there is something you can do for me, after all." The corners of his lips started to curl in a smile.

Daniel smiled back at him. "Shall I call that council of the generals now, then, Master?"

A chuckle passed the Master's lips. He brought up his right hand to cover his mouth and realized there was still fresh blood on it. The thought only brightened his mood further.

"No, I think not," he said finally, shaking his head again. "How's the special shipment from Zachariah coming? His so-called secret weapon?"

Daniel thought for a brief moment. "It's not ready yet, Master. He said production is taking a bit longer than expected. It will be another couple of weeks."

The Master frowned. "That's too bad," he said casually.

"It would have been an excellent test to try it out." He shrugged. "No matter. Now about that favor."

His servant cocked his head. "Yes, Master? What can I do for you? Bring around another guest?"

A sinister thought crossed the Master's mind as he thought about how much fun he could have with another prisoner. The last one had been such a joy. Surely another…

"No, thank you, my dear Daniel." He paused for a moment. "I think it's time I take matters into my own hands."

Daniel's eyes brightened. "Does that mean…"

The Master nodded. "Yes, child. That's exactly what it means."

CHAPTER THREE

"What is it?" Sariah asked Valerie. She creased her brow and stared at the older woman.

Valerie put out a hand and took a few deep breaths. "It's..."

"Out with it, woman! What's going on!" Will demanded. He had a bitter expression on his face. Sariah figured he was upset at the interruption.

"It's Ilene," Valerie spat out at last, her breathing finally slowing down to the point where she could string more than one word together. "Please, you two. You have to come quick!"

Will rolled his eyes. "What's the old bat gotten up to now?" he asked. His eyes were full of anger, and it looked like he was about to attack poor Valerie where she stood.

Sariah glared up at him. "Old bat?"

His face flushed, and he gave her a sheepish grin. "Don't tell her I said that."

Sariah grinned back at him. "Wouldn't dream of it.

Although, I'd love to be a fly on the wall for that conversation."

The two burst out laughing while Valerie looked at them dumbfounded.

At least I diffused his anger, Sariah thought.

Valerie glared at both of them. She raised one hand and practically struck Will but stopped short. "Are you two going to stand there guffawing at each other all day, or are you going to come along already?"

Will flinched away from the older lady, and his face sobered quickly. "Sorry, my dear," he stammered. He motioned with one hand for her to start walking. "Lead the way. Our guest isn't going anywhere."

Sariah flashed Will another grin. It looked like he was going to burst out laughing again, but the light in his eyes died quickly, and his serious expression won out.

The three of them sped through the corridors of Talon's Reach, Bear at their heels. Sariah tried to stop Valerie to get a better answer out of her as to what was going on, but the older woman remained stoic.

Shaking her head, Sariah kept going. It was all she could do to keep pace with the older woman.

A few moments later, the trio rounded a bend and came upon the courtyard. It opened up into a massive throng of people. It looked like every single person in the whole of Talon's Reach was there, including the recent arrivals from Chatwick.

They were all completely silent and staring at a lone figure who occupied the far end of the courtyard.

That figure was none other than Ilene, who was standing still looking out over the crowd with a somber expression that spoke of authority. She was wearing a plain black outfit that stood out oddly against her pale skin. The color choice was unusual for the woman who was usually never caught in anything but white, lacy dresses. The change in appearance made Sariah do a double-take.

"What's she doing?" Sariah whispered into Will's ear.

Will's fists were slowly clenching and unclenching, and his face was turning beet-red. "There's only one thing she could possibly be doing in an outfit like that," he said through clenched teeth.

She put a hand on his shoulder to try and calm him. "That is?" she asked in as soft a tone as she could muster.

"You'll see soon enough," Will replied cryptically.

"Well, that didn't help much," she chided him, rolling her eyes.

"Hmph," was all Will said in reply. His eyes never once left Ilene's position.

Sariah thought about waving a hand in front of his face to get his attention but decided against it. She'd managed to calm him down with humor once today already and didn't think she would be as successful a second time.

She opened her mouth to say something further, but never got the opportunity. Ilene began to address the crowd.

"Welcome, one and all," she said. Her tone was every bit as cool and firm as it usually was, with not a single hint of warmth, despite the cheery words. "Thank you for coming."

An odd thought came to Sariah, then. She wondered why Ilene was the leader of the Eagle's Claw, given that she wasn't precisely charismatic. She shook her head and let the thought drop. It didn't really matter.

Ilene took a step forward and lifted her arms up in a dramatic fashion. "I want you all to know," she started, "that you are welcome and safe within these walls. Outside there are many who would move to harm one of our family solely for existing."

The cold woman lowered her hands and leveled her gaze at the throng of people as if staring into the souls of each individual. It sent a chill down Sariah's spine.

"Here, you will always have a home. Here, you may count yourself safe from the troubles and worries of the outside world."

Will snorted. The noise broke through the silence that had fallen over the courtyard. Ilene shot him an icy glare, and his visage hardened.

"What was that for?" Sariah whispered at him.

"It's the same speech she used last time," Will replied out of the corner of his mouth. "Almost word for word, too."

This time, Sariah let out a slight chuckle, though she did her best to muffle the sound so as not to get singled out by Ilene.

"If there are no further interruptions?" Ilene said in an icy tone, staring at Will. He shook his head slightly. "Good. As I was saying, it is my first priority as your leader to ensure the safety of all of my people. Each and every one of you."

Her eyes moved across the crowd. She settled her gaze on several people, who seemed to nod in reply but remained silent.

"Sadly, there are some scenarios that not even I, through my effort and wisdom, can prevent." She lowered her head, then placed her hands in front of her and clasped them together.

A low grumble erupted from Will. It was barely audible, but Sariah, as close as she was to him, caught it.

"What is it?" she asked him again, still whispering.

Will let a small sigh escape his lips. "You'll see soon enough."

Ilene raised her head again, and Sariah noticed that her lips were moving, though no words seemed to come out. As the older woman's mouth kept moving, the air around all of them seemed to shimmer and change.

Sariah let out a gasp when she realized the older woman was using mental magic in a way she'd never seen before.

Ilene closed her eyes briefly, and when she opened them again, they were pure white, even whiter than her skin. She opened her mouth again, and this time words spilled out freely.

"Recently, it has come to my attention that there was an incident outside of town. One might even refer to it as an act of insubordination."

Will balked, but this time Ilene didn't stop to acknowledge it.

"There was an incident involving our beloved fellows not two weeks prior. Like many such incidents, the consequences of the foolish act were dire."

Ilene's icy eyes went about the crowd once more, only this time there was no softness or understanding in them.

Her eyes met their targets, and the people she glared at all lowered their heads in shame.

Sariah quickly recognized the pattern—Ilene was singling out everyone that had gone on the assault of Stratton with her and Will. She lowered her own gaze before Ilene's eyes could find her, not wanting to see that look of complete disapproval for herself.

The older woman brought forth her hands and moved them in front of her as if trying to mold the air like one would a piece of clay. In between her hands, the form of a person's face came into being. It was a soft, sweet picture of a person Sariah recognized at once.

"Trevor," Ilene said softly once the face was fully formed. The older woman lowered her gaze to stare at her creation. "Such a kind soul. He was destined for far greater than the fate the Patriarch had in store for him."

Ilene moved to the side, and her hands started moving again, forming the face of another person. Sariah recognized this one, too. It was Bindi, one of the warriors that had gone to Stratton with her. Gone, and not come back.

"Bindi." Ilene looked out at the crowd again, but Sariah felt like the woman was looking directly at her. She recoiled under the pressure of that gaze. "Never a sweeter soul would you find playing in the fields at sunrise on worship day than her."

Sariah lowered her head until she was staring at her feet. All at once, she recognized what was occurring. This was a memorial service for the fallen at Stratton.

Her chest tightened involuntarily, and she thought she might be sick. Trevor and Bindi were dead, as were Misty and a handful of others. Whose fault was it?

Sariah's.

All of them were dead because of something she'd done. Whether directly or indirectly, she was responsible for their deaths. Now, she had to stand there while Ilene spoke about how wonderful they were. She couldn't feel worse about herself.

Fate is cruel sometimes, and she knew she deserved far worse. Those people had been friends of hers, too. Now they were gone.

"Misty," Ilene continued, forming another face in the air. "Her name was fitting, for she was quiet, like the mists off the fields in the morning, with soft features and an even softer touch to match." The old woman smiled like she was remembering something and paused for a moment.

Sariah's stomach churned. The thought of vomiting came to the forefront of her mind again, and she almost relented. She'd liked Misty. That girl had been kind to her on her first day of training. The two had bonded over how harsh of a trainer Will could be at times—especially toward the women in the group.

Ilene moved again and started making another face with her hands, but Sariah tried to shut it out as best she could. The whole thing was overwhelming, and she was almost at her breaking point.

I get it already. I'll never break rank again, I swear. Please let this all stop!

Will seemed to sense her unease, and he placed one of his giant hands on her back and rubbed gently. Sariah looked up at him and flashed him a quick smile. The motion had the intended effect on her.

"Noah," Ilene said then, pointing at the freshly formed

face in front of her. "Much like the man in the ancient stories of old, he was always ready and willing to help out and lead where others would merely walk."

This one hit her hard in the gut and made her double-over for a moment. Noah had been more than a fellow warrior. He'd been her teacher. She had fond memories of their time together.

They were only halfway through the memorial, and already her knees felt like they were ready to give out. She braced herself as best she could and wiped a stray tear that had managed to work itself free.

At her feet, Bear pushed his muzzle into her thigh. His cold, wet nose seemed to tell her silently that she was stronger than she thought.

She smiled at him and patted his head. I can do this, she insisted and took a deep breath.

Through sheer force of will, she remained standing as Ilene repeated the scene with the remaining four names of the soldiers who would never come back from that fateful battle.

Once all eight names had been spoken, and their stories told, Ilene let their faces wink out of existence.

Sariah breathed a small sigh of relief and let her features relax.

Ilene didn't look like she was done with her little show. She was raising her hands again to encompass the crowd. Sariah wondered what was going to happen next.

"Good people of the Eagle's Claw," Ilene called out. "Mistakes were made, and a dear price was paid for it. Now eight good, strong souls will never see their families again."

Sariah's stomach started to churn again, but she heard another low growl come out of Will, and it broke her out of her self-loathing.

What was going on with Mr. Grumpy Pants? Didn't he feel bad about their deaths, too?

Ilene started again. "Unfortunately, there's nothing that can be done about that now," she told the crowd. "What's done is done, and what's in the past will inevitably stay there forever."

The older woman's eyes took on their icy quality again, and she stared through the crowd at her and Will. "However, I will do everything in my power to make sure another incident of this caliber never happens again. As part of my duty as your leader, I can suffer no less."

Sariah's cheeks felt flushed for a moment, but then she started to catch on to the hidden meaning of Ilene's message. Her unease was replaced with fiery defiance.

"That is why I am insisting on a new policy that will ensure this type of incident never happens again," Ilene continued. "Starting today, all Eagle's Claw members will be confined to Talon's Reach and the surrounding fields where we can watch over you and help to ensure peace and tranquility for all."

Sariah's expression soured. She looked up at Will, and his cheeks were a bright red. His eyes were seething like he was about to explode. Hesitantly, she put a hand upon his shoulder, but he shrugged it off.

"It is only after great deliberation that we have come to this conclusion, but we assure you, it is in everyone's best interest to follow the new policy."

"Oh, hogwash!" Will shouted, finally losing his decorum.

An audible gasp washed over the crowd, and everyone's eyes turned from Ilene to Will. Ilene stood with her mouth agape.

Will took a few giant steps forward through the crowd. "How can you, of all people, stand up there and say that bunch of hornswoggle?"

Ilene did a double-take. "I beg your pardon, my lord?"

"Come now, Ilene!" Will sighed a little. "What happened to the lads and lasses was tragic, but I assure you, they wouldn't have had it any other way!"

The older woman straightened herself and regained her composure. " I suppose you think you can speak for the dead, now?"

Will kept advancing on her. "You're damn right I can! At least in this instance."

"How...presumptuous of you." Ilene eyed him up and down. "I fear you only say that because you do not share their fate. Something I'm sure you do not regret."

Another gasp escaped the gathered crowd. Everyone's attention was squarely on Ilene and Will.

"How dare you!" Will fired back. He raised a hand as if to strike her, and Ilene shrank away from him. Seeing her cowering, he lowered his hand just as quickly.

The big man closed his eyes for a moment. "There's not a day...no, not a minute even, that I don't mourn their loss. Them and all the others before them!" he insisted. "Still, they knew the risks before they signed onto the job. Each and every one of them. They all came willingly to help end the Dusk Raven threat."

Will turned to look at the assembled group. "Now, you'd throw all of that effort—all those poor, lost souls—all of it away in the name of a temporary peace?"

Ilene glared at Will, then she lowered her gaze. "It is the only way I can keep all of you safe. That is my utmost duty. To keep you safe. Is it not?"

Will's face reddened until it looked like it was about to explode, then he took a deep breath to calm himself. "Yes, my lady, it is your job to keep us all safe," he admitted at length.

The older woman nodded and looked over the crowd again. "Yes, my dear William. It is a sad but necessary state of affairs."

"How long will this new policy buy us?" Will demanded. "Just how much peace can we win, before the evils of the Dusk Raven clan come to our doorstep? Left unchecked, they will only grow stronger."

Ilene raised her hands to encompass the group again. "So shall we. I'm not suggesting we stop growing, only that we are more careful. We cannot afford to lose even one more soul to this madness."

A few of the heads in the crowd nodded their assent. Several others started whispering amongst themselves.

"I can't believe this!" Will balked. "You take a tragedy— nay, a bold sacrifice—and you twist it to serve your own ends! Unbelievable!" He threw his hands up and walked away from her.

"Why don't we ask the good people of Talon's Reach what they think?" Ilene offered. "Whose side they think is right?"

Will harrumphed. He shot Ilene an icy glare over his shoulder.

"Very well," Ilene continued. "We shall put it up to a vote. Let it not be said that I am anything but a just and understanding ruler." She smoothed out the fabric of her dress and cleared her throat. "All in favor of the new policy, please raise your right hand."

A couple of the assembled people raised their hands, then a few more followed suit. One by one, more hands joined until it was obvious that the vast majority of the assembled were in agreement.

Ilene smiled at the group. "There," she said in a haughty tone. "You see? The people like my plan."

Will turned to face her and wagged a finger. He opened his mouth, about to yell at her further, but something stopped him.

Sariah looked around to try and figure out what it could be but didn't see anything out of the ordinary.

Then she caught sight of the disturbance. A single arrow, sheathed in flames, whistled through the air above them. It landed on the ground, not inches from where Ilene and Will were squabbling.

Another hush fell over the crowd as everyone stared with a mix of awe and dread on their faces.

Sariah cocked her head and stared too. Where on Irth had that come from?

Moments later, it was joined by another burning arrow, then another. Soon, the sky above them was alight with dozens of the fiery brands raining down.

A few of the assembled townsfolk screamed and started

running for cover while Ilene and Will tried to calm them, but to no avail. It was pandemonium.

The gate guard Lester came running toward them, a look of sheer terror on his face.

"Invaders!" Lester shouted. "The Dusk Ravens are here!"

Sariah's stomach churned again, but for a different reason. She spared half a glance at Ilene and Will, who both stood looking dumbfounded. She scoffed at them, then started toward the weapons rack.

There was no denying the truth. All that bickering had been for naught. In the end, the answer had been made for them.

Talon's Reach was under attack.

CHAPTER FOUR

"Warriors, rally to me!" Will's voice cut through the din of the helpless cries of panic that surrounded him as he called out to his soldiers.

He watched as the heads of several people jerked up, and they looked in his direction. He'd reached most of his soldiers with that one call.

"To me!" he shouted again, motioning wildly with his arms. They complied, breaking through the ranks of citizens running around like they were the ones on fire instead of the arrows.

Within moments, he was surrounded by a wall of strong, able-bodied soldiers. To his left stood Albert, Sean, and their friends, and to the right stood Sariah, Harvey, and a few brave faces from Chatwick that had come with them, including a rearick whose name he couldn't remember.

Will's face broke into a broad smile at his well-trained troops standing fast amidst the chaos.

At least I've done something right, he thought.

He began barking orders to the assembled troops. He wasn't quite sure what to do about a pending invasion any more than the rest of them, but he knew they'd look to him for guidance.

"You three!" he said to a group near Albert. "Take Ilene and the townsfolk somewhere safe. Bar the doors and passages. Don't let anyone in until the conflict is over and guard them with your life."

Three curt nods from those soldiers greeted him. "Yes, sir!" one of them said, then they were off.

To her credit, Ilene went with the soldiers willingly and didn't put up a fight. She didn't even speak against him. He rubbed his chin. Sometimes she could do the right thing, after all.

He turned to look at Sariah and Harvey. "You two!"

"Yes?" Sariah replied. There was a fierceness in her eyes that he appreciated, especially during times like this.

"Go to the main gate. Survey the troops attacking us and send back word, so we know what to expect. Take Sean and several men with you. Then lend the defenders whatever aid you can."

Sariah and Harvey both nodded. Sariah threw in a mock salute. "You got it, boss," she said. Then she flashed him a grin, and the two were off, thick as thieves, with Bear and most of the rest of his soldiers in tow. He watched them go and hoped they wouldn't get into too much trouble.

He surveyed the remaining troops standing at attention. There wasn't much left—just Albert, the rearick, and a couple of men from Chatwick. Hopefully, it would be enough, and the battle would never get past the main gates, but he couldn't depend on that.

"You there!" Will shouted at the rearick.

Padron looked straight at him. "Aye, sir?"

"What's your name, lad?"

"Heh," Padron replied. "Look who yer callin' a lad, young one."

Will rolled his eyes. "I don't have time for games, rearick."

Padron shrugged. "Me name's Padron. I dare say I've seen more combat than ye."

Will nodded. "Padron, eh?" A nod. "Padron, I've got a special mission for you. The children in town are sequestered in the old pastor's home this time of day. I want you to go there and guard them with your life. Don't let anyone get into that building, no matter the cost. Am I understood?"

The rearick nodded. "Aye, Sir William. I got ya." With that, he ran off in the direction of the pastor's home. Will sent almost all of the rest of the men with him, just in case. He really didn't want to lose any children in this encounter.

Lastly, he turned to Albert. The kid had proved himself well enough at Stratton, but he was still uncertain of the boy's potential. He needed a task for the kid that he couldn't screw up.

A thought came to him then and he pounced on it.

"Come here, lad," he told the kid.

Albert looked around and then stared at him with a shocked expression. "M-me?" he squeaked.

Will nodded. "Mmhmm. Come over here."

The poor kid looked bewildered, but he complied. Will put one of his arms around the boy's shoulder to comfort him.

"Albert, I've got a very special mission for you. Come with me, and I'll explain on the way."

———

The Master stepped out from his tent and surveyed the assembled troops in front of him. He was very pleased with himself.

He had to admit, he'd been impressed by the speed with which Daniel had assembled the army. There weren't many troops overall—perhaps two hundred—but many of them were mages in their own right. It was an amazing sight to behold.

Too bad my secret weapon isn't ready yet, he mused. Then this would really be a massacre. Alas, it would have to wait. He couldn't waste this opportunity.

He had been surprised that the Eagle's Claw base was so close to his own. Just a week's hard march away, and they'd remained hidden all this time. He'd have to punish some spies when he got back to his stronghold.

That was a treat for later. Right now, he was about to crush the Eagle's Claws' pathetic band and end their threat once and for all.

It was enough to bring a smile to his face.

A gruff looking soldier approached him. Was his name Sergeant Dickerson? No, it was Richardson. He was pretty sure it was Richardson.

"Sir?" the sergeant asked him.

The Master cleared his throat. "Yes, sergeant? What is it?"

"The troops are ready to begin the assault proper. Shall I give the order?"

"Hmm." The Master rubbed his chin thoughtfully.

Is she here? he wondered. She had to be here. The rest of Darla's information was on point. Surely this would be, too.

He doubted the intelligence just a bit. It was why he'd put his other plan into motion at the same time. With the might under his command, he didn't have to be picky, but he really hoped the girl would be here. That's why he'd picked this army to lead personally.

"What's the front gate situation like, sergeant?" the Master demanded.

Richardson gave him a stiff salute. "Sir, they have several men on the top of the gates, but it doesn't look too well defended. We could probably have the gate down in no time if you let us."

The Master shook his head. "No. I want you to take it slow. I want the people in the town to know fear before we destroy them."

Another stiff salute. "Yes, sir. Of course, sir."

With that, Sergeant Richardson turned and left his sight, to relay his orders to the troops.

The Master inhaled a deep breath. There was the slightest hint of the smell of smoke in the air from the earlier volley of fire arrows. It was faint, but there. He smiled at the thought of all the carnage to follow. It would be beautiful.

Sariah would bear witness to it all.

Sariah looked over the wall of Talon's Reach. From her vantage point, she could see the entire Dusk Raven army. There were a lot of soldiers, and somehow she was sure that unlike Will's ruse back in Stratton, each and every one of them would be real.

A knot formed in her stomach, and she did her best to gulp it down. It wouldn't do to give in to fear.

She turned to face Harvey. "Why aren't they attacking?"

Harvey shrugged. "You're asking me?" He let out a chuckle. "I'm the wrong one to be asking about military strategy."

"Oh yeah?"

He nodded. "Yeah. I've no more experience with this sort of thing than you have. Less even. You stormed Stratton, remember?"

A smile crossed Sariah's lips. "Did I?" she replied demurely. She winked at him. "Well, you did a pretty good job ridding Chatwick of its raven infestation if the tales are to be believed."

Harvey flashed her a big, dopey grin. "Is that what they tell you?" She nodded. "Luck, I tell you. It was all luck."

"Uh-huh. Sure it was." She punched him lightly on the arm, and he recoiled from the hit.

"Hey! What was that for?"

"For being you." She shrugged and gave him another wink.

Harvey furrowed his brow. "What's that supposed to mean?"

The answer never came. At that moment, the two saw

movement in the enemy camp below as the troops started forward. They approached the small fortress, marching in lockstep like the seasoned warriors they were. It was a frightening sight to behold.

Sariah readied a fireball in her hands to send hurtling into the assembled troops, but someone took hold of her arm and held her back.

She turned to see who it was. It was Lester, the gate guard.

"Easy now, miss," he told her in a gentle tone. "Let's wait and see what they're planning first."

Sariah cocked her head to the side. "What do you mean?"

Lester shrugged. "Don't see no ladders nor climbing gear," he replied. "How are they planning on getting up here?"

She let that thought simmer and realized he was right. All of the defenders were assembled on the walls, but the enemy force wasn't going to be coming up there with them. So just what were they planning?

Albert stood by the old iron door, waiting for the sight or sound of someone coming. There was no one anywhere near him.

Why would they be? He was standing guard outside the dungeon door. The absolute last place an enemy would come in an invasion would be the dungeon. Why would they want to risk freeing whoever was locked up in there?

It didn't make sense to him to have him guard the door.

Unless it was a ruse and Will was giving him a menial task he couldn't mess up no matter how hard he tried.

He worked just as hard as everyone else at Stratton and had even taken out a few of their number there before the fighting had gotten really thick. Certainly, that earned him a fate better than this.

In the distance, he heard the sound of shouts and metal clanging. The fighting was starting, and he was nowhere near it.

He wondered if he should leave his post, then shook his head. He'd stand guard, just like Will had asked him. He wouldn't abandon his duty, even if he didn't agree with it.

Just then, he thought he heard the sound of metal rattling behind him. His blood froze. What was he supposed to do if the prisoner attempted to escape?

As suddenly as the noise started, it ended. Albert breathed a sigh of relief. He wouldn't abandon his post, but he really didn't want to face the prisoner alone, either.

"They're still coming!" Sariah shouted. The Dusk Ravens were within a few feet of the walls and showed no sign of slowing down. It was almost as if they were planning to run right through the walls.

A chilling thought came to her. What if that was their plan? If they were mages, they very well could go right through the walls or, at the very least teleport beyond them.

She took a last look at the defenders up on the wall,

then tugged on Harvey's shirt. "Come, Harvey! We're going."

Harvey scoffed at her. "Right before the fighting starts? What are you thinking?"

"Mages!" Sariah replied. "They're going to teleport through the walls!"

The blood drained from Harvey's face. "Lead the way."

Sariah dragged Harvey with her as the two made their way down the nearby flight of stairs. Bear nipped at her heels and followed suit.

She was upset she hadn't figured it out sooner, but it wasn't her job to know strategy. It was her job to do the killing. She'd get that chance soon enough, she was sure of it.

Up above her, she heard the sound of shouting and someone casting a fireball. The thing must have been massive as she heard it impact the ground just outside the walls.

She frowned, re-thinking her plan for a moment and wondering if she were on the right track. Please, Matriarch, let me be right about this.

The two had barely left the stairwell before a Dusk Raven mage materialized in front of them. Sariah was so shocked she barely raised her weapon in time to deflect his own.

Sariah locked blades with the enemy soldier, trading blows, then a fireball from Harvey cut the man down to size.

She shot him an icy glare. "I had him, you know. Why don't you find your own targets?"

Harvey shrugged and flashed her a dopey grin. "Speak

for yourself. That's one for me and zero for you." He gave her a light shove and a wink. "Better start keeping up."

Another enemy mage appeared not ten feet away. This one got off a poorly aimed fireball of his own before meeting a similar end.

"Two to zero!" Harvey taunted with a chuckle. "This is too easy."

Sariah nodded. "Indeed. They're not so bad one at a time, but what if more of them start coming?"

The sounds from above grew louder. Then came the sound of metal clanging on metal and surprised shouts.

Were mages teleporting to the top of the wall? Sariah wondered. Seconds later, the fallen body of an Eagle's Claw defender came crashing down, answering her question.

"*Scheisse!*" Sariah and Harvey both shouted.

Sariah backed up to look at the battlement above her. Several soldiers were fighting, locked in close-quarter combat with Dusk Raven mages.

Reaching into a sheath at her waist, she took out a dagger and sent it flying with the aid of her magic for the nearest Dusk Raven. It hit with a satisfying thunk, and the enemy soldier fell back off the wall to his death.

"One to two!" Sariah shouted back to Harvey. "I'm catching up!"

A massive wave of flames floated over her head and careened into another Dusk Raven.

"Three to one now," Harvey chided her playfully. "Not seeing much of a difference."

Before she could think of a witty reply, three more

Dusk Raven mages appeared, weapons drawn and at the ready.

Sariah's lips curled into a smile. At her side, Bear snarled, eager to start his own tally.

Finally, something challenging.

Will paced. He could hear the tell-tale sounds of combat coming from the gate. The assault on Talon's Reach—the only home he'd ever known—had begun in earnest.

He ached to go to the front gates himself and see how the scene was playing out and lend much-needed aid to the defenders there.

He was positive they'd need him. Instead, he stayed put. He was in a central location in the courtyard and could react to any threat and provide updated instructions to the runners from here.

It was a good call, he told himself—the right call.

A runner approached. It was one of the men from the wall. "The fighting has begun!" the runner shouted, panting.

Will wanted to roll his eyes at the man, but he stopped short. He was only doing his job.

"Any news from the front?" Will asked him.

The runner nodded. "The enemy has several mages with them. A few of them teleported to the top of the wall to bring the battle to us directly. Sadly, we weren't prepared, but we're fighting them back now."

Will's hair stood on end. Enemies teleporting to the top

of the wall? If they were doing that, who knows where else they might teleport?

This was dire. He needed to go to the main gate now and help.

He grabbed hold of his blade and started moving but stopped himself. No, my place is here, he reminded himself. This is where I can be of the most use.

"Thank you, Josef," he told the runner. "Now, go back and bring me any reports you can."

Josef saluted him once, then ran off.

Will sighed. He envied the runner, going off to the middle of combat. How he wished he could join them.

A moment later, he heard the sound of a giant crash come from the direction of the main gate.

His blood froze. There was only one thing that could have caused that much noise.

"They've breached the main gate," Will said aloud.

He looked down at his blade again. Looks like he'd get his wish after all.

***

Sariah ran her blade through the last of the Dusk Ravens who had teleported through the wall. She tried to get her blade loose, but it was stuck, and she had to put her foot on the man's chest to pull it free.

At last, it came free, pulling bits of the man's clothing and who knows what else with it.

"Eww," she said. Then, turning to Harvey, she added, "That's three to four now. None too shabby."

Harvey laughed. "I'm still ahead, though."

Bear let out a sharp bark. There was blood dripping from his teeth, and his paws looked messy, too.

"See? Even Bear has racked up a couple of kills," Harvey chided her.

She rolled her eyes. "Well, if things keep going like this, I'll catch up to both of you soon enough."

He flashed her a dopey grin, then his eyes scanned their surroundings.

She did the same. A gnawing thought kept at her that if the mages could teleport through the walls, they could technically teleport to anywhere else in the town —even the secluded areas, like where they were hiding Ilene.

Desperately, she ached to know more about the enemy's plan. She tried casting about with her magic to see how many people were in the vicinity, but there were so many hits she couldn't make any sense of it.

She bit her lip and waited.

Moments later, she heard the sound of a giant crash coming from the direction of the main gate. She looked over at the massive door. It appeared to be smoking around the edges.

"Eek!" she screamed.

Harvey looked over at the gate as well. He winced. They both had the same thought—that thing wouldn't survive another blast.

Sariah started toward the gate, but Harvey held her back with one of his hands.

"Wait!" he implored her.

She growled at him but did as he asked.

Another crashing noise came, and this time the main

gate came flying inward, passing right through the spot where she would have been if Harvey had let her go.

Sariah looked up at Harvey. "Thanks," she managed. "I guess I owe you one."

He flashed her another grin. "You can make it up to me later." He pointed to the now wide-open gateway, where Dusk Raven soldiers were starting to pour through. "We have company."

Padron heard a loud crashing noise coming from outside and shuddered involuntarily. He shook his head. It didn't sound like the fighting out there was going so well.

I should be out there with 'em, he thought for the hundredth time. Not stuck with tha kids.

A promise was a promise, and there were at least a dozen children in the room with him. If anything did happen, it would be a massacre without him and his trusty axe. He couldn't bear to think about that.

He heard the sound of crying from the corner of the room, and it drew his attention. Slowly, he walked over to where a young boy, perhaps six, was huddled in the corner. Another child, maybe eight or nine, had her hand on the boy's back and was trying to comfort him.

Padron knelt beside the boy and put his hand underneath the kid's chin. "Easy now, lad," he told the child. "There's nothin' ta worry about."

"I'm s-s-scared," the child admitted.

The rearick smiled at the small child. "Tha noise out there a bit much for ye, eh?"

Slowly, the child nodded in response. "Y-yes, sir."

Padron rubbed the child's cheek. "What's yer name, boy?"

"S-simon, sir," the boy replied.

"Now that's a strong name, there, Simon," Padron replied with a wink and another smile.

Simon gave him a weak smile in return, then buried his head back in his hands.

"Now, now, Simon, lad. I won' let anything happen to ye or any o' yer friends while I'm here. Ye can count on me word, lad."

Simon sniffed a few times. He looked up at the rearick and held his gaze. "What about my dad?"

Padron rubbed his chin. "Is he out there in tha fightin?" The boy nodded again. "Well now, me mates Sariah an' Harvey are out there. They won't let nothin' happen to no one if they can avoid it. I think yer dad'll be just fine."

Simon gave him a weak smile. "I'm sure you're right."

The doorway to the small room he shared with the children creaked, then, like someone was trying to open it.

Simon started to say something, so Padron put his hand over the boy's mouth. "Shh," he whispered. "Be real quiet now."

The rearick started to inch his way toward the doorway. In the same instant, the noise came again. Then the door shook in its frame, and all the children in the room jumped.

Padron shushed the children, then turned his attention back to the door. He took the battle-axe out of its sheath. Perhaps the battle would come to him after all.

Will heard another loud crashing noise from the direction of the main gate.

His face soured, and the blood drained from his cheeks. Only another few seconds and he'd be there. He picked up his pace.

Rounding the corner, the gate area came into view, and the sight made his jaw drop. The front gate was gone, with nary a stone still hanging in the giant opening that lay before him. In its wake were dozens of Dusk Raven soldiers infecting his town like parasites.

He strained his eyes to see through the gate to the end of their force, but their numbers seemed to go on forever.

He could barely make out the silhouettes of a few of his brave defenders fighting in the thick of the enemy combatants but couldn't tell who they were.

With an unhappy grin, he studied the sword in his hand. "You'll taste your fill of blood today, friend," he told it. Then he ran toward the crowd of soldiers.

Two of them fell to his blade before he even closed the gap, and another shortly after. There were far more of them than there were of him, and he knew he wouldn't be able to keep this up for very long by himself.

He wanted to reach the defenders up front to back them up. There were also more soldiers on the battlements, and they'd surely come to help soon as well.

A soldier to his left came at him with a high blow aimed to take his head off. He parried with practiced ease and used his momentum to run the man through. The Dusk

Raven's body fell to the ground seconds later, only to be replaced by another.

This pattern continued for several minutes as he hacked and slashed his way through the horde. It felt like he was holding off the entire army, though he'd seen at least a few Dusk Ravens slide past his guard.

A high-pitched scream from behind him pulled his attention away from the battle for a moment. It was almost a second too long. The soldier in front of him used the momentary confusion to get past Will's guard and land a glancing blow across his middle.

Will hissed and slashed at the Dusk Raven, felling him with one massive strike.

The scream nagged at him. He thought he'd recognized the voice.

Then it hit him. "Sariah!" he yelled. There was no answer.

Will hacked at another soldier, then started retreating into the town. Sariah was in there somewhere, and she was in trouble!

The Master walked behind the main force. Let them get their fill of death first before I get mine, he thought. It didn't hurt that they served as a decent shield as well.

He watched some of his mages cast a massive fireball through the main gate to Talon's Reach like it was nothing but a piece of paper. A small smile crossed his lips. He'd trained his men well, and it was really starting to show. He'd have to reward them later. If any of them lived, that is.

With the gate down, his non-magical forces made their move, swarming into the town like locusts. It was a wondrous sight to behold. All those innocent people inside, suddenly without their protection. It would be a massacre.

One of the sergeants came up to him. "Sir, we've breached the town gate and started the assault. Do you have any orders?"

The Master rubbed his chin. "No, sergeant. Do as you like with the inhabitants. Rob them, kill them, whatever you like. Your men have free reign in there."

"Yes, sir," the sergeant said. He gave the Master a stiff salute.

"Oh, and one more thing, Captain."

The sergeant gave him a confused look. "Captain?"

"Are you disagreeing with the promotion, Captain?"

There was a second of doubt, then a firm shake of the head. "No, sir."

"Good." The Master nodded. "While you're in there, Captain, remember that while you can do what you like with the populace, Sariah is mine and mine alone. Understood?"

Another salute, and then a wry grin. "Yes, sir."

CHAPTER FIVE

Albert watched in horror as a pair of Dusk Raven soldiers passed in the alleyway in front of him. The town had been breached, and all he was doing was sitting on his thumbs guarding a stupid door!

He looked at the old piece of iron in disgust. He wanted to spit at it, but he knew it wouldn't do him any good. Surely the old door would be more than enough to keep their prisoner at bay, wouldn't it? It looked sturdy enough. Plus, it was locked, and the prisoner's cell was locked, too.

He couldn't think of anyone who could manage to escape two pairs of iron locks like that.

The acrid smell of smoke filled his nostrils, and he wrinkled his nose. He didn't want it to be his fate to waste away while his town burned.

The Patriarch would not be that cruel to him.

His eyes darted around again, and he saw another Dusk Raven come to the entrance of the alleyway. This one had his weapon drawn and was concentrating on something close by.

Albert's eyes gleamed, and he reached for his own blade. Finally, a chance to prove himself.

Then another figure came into view. This one did not wear the brown uniform of a Dusk Raven. He recognized the other combatant at once—it was Sean.

Sean's blade moved up and down in response to the Dusk Raven's own weapon. The two looked to be evenly matched, but Albert knew his friend could handle this on his own.

His hopes were dashed, but he watched the combat unfold anyway. At least it was more interesting than guarding a door.

A few moments later, he caught sight of another Dusk Raven coming their way. This one had a dagger out and was attempting to sneak up on Sean.

From his vantage point, Albert could easily make him out, but Sean would be caught unawares.

His mind raced. He had to do something to save his friend. A fireball could easily hit Sean instead of the assailant.

An idea came to him. He grabbed his own dagger from his belt and used his magic to guide its path. The blade flew through the air and plunged into the unseen attacker's chest.

Sean heard the commotion, and he looked around in confusion, wondering what was going on around him. The momentary lapse in judgment was enough for the remaining Dusk Raven to get a cut in on him.

Albert shrieked and threw a fireball at the Dusk Raven. It engulfed the man, and he fell to the ground, writhing in flames.

The iron door momentarily forgotten, he ran to his friend's side. Sean was on the ground, not moving.

He placed a hand gingerly on Sean's temple, feeling for a pulse. It was there.

Albert breathed a sigh of relief and looked his friend over. The big man had a fresh wound on his leg but didn't look too much worse for wear.

"You gave me quite the scare there," he told his friend.

Sean nodded. "Yeah, well, you seemed to hold your own well enough." He motioned behind him with his head. "Thanks for the save back there."

Albert smiled at him and shrugged. "You'd have done the same."

Sean looked down at his own body, then stuck out a hand. "Mind helping me up?"

"Of course!" Albert took his friend's hand and helped him to a standing position.

Sean leaned a little on his uninjured leg. He looked to be in a lot of pain.

"You okay?"

The big man waved a hand at Albert dismissively. "Couldn't be better." He gave Albert a wink. "Now, let's go hunt down some more Dusk Ravens, shall we?"

Albert's face burst into a wide grin. "Absolutely."

Padron watched as the door to the little room shuddered once again. Someone on the other side was determined to get in.

He'd put a large dresser in front of the door to block it

earlier, but he knew it wouldn't hold much longer. Not much would if the attackers were determined enough, and it seemed they were plenty determined.

The rearick fingered the blade of his battle-axe, then he looked at the scared faces of the children all around him.

What am I going to do with all of them? he wondered. He could handle a few attackers well enough, but he was worried the little ones might get in the way and get hurt by accident.

With a look of desperation, he scanned the room. There was a large bed in one corner, but not much else.

He shrugged. It would have to do.

"All right, children, now listen ta yer uncle Padron," he told them in a voice barely over a whisper. He didn't want to chance that the people trying to knock down the door would hear him.

The children gathered in close, all but Simon, who barely budged from his spot. Padron shook his head but kept talking. "See tha' bed over there, children? I want ye all ta cram in under it and hide. No matter what happens out here, ye stay there and don' make a sound. Got it?"

Several of the children nodded. Simon remained frozen. "Good. Now git."

Behind him, the door shuddered again as something battered into it. He turned and practically shoved the children under the bed.

Then he turned his attention to Simon. The boy was still frozen in place.

"Get, I said!" Padron insisted. The boy didn't move.

Padron let out a low grumble, then he picked up the boy and placed him on the bed facing away from the door.

"I don't have time fer this," he said with another shake of his head. "Just stay put, lad."

With the children out of harm's way, he took out his axe and faced the door once more. It moaned and started to splinter as the attackers had their way with it.

One more massive push from the attackers and the door blew off its hinges, forcing the dresser out of the way in the same motion.

"That was a big mistake," Padron said in a level voice. "Now yer gonna pay."

Padron hefted his axe and made a broad-sweeping vertical swipe toward the first attacker. The man was so shocked to see any real resistance that he was cut down in seconds. Two more men spilled into the room, swords at the ready.

The rearick grunted and mumbled something about having to work in cramped conditions, then he swung his axe again. This time, it was met with some resistance by the first assailant, and the blade didn't find purchase.

Attacker two made a low thrust, aiming for Padron's midsection. He side-stepped the blow and pushed out with the head of his axe. It hit the attacker and sent him into the wall.

The Dusk Raven hit the wall with a grunt and fell to the ground.

Padron eyed the remaining standing attacker and smiled at him. "Ye picked tha wrong door, friend," he told the man. Then he swung his axe right for the man's stomach. The blow had such force that it went right through the man's sword blade that he'd raised in defense and practically split him in two.

With the immediate danger averted, Padron turned his attention to the last attacker. He was still half-propped up against the wall and looked dazed.

He shrugged his broad shoulders. No matter.

Padron didn't want to give the Dusk Raven a chance to recover. He hefted his axe and swung downward, severing the man's head from his spine.

Taking a few deep breaths, he ventured a few steps into the hallway beyond. There didn't seem to be any other soldiers—friend or foe—in the vicinity, so he went back into the room to check on the kids.

Standing on the bed, facing him with a stunned expression on his face, was little Simon. There was a wet spot below the lad like he'd peed himself.

Padron knelt and looked the child in the eyes. "See all that, did you?" he asked.

Simon nodded. His wide eyes didn't leave Padron's.

"I'm sorry, kid. There're some things a young lad like yerself just shouldn't see."

Another slight nod answered him.

He placed a hand gingerly on the boy's shoulder. "What say ye that when this is all over, we find yer father an' talk ta him about it?"

Simon's lips curled into a bit of a smile, and his eyes brightened.

"Good," Padron said. He held out a hand. "This room isn't safe fer us anyway. How about we go lookin' fer a new one?"

The young boy took his hand. The tiny appendage felt small and breakable in his own massive hand. He motioned toward the rest of the children still hiding under the bed.

"Come, children. Let's find a new place ta lie low for a bit."

Sariah parried another sword blow. This one had been aimed at her head. She swung her own blade at the attacker and scored a glancing strike on his sword arm.

The man howled and dropped his weapon. She used the opening to skewer him and let his body slump to the ground.

Huffing a few times to slow her breath, she looked around her. How many was that now? Ten men? Twelve? Somewhere along the way, she'd lost count.

She looked around for Harvey and Bear but didn't see them.

In all fairness, after the main gate had blown and the soldiers had come rushing in, the whole scene had been pandemonium. Who could blame them for getting separated amidst the chaos?

Sariah bit her lip and scanned her surroundings again. Another two Dusk Raven soldiers were heading her way, but there was no sign of Harvey or Bear.

In fact, there was no sign of anyone she recognized.

She wondered where Lester and the rest of the gate guards were. They should have come down by now.

There was no one—just her and more of the enemy.

She gritted her teeth and braced herself for another round of combat. To even up the odds, she readied a fireball and flung it at one of the two Dusk Ravens. He howled and fell to the ground as the mass of flames overtook him, but the other soldier stupidly kept coming.

Groaning, she raised her blade. She lunged at the man, but he parried the blow easily.

This soldier was fresh and ready, and she was starting to feel the toll of all the combat. Sariah grumbled. This confrontation would not be fun.

Dusk Raven two swiped low at her feet, and she jumped backward just in time, lashing out with her own blade to keep him at bay.

She followed it up with an upward stroke that the soldier batted away like he wasn't even trying.

Another swipe came at her, this one aiming for her sword arm. She managed to deflect the blow, but it left her open.

Fortunately, the Dusk Raven wasn't practiced enough to realize this, and he made another wild swipe instead.

This one she easily dodged, then stepped forward on her right foot and lunged again, coming in from under his guard. That blow connected, and another Dusk Raven fell at her feet.

"That's fourteen!" she shouted, hoping to catch Harvey's attention. It was probably really twelve, but he didn't need to know that.

No answer came.

Through the haze of combat, she saw another attacker. This one looked different from the others. He wore robes like he was more wizard than a fighter.

Sariah shrugged. The Dusk Ravens had plenty of mages. She'd already taken out a few. What was one more? She readied another fireball, but something about the appearance of this particular man stuck out.

The new assailant took another few steps toward her, and all the blood drained from her face.

Somehow, she knew this man. Or knew of him, at least. His appearance was unrecognizable at the moment, but deep down she knew who it was.

A chill ran up her spine, and she stood frozen in place, staring at the strange man. She didn't know how she knew, and yet there was no mistaking it.

Sariah had come face to face with the Master.

Harvey grunted and pushed another dead body off his sword. "That's thirteen for me!" he yelled at the air.

As the dust started to clear, he realized there was no one around him. Somehow, during all the fighting, he and Sariah had gotten separated.

"Sariah!" he shouted. There was no answer.

He shook his head. If Sariah had been killed, he would have felt it. He wasn't very good at mental magic tricks, but somehow he knew he'd feel it if that happened.

She was alive, then, but where? He scanned his surroundings again, but there was nothing but dead bodies as far as the eye could see. Mostly Dusk Ravens, though there were several Eagle's Claw bodies mixed in with them as well.

To his left, he could see someone fighting with the mass of soldiers at the gate. It looked like Will, though he couldn't be certain.

To his right, there was nothing. Not a soul moved in that direction.

Harvey decided to help out Will with the remainder of the troops at the gate. He'd catch up with Sariah later and brag about his kill numbers over a nice drink or something.

Just then, a shrill cry broke through the stillness.

The hair on his neck stood on edge and bile rose to the back of his throat. That voice was Sariah's. She was in trouble.

Harvey took off in the direction of the scream as fast as his feet could carry him.

After making his way down a couple of corridors, he groaned. "Which way?" he asked aloud. He hadn't been at Talon's Reach long enough to really know. He picked a random direction and kept going.

Up ahead, he saw five Dusk Raven soldiers blocking his path. Each of them had a weapon and looked untouched by the recent combat.

He groaned. "I don't have time for this!" he shouted at them.

Thinking fast, he used his magic to pick up several sword blades that had fallen to the ground from other attackers. With a few twirls of his fingers, he spun the blades in a circular pattern in front of him and sent them hurtling toward his foes.

The Dusk Ravens seemed so shocked by the suddenness of the action that they barely brought their own weapons up in time to block the onslaught. Two of them fell right away, while the remaining three remained standing with only minor cuts.

Harvey gritted his teeth and summoned more blades. There were probably fifty to spare on the ground around him, plenty of ammo.

He sent the new blades speeding toward the last three Dusk Ravens. Two more fell. Only one was left now between him and Sariah.

Using up almost the last of his reserves, he brought even more blades up from the ground and sent them flying. The mass of weapons proved too much for the lone Dusk Raven, and he fell, skewered by a dozen or so sword tips. It was a bit of a gruesome sight.

Another cry came then, once again breaking through the stillness of the air and giving Harvey a direction to go.

"I'm coming, Sariah!" he shouted. Then he took off.

"You," Sariah said to the person approaching her. It was more of a statement.

The Master smiled at her and nodded. "Yes, child, it is I. The one known only as the Master."

His tone was icy and cold, but in a way that was different from Ilene's. Ilene's voice had a certain warmth and kindness to it. This voice was utterly devoid of such emotions. It almost wasn't even human.

"So we meet at last," Sariah continued. She looked down at her sword briefly, then back up at the Master.

Will this puny weapon protect me from him? Another chill ran down her spine. She knew the answer.

The Master waved his hand, and her blade was wrested

from her grasp. It flew into a nearby wall and clattered to the ground.

A lump formed in Sariah's gut, and she did her best to suppress it. Magic it is, then. She was growing tired from the earlier combat, and the Master looked so rested, untouched by the carnage.

It was an illusion, most likely, but still, it was enough to make her shake.

"You're smaller than I imagined," the Master told her, taking another few steps toward her.

"Yeah?" Sariah answered. "Well, no one told me you looked like a stuck pig!"

The Master scowled and lashed out with a bolt of energy. She brought up her shield to defend herself, and the magic bounced off harmlessly.

"Heh," the Master said. "Guess your little boyfriend taught you a few tricks." He cocked his head to the side. "Where is he, anyway?"

"My boyfriend?" Sariah fired back. He was referring to Gabe. She shrugged and tried to make it look casual, even though it was anything but. "I killed him. He was useless to me."

The Master let out a slight chuckle. "Seems we can agree on something, at least."

Another wave of energy came at her, and she blocked it with her magical shield once more. It was a little harder the second time, but she managed.

"Humph. Bet you won't do so well without your little spells to protect you," the Master told her. Then his eyes flashed black, and before she knew it, he was on top of her.

He reached out and grabbed her by the neck, squeezing hard.

Despite herself, Sariah let out a gargled scream.

"Yes, child," the Master said with a gleam in his eyes. "That's more like it."

Sariah readied a fist and punched the Master in the gut. He let go of her, clutching his stomach.

"You bitch!" he roared. He lashed out with another wave of magic that she managed to block, but only barely.

"You'll pay for that!" He was on her again, only this time, he didn't grab her neck. He grabbed her arm. Then his eyes turned an intense shade of red.

Pain washed over Sariah, unlike anything she'd ever felt. It rocked her to the core, and she screamed again louder this time. Then she started to feel weaker than she did even after casting several spells.

"You stupid little wretch," the Master said. His face was inches from hers, and she could feel the heat of his breath on her cheeks. "You will learn your place before I'm done with you."

Sariah gasped and tried to ready a spell to attack him but couldn't. She felt completely drained of energy. The spells wouldn't come. "S...screw you!" she managed, then she spat on his face.

The Master wiped the spittle off with one hand, then slapped her hard. She fell to the ground at his feet.

"Insolent whelp," he muttered. Then he slapped her again. "You will know true pain before I'm done with you. You and everyone you know will face my wrath."

Sariah looked up at him. There were stars in her eyes, and she felt so weak it was all she could do to breathe, but she was still defiant. "P...piss off," she mumbled, knowing it would cause him to lash out again.

She wasn't wrong. The Master laid into her, punching her several times. The pain was bad, but it paled in comparison to his earlier spell, whatever that had been.

The Master hovered over her with a menacing expression. "Any last words, bitch?"

Sariah looked around. Her vision was starting to slip, but out of the corner of her eye, she thought she spotted something, or rather, someone.

Her lips curled into a smile. "H-harvey," she said. Then she laid her head down.

The Master paused and cocked his head to the side. "Harvey?" he repeated. It didn't take long before he realized what that meant.

"Get away from her!" Harvey's voice rang out. Suddenly he was there, standing not ten feet away from the Master with at least a dozen swords swirling in the air around him.

The Master turned to face Harvey. He scowled. "Ready to face your death so soon, whelp?" he asked. He raised a hand as if to cast a spell, then lowered it a second later.

"He said, get away from her!" another voice called out. This one was Will's. He had two fireballs at the ready, one in each hand.

"That's right!" a third voice called out. Sariah craned her neck to look at the new person. It was Albert. He was there with what looked like a wounded Sean next to him. The two had fireballs in their hands, too.

Bear materialized a second later, barking and gnashing his teeth, ready to pounce.

The Master looked at these new threats, his eyes darting between each. "Heh," he muttered. "Another time, perhaps." Then he disappeared in a puff of black smoke.

"Sariah!" several voices said in unison. They all rushed toward her.

"My saviors!" she replied in a voice so weak she barely recognized it as her own. She smiled at them, then everything went black.

CHAPTER SIX

When Sariah woke next, it was in a strange bed. She slowly rubbed her eyes and started to take in her surroundings. She could barely make out the forms of two people hunched over in chairs.

At least I'm not alone this time, she thought dryly. She'd had her fill with waking up in strange beds by herself.

Once her eyes came into focus, she recognized Will and Harvey. They both looked to be napping, waiting for her to wake up.

Bear, of course, lay at her feet, snoring away.

She supposed she couldn't blame them, given the intense battle they'd all just survived.

Memories of the battle and her confrontation with the Master came rushing back. One hand went up to her throat unconsciously. She could still feel his cold, lifeless hand clutching her there.

The memory made her shiver, and she pulled the blanket around her a little tighter.

A moment later, one of the two men started to stir. It was Will.

Sariah sat up in bed so she could talk to him. "Will!" she said in a whisper. She didn't want to wake Harvey if she could avoid it.

Will roused himself the rest of the way and looked at her. A big smile crossed his lips. "Sariah," he replied warmly. "It's so good to see you awake at last." There was a gleam in his eyes as he spoke.

He motioned to Harvey, who was still sleeping away. "We were very worried about you after that last encounter," he told her. "Who was that, anyway?"

"That," Sariah said slowly, "was the Master." She could barely even say his title without the feeling of helplessness he'd brought on her coming back.

"The Master?" Will replied. He looked confused.

Sariah nodded.

"Are you sure?" He gave her an odd expression like what she was saying didn't make any sense.

"Oh, I'm sure all right." She paused for a moment. "I know what you're thinking. He didn't look anything like I expected him to, either. Then again, I was expecting a grade A dickwad," she added with a smile.

Will chuckled. "A grade A dickwad, huh?" Sariah nodded again. "I guess he did look a little dickwad-ish."

They both laughed at that, and Sariah felt the skin around her chest start to loosen as the tension faded. She felt a little better now that she was safe in Will and Harvey's presence. Both of them did so much to help her and had given so much. How could she ever repay them?

She shook her head to clear her thoughts. It wouldn't

do to think like that. There were far more pressing matters to deal with.

"Is the battle…"

"Finished," Will replied with a nod.

"The Dusk Ravens?"

"Most of them were killed off in the invasion. The few that survived managed to run away, but I don't think they'll be coming back anytime soon." He let out a long, slow breath. "We're safe enough. For now."

Sariah's features softened, and she let her shoulders relax, only now realizing how tense they'd become. "What about the rest of us? The Eagle's Claw? Did anyone…?"

Will's face darkened, and he lowered his gaze. "We lost about thirty soldiers in the attack. Given the damage done to the Dusk Ravens, I'd say it was more than an even trade. It's not like we could afford the losses, though."

"What about Albert and Sean? Jennie and Susan? Bertrand and Ellie?" She let out a gasp and clapped her hands to her mouth. "Ilene?"

Will put a hand on her shoulder. "Whoa, slow down there, missy. One thing at a time, will you? You're still weak from the fighting. You need your rest."

Sariah furrowed her brow. "You're not giving me an answer." Her cheeks flushed. "Does that mean they died in the attack? It does, doesn't it?"

Will shook his head and let out a sigh. "Hey, I said slow down. All those people you just mentioned are perfectly fine. It was mostly the men at the gate that got taken down. Hardly anyone you know."

Another name came to her. "Lester?"

Will laughed out loud. "That old coot? Heck, nothing

could kill that guy. I'm pretty sure he'll still be alive when the Irth itself finally gives up the ghost."

Sariah let out a small sigh of relief. Lester was such a gentle soul. She couldn't bear it if something happened to him. After all, the whole attack had kind of been her fault.

"I'm sorry," she said at last, lowering her own head and trying her best not to look at him.

Will cocked his head to the side. "Sorry? For what?"

"For bringing the enemy here. For provoking them. After the Battle of Stratton, they were bound to come here looking for revenge. It's all my fault, I..." Tears started to stream down her cheeks, and she put her head in her hands.

"Hey," Will said softly. He brushed her hair with one of his hands and pushed her head up a little so they were looking eye to eye. "You've got it all wrong, missy."

Sariah bit her lip. "How?"

"The Dusk Ravens were our sworn enemy long before you came along, remember? You joined us, not the other way around. They would have found us eventually. Maybe you sped it up a little, but what happened was bound to happen."

Another tear fell down her cheek, and she wiped it away with her hand. She sniffed once to keep the snot from coming out of her nose. What a look that would have been. Then she chided herself for thinking about her appearance when she should be thinking about how to avenge the fallen.

"I suppose you're right," Sariah said at last. "Maybe Ilene was right. If we'd just stayed put, maybe things would have been better."

Will scoffed and got to his feet. His cheeks burned bright red. "Now don't you go falling for her tired old rhetoric, too!" He paced, then sat back down and looked her in the eye, leaning forward a bit. "Listen. Ilene has been around far longer than I. She's seen a lot of loss, and it's hit her hard, but we're not going to win this war by closing our borders. We need to get more people involved in this conflict, not less."

Sariah nodded. His words made sense.

"Besides," he continued. "If we'd let the Dusk Ravens have their way with Stratton, even more people would have suffered." He rubbed his chin, then shook his head a few times. "No, we made the right call there. Don't ever doubt yourself like that again."

She smiled at him and sniffed again. "You got it, mister."

A knock came at the door and it opened, spilling light from outside. Sariah could make out the outline of an older woman in the door frame.

"Come in," she said, beckoning with her hand.

Valerie walked into the room. Padron was behind her, though he didn't enter. He had a dark expression on his face and looked away when Sariah tried to look at him.

"Sorry to interrupt you," Valerie said as she entered.

Sariah smiled up at her. "Nonsense! You're not interrupting anything. What's up?"

Valerie took another two steps, but Padron didn't budge. Sariah found his behavior odd but ignored it for the moment.

The older woman frowned at them, and her eyes searched the room. "Have either of you seen a little girl running about? I'm sorry to ask, but I know she took a liking to you earlier, Sariah, and I thought she might have snuck in here."

Sariah's eyes went wide. "You mean little Heather? She's missing?"

"You've met Valerie's granddaughter?" Will asked. He looked surprised.

Sariah nodded. "Yeah, I met her a while back while I was out...taking a walk. So what?"

Will shrugged. "Just surprised is all."

"Back to the matter at hand," Sariah said, giving Will a dirty look. "Heather is missing? What happened?"

"It's all me fault, it is!" Padron blurted out. His cheeks were red, and his eyes were puffy like he'd been crying. He ambled into the room. "Please, forgive me, Sariah!"

"What's all your fault?"

Padron started crying in earnest. "The kids was my responsibility!" he said through sobs. "'Twas my duty ta protect 'em. Only I got caught up in tha fightin' and...I'm so sorry!" He broke down into more wild sobs.

"There, there," Sariah said, getting up and walking over to him. She put a hand on the rearick's shoulder. "I'm sure you were only doing what you thought best."

Padron nodded. "Aye, lass. That I did." He wiped the tears from his eyes and started to calm down.

"There's still a child missing. Tell me, Padron, when did you see her last?"

The rearick started to sob again. "I dunno, Sariah! First tha Dusk Ravens came, then I got ta fightin', then we moved around a bit. I'm not sure when she got lost or where."

Sariah patted the rearick on the back. "It's okay,

Padron. You did your best." She turned to look at Valerie. "We'll go look for her. You two stay here in case she shows up."

Valerie's jaw dropped. "Are you sure? No, it's more than I could ask."

Sariah shook her head. "Nonsense. It's the least I could do after all you've done for me."

The old woman put a hand on her chest and bowed her head. "Bless your heart, child."

"Come along, Will," she barked at him. "You're helping, too."

Will groaned a little, but he got up and nodded. "Of course. Anything to help."

She looked at Will, then spared a glance at Harvey and Bear. They were both still sleeping, in spite of all the commotion.

A slight frown creased her lips. "Should we wake them?"

Will shrugged and let out a slight chuckle. "Nah. Let those two have their little nap. If they've managed to sleep through all this racket, they've earned it. Besides, it'll be quite the shock when Harvey and Bear wake up to find Valerie here in your place."

She shot him a wicked grin. "Now that sounds funny as hell."

"Heather!" Sariah shouted. It was about the hundredth time in the last hour she'd done so. No one answered, not that she'd expected anyone to.

"Come on, Heather! I've got some new tricks I want to show you, but you have to come here!" It was a long shot, enticing her with the promise of combat moves, but she'd tried just about everything else, and nothing had worked so far.

She bit her lip and looked around. The town of Talon's Reach had certainly seen better days. A lot of the homes she passed had broken windows or doors torn off their hinges. Several large stones that had previously been on top of the walls riddled the ground. It was a huge mess.

A sigh escaped her lips. Talon's Reach had been an imposing place to search before the attack had come. After, there were even more places for a little girl like Heather to hide now.

That was assuming she was still alive.

Sariah shook her head. She couldn't afford to think like that. Heather had to be alive. After all, Valerie had done and given up helping her out, she couldn't bear it if the old woman lost her granddaughter, too. No, she'd find the girl one way or another.

"I've got a treat for you, Heather!" Sariah cried. She waited a full minute after that one, but no one came running.

She was starting to doubt her earlier decision to split up and have Will look outside the town. Certainly, he'd be better equipped to look inside the walls.

She had been there for almost two months now, but still.

A chill autumn wind came rolling down off the walls, and Sariah shivered a little. She rubbed her arms to warm them and thought about how cold and alone little Heather must be, wherever she was.

"Come on, Heather! We're all worried sick about you!"

There was no response.

"Ugh," Sariah groaned. "This is hopeless." Then she smacked herself.

Come on, Sariah, you can't give up that easy. This is Valerie's granddaughter you're talking about. You'll search all day if you have to.

Her little pep talk seemed to do the trick. She felt much better and more confident that she'd find the little girl somewhere, assuming she hadn't run back home to her grandmother by now.

Which is entirely possible, she thought as she peered around another downed boulder. She should go back and check with Valerie.

The thought seemed like a good one. She'd stop by for only a moment, then she'd get back at it if Heather wasn't there. She started back to the house they'd all congregated in. She'd learned that it was Valerie's house, and it only made sense that Heather would go back there.

On the way, she passed by the alleyway that contained the dungeon. Another shiver passed over her as she started to walk past, this one having nothing to do with the cold winds.

Sariah was shocked to find her feet walking toward the old iron door to the dungeon almost all by themselves.

Stupid feet, she chided herself. What do you want with him anyway?

Even so, she kept going when something odd caught her eye. The iron door was ajar.

The hairs on the back of her neck stood on end, and she had to take a moment to calm her nerves. If the door was open...

She had to find out for herself. She braced herself for whatever she might find inside and pushed the door open a little further so she could squeeze through it, then darted inside.

She wondered once she was inside if she should close the door behind her. If he was already gone, it wouldn't do any good, and if he wasn't... She wasn't really prepared to face him alone again so soon.

An involuntary shudder ran down her spine. Hastily, she snatched a torch from the wall and lit it with her magic, then started down the stairs.

The dungeon was every bit as dark and musty as she'd remembered it. Only this time, it seemed even more imposing, even though Gabe was probably nowhere near the place.

When her feet touched the bottom of the stairwell, she thought she heard the sounds of labored breathing coming from within the chamber just beyond. There was a torch still burning, too.

That's odd, Sariah thought. She dowsed her own torch, not wanting to bring attention to herself if she could avoid it, and made her way around the corner to face the inevitable.

As she rounded the corner and looked in the cells, she saw Gabe's cell door was wide open, but Gabe himself was nowhere to be seen.

Sariah let out a sigh of relief. He had escaped. Part of her felt like she should be sorrier.

She was still confused about the lit the torch and who the breathing belonged to if Gabe was gone. She inched forward.

"Hello?" she asked. Out of the corner of her eye, she thought she caught a glimpse of a pair of eyes glinting in the firelight, then they were gone again just as quickly. The eyes couldn't have belonged to an adult.

A smile started to creep upon Sariah's lips.

"Heather?" she asked. The flash of eyes appeared again for another second, then they darted behind the bunk in Gabe's cell.

Sariah took several steps forward. "We've been worried about you, Heather," she continued. "Your Gamma and me, that is. Worried sick."

She saw Heather's head bob up from behind the bed, and the girl's big eyes stared at her. "You have?" The voice was barely over a whisper.

"Mm-hmm," Sariah said. "We've been looking for you everywhere." She was almost to Heather, and she knelt next on the floor. "What happened, sweetie?"

"A bad man came," she uttered. "He wanted to hurt us, but Uncle Padron made him go away."

Sariah took the young girl's chin in her hand and pulled it toward her. "He did, huh?"

Heather nodded. Sariah could see tear tracks running down her cheeks. The little girl sniffed. "Uh-huh. I was still scared so I...I didn't mean to, I swear."

"You what, sweetie?" She stroked the girl's hair a few times. "It's okay. I'm not mad. You can tell me, honey. What did you do?"

The girl sniffed a couple more times. "I was just so

scared, Sariah! I tried to remember everything you showed me in your fights, but I couldn't! I...I ran away."

"Hey," Sariah offered. She grabbed the girl's face in her hand again. "It's okay, sweetie. You're too little for all of this. You did nothing wrong."

Heather sniffed again and rubbed her nose with her shirtsleeve. "I didn't?"

Sariah shook her head gently. "No, honey. You did great. You went somewhere safe. That was the right thing to do in that situation."

"It was?" Heather's face brightened at the revelation.

"Mm-hmm." Sariah held a hand out to Heather. "Now, what do you say we take you back to your Gamma?"

Heather grinned at her, then she took Sariah's outstretched hand. The two started walking when Heather turned and waved at something. "Goodbye, ghost," she said cryptically.

Sariah furrowed her brow. "Ghost? What ghost?" She looked around but saw nothing.

"The friendly ghost down here. He helped me when I was sad and lit the torch, then he stayed with me for a while. He said adults can't see him, though, so it's okay that you don't."

Sariah bit her lip. Could the ghost have been Gabe? She shook her head. It didn't matter. Her mission was done. She had a child to reunite with her family.

"When we get back, we'll tell your Gamma all about your big adventure." She leaned in close. "Let's leave the ghost part between us, okay?"

Heather smiled at her. "Okay."

Gabriel watched Sariah and Heather leave his little cell. He thanked the Patriarch he'd had the wherewithal to cast an invisibility spell over himself before Sariah had made it down the stairs. He didn't want to think what would have happened had she seen him down here.

He didn't know why he was still down there and hadn't left the moment the combat had started. It had been easy enough to open the cell door, and with all the commotion, he could have escaped easily.

He still could, in fact. Maybe he was hoping to prove something to Sariah by being a good little boy and staying put. That didn't explain why he hadn't been willing to show himself to her when she'd come down. Nothing made sense to him anymore.

He told himself it was because of the little girl. He'd stayed put for her, to help her out. He was an orphan himself, and there were plenty of nights when he'd been cold and alone. Helping the little girl Heather was a way of paying back the world.

He nodded to himself, semi-satisfied by his answer.

Yet, it continued to gnaw at him. The little girl was gone and Sariah with her. Why didn't he just leave? No prison could hold the great Gabriel without his permission, or so he'd always told himself. Yet here he remained.

What on Irth is wrong with me? he wondered. It was a question that would continue to eat away at him for some time.

CHAPTER SEVEN

"How could you let this happen?" Will asked Sariah. His face was flushed, and his brows were furrowed.

Sariah reared back. "You think I did it? I didn't want Gabe running free any more than you did!"

Will put his hands on his hips. "Well, you were the last one to see him, and there was no evidence of tampering on the locks."

"Pfft." She crossed her arms and gave him a defiant glare. "Like that means anything. He's a better wizard than either of us. He could have easily manipulated the locking mechanism."

He raised a finger and wagged it at her but said nothing. After a few moments, he turned his back to her. "You were still the last one there," he called over his shoulder.

Sariah growled. "Well, you were in charge of guarding the dungeon, and we all saw how that turned out."

Will spun on his heels and stomped one of his feet. Heat rushed to his cheeks. "Now listen here! Albert is one of my best men. I put him in charge of the dungeon because I knew I could count on him to do anything. Besides, you certainly seemed to be fond of him when he came to rescue you."

This time Sariah stomped. "Humph. Some guard he turned out to be then."

Will's jaw dropped, and he sat stunned. After several moments, he straightened up and broke the silence. "Well, I guess it's really no one's fault, then, is it?"

Sariah gave him an "I told you so" look.

His features slackened and he cocked his head. "What are we fighting for again?"

She shrugged. "Beats me. You just got all huffy for no reason. What choice did I have but to rise to the bait?"

Will's cheeks started to turn red again, but he forced himself to calm down. Sariah was really good at getting on his nerves, and yet he kept coming back for it anyway.

"So now our prisoner is on the loose again, and we have two major enemies out there wanting us dead."

"That about sums it up, yeah. We're so screwed." She smiled and gave him a wink.

That brought a grin to his own face. "Not yet," he reasoned. "We just need a plan."

Sariah yawned for the second time. It was early in the morning of the next day. Too early if you asked her. The sun was barely peeking out in the sky, and the air was a little crisp.

She was standing huddled in the corner of the court-yard with Will, Harvey, Padron, and Albert. Sean was still in the infirmary, or he would have been there, too. Albert and Sean tended to be pretty inseparable.

"We need a plan," Will said quietly.

"Agreed," Harvey added with a nod.

Sariah rolled her eyes and stifled another yawn. "We all know that much, geniuses," she said. She was still a little annoyed with Will for accusing her of letting Gabe go yesterday. Getting back at him with petty comments felt altogether appropriate.

Will looked a little red and opened his mouth but didn't say anything. Instead, he lowered his head and studied the map he had laid out in front of them.

"So, anyone have a place to start?" Sariah continued. "We got a big surprise from the Dusk Ravens last time." She shuddered. "I'm not eager to repeat that experience."

"We need more men," Padron chimed in. "And better weapons."

"That much is obvious," Will said in a huff. "It's not like troops and weapons are falling from the sky. Just where do you think we can get these magical troops and weapon stores from, anyway?"

Padron shrugged. "People I can't help with, but me trusty arm can forge a mighty weapon." He flexed his muscles to accentuate the point. "Just point me to a forge an' I'll be happy to help ye there."

"That will only do so much. Good steel is no match for the Dusk Raven mages, even in the most skilled of hands. We saw that all too plainly in the invasion," Will replied. He pulled on his face and shook his head. "They'd have to be the best weapons I've ever seen."

The rearick rubbed his beard a few times. "Perhaps they

can be," he said. He snapped his fingers. "Back at home tha mages used amphoralds fer magitech weapons. Those were a thing o' beauty. With a magitech weapon in hand, even the lowliest of yer soldiers would be a match fer a mage or two."

Will's eyes brightened. "That's not a bad idea, rearick," he answered slowly. "But no one here knows how to power amphoralds, so that option is closed to us. It was a good idea, though."

Padron's face darkened a bit and he lowered his head. "Bah." He threw up his hands in defeat.

The five of them sat in their little huddle in silence. Sariah was doing her best not to look anyone in the eye. She had to admit, she was fresh out of ideas. Besides, her attention wasn't completely on the meeting.

Her mind was still consumed with thoughts of her meeting with the Master. It had gone so poorly. He'd reduced her to a useless puddle with nothing more than a touch. What kind of power could stand against that?

She shook her head and let out a low sigh.

"I still think Padron's idea is worth looking into," Harvey said at last, breaking the quiet. "We've got loads of amphoralds from the mines in Chatwick. Given some time, I'm sure one of us could figure out how to power them."

"Aye, ye might lad," Padron added. "Will might be right on this one. Do it wrong, an' tha amphoralds will blow up in yer face. I don't think ye be wantin' that."

Harvey looked crestfallen. "It's still the best idea we've got going for the moment."

"Maybe not," a chill voice broke through the air. It was Ilene.

Everyone turned to face her. She looked disheveled like she hadn't slept a wink in the three days since the attack. Sariah figured she probably hadn't. While she had no idea what it was like to lose that many people, she had lost enough to be empathetic.

A collective gasp came from the group.

"My lady," Will said at once, bowing low.

Ilene waved at him dismissively with one of her hands. "Please, dispense with the formalities," she implored him. "The time for such frivolities is long past."

"Apologies, my lady," Will said with another bow of his head. "We were just..."

"Having a war council without me?" Ilene finished for him.

Will's cheeks turned bright crimson, and he gave her a weak grin. "My lady, we would never."

She waved at him dismissively again. "Of course you would. After my actions the other day, who could blame you?" She lowered her gaze, and her voice broke a little as she spoke. "I am the one who should be apologizing."

Will looked confused. "For what, my lady? I went directly against your orders. I brought this attack upon us. I deserve to be stripped of rank."

"Nonsense. We had already stirred the hornet's nest. The attack would have come in due time anyway. I see that now with a clarity that I lacked before. My isolationist tendencies are not going to win us this war."

She raised her head and looked at each of them in turn. "I am the one that should be apologizing. To each and every one of you. I only hope you can someday forgive me for my lack of action."

Albert was the first to chime in. "You did what you thought was best, my lady." There were several nods at this. "In your place, I likely would have done the same."

Ilene smiled at him. It was an odd smile that didn't look like it belonged on her face. "Thank you, Albert." She reached out and touched his face. "Your words are too kind."

Albert beamed at her and bowed his head, then she withdrew and faced the group again. "Anyway, back to the war council. I think I may have a solution to our amphorald issue."

Her eyes sought out Sariah's. Sariah felt like Ilene was staring through her more than at her, and it was a little unnerving, but she did her best to stand strong.

"Sariah dear," Ilene said, her voice a little shaky.

"Yes, my lady?" she replied.

"Do you remember that little incident a few weeks ago with the Dusk Raven contingent from the south that you so conveniently...helped with?"

The memories came flooding back, and she gave Ilene a sheepish grin. That was when she'd gone off on her own to steal tech secrets from the Dusk Raven caravan. Only the secrets had turned out to be a person who had later escaped.

A light went off in her head. "Do you mean to say that man's still alive?"

Ilene nodded. "If our latest scouting report is to be believed, yes. There's a small Dusk Raven research facility due east of here. Word is your little escapee is holed up there, hard at work on amphorald research. If he could be persuaded to join us instead..."

"Then we'd have just the weapon we need to turn the tide in this conflict!" Will finished for her. His face had brightened considerably. "My lady, that's a masterstroke. We must plan an assault at once!"

"I'll come!" Albert chimed in. He had his hand raised high in the air.

Sariah smiled at him, then at Will. "I'll go, too. I've been a little bored standing around here waiting anyway." In truth, she was scared the Master would come back to finish her off, so being somewhere far from here sounded really nice.

Will flashed her a grin and nodded. "It's settled then." He turned to face Padron. "Rearick, while we're gone, I want you to start building weapons for us that can house amphoralds. I want to have a mountain of arms waiting when we get back."

Padron gave Will a stiff salute. "Aye, sir. Ye can count on old Padron."

"That only solves one of our problems. We still need more people," Will said. "Anyone have a grand suggestion on that front?"

Sariah looked around at the assembled group. Everyone was lost in thought, but no one was piping up with a solution. After a few minutes, an idea came to her.

"What about recruiting in Stratton?" she asked. "The Dusk Raven presence there is all but gone now that we liberated it. I'm sure there are some people there who would love to join our cause."

"Hmm." Will rubbed his chin a few times. "It's an interesting thought. The thing is, we're not really sure what the current situation is in Stratton. All of our eyes there went dark shortly after we attacked." He threw his hands up. "For all we know, the Dusk Ravens have redoubled their guard efforts in the last couple of weeks. It could be a veritable fortress, and we'd have no clue."

Sariah felt deflated. "I didn't realize," she mumbled. "Sorry."

Will shook his head and placed a hand on her shoulder. "No, no, nothing to be sorry about. It was still a good idea. We will send a few scouts to investigate and report back. Just a few, though. We don't exactly have a lot of people to spare at the moment."

Harvey raised his hand. "What about Chatwick?"

Several heads looked up.

"What about them?" Will asked after a moment.

Harvey shrugged. "Maybe the townsfolk could help. I could go and check it out."

"It's a thought, but I'm not sure kid," Will countered. "That town has already suffered a lot, and you already brought some of their most able-bodied with you the last time. We need warriors, not more mouths to feed."

Harvey's eyes went wide, and he stood a little more erect. "I know my people! When the chips are down, they'll help. Every last one of them."

Will looked at him for a moment, then sighed. "If it's our last resort, maybe. Let's give Stratton a chance first. There are far more people up there, anyway, and we're in desperate need of people right now."

Harvey continued to lock eyes with Will, then finally he nodded. "Fine. We'll do it your way."

The two kept chatting for a moment, with Ilene butting in from time to time, but Sariah didn't hear any of it. The mention of Chatwick had stirred a memory of something the Master had said to her, and it was clouding her thoughts, refusing to let go.

What was it he'd said? *"You and everyone you know will face my wrath."*

She bit her lip almost hard enough to draw blood. The pain brought her back to the conversation briefly.

"You can't afford not to send me," Harvey was telling Will. "I'm the best magic-user you've got. I can get up there and back in no time."

"True," Will replied, eyeing him cautiously. "But your mental magic game sucks. Stealth is required for this recon mission. If you need to go invisible at a moment's notice, then what?"

Harvey looked defiant, but also a bit defeated.

They argued further, but Sariah blocked them out and returned to her earlier thought. What had the Master meant?

At the time, she'd been convinced it was just puffery said in anger. She had been pretty defiant and had practically been done for right then. What did it matter what the man said? Now she wasn't so sure.

She was fairly certain there had been a deeper meaning, and she thought she knew exactly what he'd meant.

"Chatwick!" Sariah shouted.

All eyes turned on her at once. She felt her cheeks redden, and she gave them a sheepish grin.

Will rubbed his head. "We already agreed Chatwick was a last resort, remember? Please, stay with us for the whole conversation."

Sariah steeled herself to remain firm. "No, you don't

understand." She took a few deep breaths, then clenched and unclenched her fists. "Chatwick. The people there are in danger!"

Will and Harvey cocked their heads, and it was Will who spoke first. "How can you be so sure?"

"It was something the Master said to me. He said everyone I know would suffer." She locked eyes with Will. "Chatwick. He's going to attack it. That's what he meant. I'm sure of it."

Will rolled his eyes. "Look Sariah, I'm sure you're still a little traumatized by your meeting with the Master." He looked around at the group and waved his arms to encompass them. "Heck, we all would be, wouldn't we?"

Everyone nodded in agreement.

"He could have meant anything by that. He had you right where he wanted you and was just trying to instill fear in you before he finished you off." A sigh escaped his lips. "There's no reason to think he meant anything by it."

Sariah shook her head. Will's words made sense, but she was sure she'd interpreted things correctly. "No. No, you weren't there. You didn't see how much he hated me. You didn't feel it. I did. I'm right on this one."

"I believe her," Harvey chimed in.

She looked at him. He was standing tall, and he shot her one of his signature dopey grins.

Will opened his mouth to argue, but Harvey cut him off. "Look, has she ever given you a reason to doubt her in the past? If she says Chatwick's in danger, then Chatwick's in danger."

Sariah beamed at Harvey, then shot Will an icy glare. "See? Harvey agrees with me."

Will looked at both of them, mouth agape. Then he threw his hands up in defeat and sighed. "Fine. If you two are so sure about this, we'll send someone to check on Chatwick. We can only spare a few people."

"I'll do it," Sariah said. "It's my idea. I'll go."

"No, my dear," Ilene replied. "You must go with Will to the Dusk Raven stronghold. Your talents will be needed there." She smiled at her. "Besides, you are the only one who has seen the amphorald mage's face. How else are we to recognize him if not with your help?"

Sariah bit her lip. Ilene was right, of course, but she really wanted to check on the people of Chatwick. Mrs. Hensworth, the Thomassons, Harvey's father. They were all in danger, and it was her fault. How could she abandon them in their hour of need?

"It's okay, Sariah," Harvey said. He walked up and put a hand on her shoulder. "I'll go to Chatwick. I'll bring everyone back safe and sound. You can count on me."

She looked up into Harvey's eyes. There was a grim determination there, and also a certain gleam. He was happy to be going home, if only for a few days.

A smile broke out on her own face and she nodded. Harvey would keep them safe. He'd keep them all safe for her. They were his people, too.

"Okay," she said after a moment's silence. She knelt and looked at Bear. "Go with him, Bear," she commanded. "Protect them."

The animal whined but walked over to Harvey.

Sariah's chest eased a little. The two of them would do everything they could to protect their friends back home.

"What about the Stratton recon op?" Will demanded.

His face was bright red, and he had a death glare. "Who's going to man that now?"

"I will," a voice called out from behind the group. Everyone turned to look. It was from Sean. He looked well-rested and much better than he had three days ago. The healers had done their work well.

Will smiled at the young man. He went over to the lad and clapped him on the back. "Sean! Good to see you out and about. You should be resting, not running a stealth mission."

Sean waved at him dismissively. "Nonsense. I'm fit as a fiddle." He pounded his chest a few times for emphasis. "Besides, I can move quietly enough. I know my way around an invisibility spell." He smiled broadly, showing his teeth.

Will eyed him carefully. "Are you sure, lad?"

The boy nodded. "Doubly sure. Can't take no more sitting around and waiting, anyway. I've friends to avenge. Can't do that from a hospital bed."

"Heh." Will clapped him on the back again. "That's my boy! Fine, you'll manage the Stratton operation."

He looked out over the assembled group. "Does everyone have their marching orders, then?"

Everyone nodded.

"Good." He paused for a moment. "We'll meet back here in a week once the missions are complete and go from there." He looked at Padron. "In the meantime, I expect great progress from you."

Padron saluted him again. "I won't let ya down, William."

Seemingly satisfied, the group broke up. Padron went

one way, Sean and Ilene another, and Harvey in yet another. Sariah, Albert, and Will stayed put.

After a few moments, Will spoke again. "So. Who's ready to go storm a Dusk Raven base and get some payback for the last few days?"

Sariah's eyes brightened, and she gave him a broad smile. "Let's do it."

CHAPTER EIGHT

Harvey stifled a yawn. It was nearing the end of his watch, and the sun was peeking over the horizon through the tops of the trees.

Damn if he wasn't still tired. The last three days of marching had taken their toll, but their end goal was almost in sight.

He looked at his sleeping companions. Bear had stayed glued to his hip the whole time and was still just inches away. Justine had insisted she come with him for some odd reason, along with one of the miners from Chatwick that he'd liberated named Ben.

Ben's reason for coming along, he understood. The guy had a wife and kid back in Chatwick. But Harvey didn't know why Justine always wanted to follow him around everywhere.

Another yawn threatened to interrupt his thoughts, and he did his best to keep it from coming to fruition with a vigorous stretch or two.

Then he got about the task of waking his companions.

Bear was already yawning, and Ben was easy enough. He walked over to the man and shook him gently, and the man roused from his slumber.

Justine, on the other hand, was a problem. That girl liked her sleep a lot.

"Hey!" he called, poking her gently with one finger. "Hey, it's time to get up."

The sound of a half-snort, half-snore greeted him in response.

Harvey groaned. He was going to have to do more. He placed his hand gingerly on her shoulder and shook it. "Wakey-wakey," he said. "Time to get up."

This time he got a wild hand wave in his direction, but the girl stayed put, and her eyes remained shut.

He rolled his eyes. He hadn't wanted to resort to this, but he had little choice. He crouched down close to her ear and shouted. "Bacon's ready!"

That got the desired reaction. Justine shook a little, then shot up into a sitting position faster than Harvey would have thought possible. She looked around bleary-eyed for a moment, then rubbed her eyes and let out a yawn while her arms stretched.

It was an odd sight to behold. Harvey remembered thinking Sariah woke so gracefully when they were together, but this? This was another thing entirely.

"Where's tha bacon?" Justine asked, looking around confused.

Harvey's cheeks turned red and he shrugged. "Ben must have eaten it all," he lied, pointing to their companion.

Ben's eyes went wide, and he reared back a half step. "I did what now?"

"Aww damn," Justine said, snapping her fingers together. "Ain't that a rub. Ah well, nothin' ta be done about it now." She stretched again, then got to her feet and started to put away her sleeping roll.

"Yeah, Ben sure loves his bacon," Harvey continued. His cheeks were flushed and he had a dopey grin on his face, but Justine didn't seem to notice.

Ben leaned in close and whispered in his ear. "I can't keep being your fall guy forever, you know."

Harvey shrugged. "We reach Chatwick today. No need for longevity," he whispered back, covering his mouth with his hand so Justine wouldn't see.

His companion's face brightened, and he let out an involuntary chuckle. "Aye, sir."

"Anyway," Harvey said. "Let's clean up and get a move on. We're about an hour from Chatwick, and time's a-wastin'."

Justine and Ben both nodded. The three cleaned up their camp quickly and set about marching with Harvey in the lead.

While they walked, Harvey wondered what they'd find when they got back to Chatwick. He'd left the town in pretty good shape. The Dusk Ravens were all dead, except Jeffrey. No one knew where that man had gotten off to, anyway, but without his army, he was as good as dead.

He didn't know if the town was really in danger once again. He wanted to believe Sariah, but he couldn't be sure.

It's not like the town provides any military advantage, he thought. At least, not anymore.

Chatwick undoubtedly still had stores of amphoralds buried under the dirt somewhere, but with the town's miners all but vacated, there was no one to unearth them. That left it just a simple town in the middle of nowhere. Not exactly the kind of place a military genius like the Master would dedicate troops to.

As they got closer, Harvey thought he could smell the fires of the Thomassons' bakery firing, cooking bread and other baked goods for the town. Their bakery was famous, and one could often smell their wares from miles around in any direction.

The smell brought him back to when he was a young child, trying to convince his parents to buy him some sort of pastry and failing miserably.

A smile crept across his lips. Those were good times.

As they kept going, the scent of the flames only intensified, and with them came the smell of ashes and soot, stronger than anything one tiny bakery could create.

Harvey's blood ran cold, and a shiver ran up his spine. He reached out a hand to stop his companions and they complied. "Do you two smell that?"

Justine whiffed and her nose wrinkled. "It smells like..."

"Death," Ben finished. Justine nodded.

A sinking feeling washed over Harvey as a knot formed in his stomach. He thought he might be sick, but then it passed.

He looked up ahead and scanned the horizon. He could see the haze of smoke filtering through the tops of the trees coming from Chatwick's direction.

Bear shot forward in between his legs, faster than he could blink.

"Wait, Bear!" he cried. But the dog was gone. Without a thought for his safety, Harvey bounded through the trees after him. Sariah would never forgive him if harm came to Bear under his watch.

"Harvey, wait!" Justine called after him.

He ran as fast as his feet could take him, wild thoughts running through his head.

Please, Patriarch. Please don't let me be too late.

Soon, the trees cleared and Chatwick came into view. Bear had stopped well short of the outskirts. Harvey breathed a quick sigh of relief, but it didn't last as his eyes took in the rest of the scene.

Thick, black smoke filled the air. It made it hard to see anything other than the town gate, which hung in tatters. There was an intense wave of heat that forced him back into the cover of the trees.

All the color drained from Harvey's face. He was too late. Chatwick was in flames.

The sound of someone moaning interrupted the Master's concentration. He looked down at the broken body on the ground at his feet and huffed at it.

Moments later, the body let loose its final death wail and stopped moving altogether.

The Master sighed, then tsked at the dead body before shoving it out of the way. "These local townsfolk just don't have the same level of power as their city-bound counterparts," he said to the air around him.

"No matter. There's more of you filth around here. Enough to help me keep these flames going for hours."

He looked up at the sky and noted that the fires

surrounding him were climbing higher even though the fuel for them had all but died out an hour ago. It was a wonder the things magic could accomplish.

Especially when he wasn't the one expending energy to fuel it.

A wicked smile played on his lips. He loved how powerful it made him feel to bend another's nanocytes to his will. It was the ultimate form of control, and it gave him the ability to accomplish things no other mage had ever dreamed of.

Things like this current trap. He'd told Sariah her town would suffer, and just in case that hadn't been clear enough, he'd sent a message to that base of hers, too. She would come for him eventually.

When she did, she'd realize how powerless she was against his might.

Now all he had to do was sit and wait. He used his magic to pull another of his prisoners over and grabbed her forcefully by the arm. He began weaving his spell so he could drain her, too.

Just a little bit longer, now. With his magic, he'd sensed a few new people pop up at the edge of town, not a half-hour ago. One of them had to be her. Just a little more.

Harvey watched in horror as the flames licked higher, consuming the entire town in their path. The fire was immense—bigger than any he'd ever seen or even imag-ined—and nothing had been spared from its terrible wrath.

From behind him, he heard the muffled cries of awe

and terror from Ben and Justine as they made their way through the last of the trees and saw the carnage for themselves.

Ben came running past him, heading for the front gate, where the fires were strongest.

"No Ben!" Harvey cried. He sprinted forward and grabbed the man by his shoulder.

The older man fought against Harvey's grip, but Harvey was too strong.

"Please!" Ben pleaded. "My wife and daughter are in there!"

"I know." Harvey put his other hand on Ben's other shoulder to try and calm the man further. "It's a raging inferno in there. It's not safe." He took a quick glance at the flames inching ever higher, then back at Ben.

"Look at me, Ben," he implored.

Ben's eyes went back to the blaze, so Harvey pulled on the man's face until they were looking eye to eye. He shook the man. "Snap out of it, man!" He was getting desperate. "Look, my father's in there, too, okay?"

A look of recognition mixed with pity and empathy crossed Ben's face. Finally, the man seemed to come out of his daze and he looked at Harvey. The older man swallowed hard once before saying anything.

"You're right. You're always right, Harvey." A tear started to form in his eye. "My family, they're...they're..."

"I know." Harvey took a deep breath and relaxed his grip on Ben, fairly confident that he'd calmed down enough not to do anything stupid.

He paced around for a moment to clear his head. "Look, Ben. The fires have to die down eventually, right? It won't be this bad forever. Then we can go in and search for survivors."

The plan sounded decent in his head, but after saying it, he knew Ben was thinking the same thing he was—by the time the fires died down, there wouldn't be any survivors to find.

A long sigh escaped his lips, and he looked at the flames again. If anything, they were increasing in volatility, not decreasing, which should have been impossible for a blaze this advanced.

There has to be a better way, he thought. But what?

He kept thinking, sparing glances at Ben, Justine, and the raging inferno in turn. Justine seemed completely calm. He admired her ability to stay calm under intense pressure.

He admired it, and also hated her just a little bit. Chatwick had been home to her too, for a time. Why wasn't she more upset? He pushed the thought from his mind. It was something to worry about later. Infighting of any kind really wasn't needed right now.

Then a thought came to him. He remembered the fire that had consumed Sariah's house all those months ago, at the start of their quest. He and Sariah had been surrounded by intense flames, and yet they'd come out unscathed. He tried to remember how she'd done it.

The answer came to him quickly. Though neither of them had known it at the time, she'd used magic to control the flames and force them away.

If he could use magic to summon fire, why not use it to control it?

He rubbed his hands together and started focusing on the new plan. Eyeing the town, it was immediately obvious that the blaze was too widespread for him to control the whole thing. Perhaps he could control a part of it, just enough to let one person through unharmed.

Harvey looked at Ben and Justine. "Stay here," he implored. "I have a plan. It's risky, but I think it will work."

Justine side-eyed him. "Yer not thinkin' o' going in there, are ya?" Her tone sounded almost comical.

He flashed her a big, dopey grin. "That's exactly what I'm thinking. I'm just going to scan the area for any survivors. You three stay put, I'll be back in a flash."

Justine opened her mouth and started yelling something, but he didn't hear what it was. He'd already turned and started moving toward the town gate as fast as his feet would take him, and the sound of the roaring flames filled his ears instead.

"Here goes nothing," he said aloud, though likely no one could hear him, either. "Patriarch, if you're listening, please let my magic be enough."

Then he took a deep breath and plunged into the flaming maw that was the front gate.

Jeffrey huffed once and gave the Master a wry grin. "You sure they're going to come?" he asked the older man.

The Master gave him a broad smile. "Oh, they'll come all right. I made sure of it."

Jeffrey shrugged and let out a slight cough. "Whatever you say, old man."

The Master raised a hand and backhanded him. The

blow had more force behind it than Jeffrey had expected, and he was forced back a step.

He reached a hand up to his cheek and felt something wet. Eyeing his hand, he saw a little bit of blood there. He looked at the Master with fire in his eyes. A fire that matched their surroundings.

"Don't talk like that to me," the Master demanded. He had an evil aura to him.

Jeffrey huffed again but backed off. The Master was ridiculously powerful, and he wasn't strong enough to cross him. Not yet, at least.

Soon enough, Master. Soon I'll be stronger than you. The thoughts of what he would do filled him with glee.

Outwardly, he just shrugged. "As you say, Master," he managed. "Any more orders for me?"

The Master shrugged. "No, you've done enough redecorating around here already. You can go."

Jeffrey gave the Master a small bow, then readied the teleportation spell that would take him away from the shattered husk that was his former town of Chatwick. A slight frown creased his face as he thought about how he'd miss Harvey's reaction. Alas. It wasn't meant to be.

Harvey coughed. It felt like his lungs wanted to come out of his mouth.

Controlling the flames had been easy enough with his magic. All it took was a gentle shove to push them out of the way.

But the smoke was everywhere. He ripped a piece of

cloth off the sleeve of his shirt and tied it over his mouth. It was rudimentary, but he hoped it would keep him from inhaling the worst of the fumes.

Passing by another house, he took a quick look inside. It appeared to be empty. So far, all the houses had been empty or at least appeared that way. It was hard to tell through the haze.

He kept wondering who would do such a thing to his little town. Of course, only one name came up —Jeffrey.

Harvey's teeth clenched as he thought about the old mine foreman. He should have made sure the man was dead when he'd had the chance, but the man had escaped, and obviously still held a grudge.

When I find you, Jeffrey, I'm going to tear you into tiny little pieces so small they can't even identify you.

The thought helped mollify him and calm his nerves.

He walked forward another few paces and pushed another spout of flame away in the process. Then he saw it. Through the smoke and haze in front of him, he could make out the shape of someone standing in the middle of the town.

Harvey's hand tightened around the hilt of one of the two swords he carried, and he inched forward just a little more.

You're a dead man, Jeffrey.

———

The Master looked around. He was tapping his foot impatiently on the ground.

Where are you, Sariah? he thought with a scowl. No answer came.

It was surprisingly hard to see anything through the smoke and the flames other than his immediate surroundings. A downside of the current trap, he supposed.

He had enough bodies to keep it stoked for hours without tapping into his own reserves. It would be worth it when he saw the delicious look of despair on her face.

Yes, he mused. That delightful look of worthlessness will make it all worthwhile.

He thought he sensed someone approaching from the edge of the flames.

A smile crept across the Master's lips, and he clenched one of his fists. Here, little girl. Come closer now—Daddy's waiting.

Harvey took both swords out of their scabbards. The strange man who looked vaguely like Jeffrey was standing still like he hadn't noticed Harvey yet. Even if it wasn't Jeffrey—and Harvey was fairly certain it was—the man was obviously controlling the flames. Ending his life wasn't even a question.

A wry grin crossed his face. This was his chance.

With all the force he could muster, he loosed both blades into the air, aiming for the strange man's center of mass.

The blades flew true on their path, guided by Harvey's magic. When they were inches from the strange man's middle, they stopped moving and fell to the ground.

Harvey frowned and tried to force the blades up again, but it was as though a force stronger than his own was keeping them down.

He growled and leaped through the fire, making his presence known. At the same time, he swept up one of the many gouts of flame that surrounded him and commanded it to crash into the strange man.

This, too, stopped inches short of its goal and dissipated into nothing.

Desperate, Harvey pulled out a dagger from his belt.

"You'll die by my hand for this, Jeffrey!"

The strange man cocked his head and put his hand out.

Harvey felt his pace slow, then it felt like two strong, invisible chains locked his legs into place. He struggled against them, unable to break free.

"Who is Jeffrey?" the strange man asked. "Oh, you must mean Humboldt. I knew he had a cover name, but not what it was."

Harvey shouted something unintelligible. He began to feel real fear. Whoever he was attacking was much stronger than he was.

His mind raced, trying to think of something, anything he could do to break free and gain the upper hand, but his mind drew a blank.

The strange man took a step forward so his face was visible. Harvey recognized it immediately, and his hair stood on edge.

"You!" he spat at the Master. "You're..."

"Not what you expected?" the Master finished for him. He shrugged. "In all fairness, you're not who I expected, either."

The Master stepped closer and pulled the cloth from Harvey's face.

"You're not Sariah," he said slowly. "You know of her. I can tell that much easily enough."

Harvey furrowed his brow. He didn't know how this stranger would know that.

Of course, with mental magic, such things would be possible. He seethed while trying to clear his mind, hoping it would break the man's spell over him.

"You're one of those brats that came to rescue her in Talon's Reach, aren't you?" the Master continued. He seemed unfazed by Harvey's actions.

"Hmm, yes, that would make sense. You and that Will character. Did I get his name right?" He glanced at Harvey, then walked around him in a slow circle without waiting for an answer. "I believe I did. Only they're not here, and you are. Such a curious turn of events."

The Master was behind him. "Where are they, hmm?"

Harvey flashed him a dopey grin. "Go to hell."

The Master chuckled. "Oh, I assure you I will. First, I think I'll stop by a certain Dusk Raven stronghold east of Talon's Reach. Base station Zebra. That sound about right?"

Harvey's blood went cold, and the color drained from his face. How could he possibly know that? Then he knew the answers had come from his own mind. He was powerless to stop the Master's cruel tricks.

Sariah! I have to warn her!

The Master let out another laugh. He was in front of Harvey again. "Of course, you would think that. You're but a puppet in a badly run play." The Master looked at him and leaned in close. His eyes got a dark gleam in them.

One of the Master's small, knobby hands caressed his cheek, and Harvey felt all the power in his body draining from him. In that slight second of contact, he felt completely helpless.

The Master gave him a wry smile. "You, child, why you're about to exit stage right."

Harvey let out a yelp and let instinct take over, stabbing upward as hard as he could without thought. The blade found its purchase in the Master's shoulder.

The Master howled in pain and staggered backward. As he did so, Harvey felt the bonds around him start to loosen.

"You little shit!" the Master screamed. He looked down at the wound, then back at Harvey.

Just a little more, Harvey thought. He was almost free of the bonds.

"Serves you right!" he shouted. "Come closer, and I'll give you a matching one for the other arm!"

The Master glowered at him. "Why you little nuisance. I should squish you underfoot like the bug you are!" He took a step toward Harvey and wagged a finger at him. Harvey could see several tendrils of flame following the Master's every movement.

At the same time, the bonds holding him in place finally gave way.

Harvey grinned up at the Master, then leaped forward, aiming for his throat. Only, his fingers never found purchase. The Master was no longer anywhere to be found. He had escaped his fate, just like Jeffrey, or rather Humboldt, had before him.

"That'll teach you to underestimate me!" Harvey called after the Master. He knew it was likely for naught. The man was undoubtedly miles away by now.

Harvey coughed and let himself fall to the ground. He was starting to feel the combined effects of both the smoke and the magic drain, and he was getting weak.

Just as he was about to close his eyes, he heard a muffled cry from close by. He opened his eyes and looked over where the Master had been. There were a couple of bodies on the ground, and one of them seemed to be moving.

"Hang on!" Harvey cried.

He half-crawled over to the moving body. It was a woman, and it looked like someone he recognized. Then slowly it dawned on him, it was Ben's wife!

She looked weak and was covered in soot, but other-wise unharmed.

Harvey breathed a huge sigh of relief. Not only had he found Ben's wife, but she was safe.

"Martha," he said. The woman's eyes opened to stare at him. "It's me, Harvey. Listen, can you stand?"

The woman looked away for a second. She shook her head. Shrugging his shoulders, he stood up, then reached a hand out to her. "Grab on, and I'll put you over my back. Come on, Ben's waiting for you."

Martha smiled up at him and took the offered hand. "My Ben came for me?"

Harvey nodded and smiled at her. "Indeed, he did." He

hefted the woman over his shoulder. She was lighter than he expected. "Come on, let's get you two back together."

He took one last look at the remaining bodies to see if any of them moved, but none did. With a grave sigh and a shake of his head, he started back through the flames.

Ben paced around the little clearing anxiously. He looked over at Justine for perhaps the hundredth time since Harvey had left.

"I'm going in after him," he told her resolutely.

"Ye'll do no such thing," Justine insisted, shaking her head.

"He could be in danger in there all alone! Someone has to help him!"

Justine tsked. "Do I need ta get me club out again?" she threatened. Her eyes dropped to the wooden mace at her side then trailed back up to him.

Ben's expression soured, and the color drained from his face. "Uh no. No, I think I'll stay put."

She grinned at him. "That's a good choice."

Ben was worried about Harvey and his family both, and as the moments ticked by, his concern only grew.

He paced for a few more minutes, then miraculously, he felt the rage of the fire start to die down.

Turning to face Justine, he grinned at her. "The fire's dying down. Now I'm going in there after him," he insisted.

Instead of arguing, Justine stood and stared at the front gate with her mouth ajar, pointing.

It took a second, but then Ben saw it too. The distinct

shape of someone coming through the flames toward them.

Harvey materialized from the flames, looking haggard and carrying someone over his shoulder.

Ben recognized her instantly. "Martha!" he cried. Then he fell to his knees in a prayer of thanks to the Matriarch.

Harvey grinned at him, then fell down to his knees. "Honey, I'm home!" he exclaimed. Then he fell face-first into the dirt.

When Harvey woke up, it was almost dark. He sat up with a start and looked around to find the faces of Bear, Ben, Justine, and Martha staring back at him.

He looked over at the town of Chatwick. The fires had died down completely, though the ground still looked hot, and smoke was still pouring into the sky. Practically nothing was left standing of the city itself.

He breathed a sigh of relief that his companions were okay.

"Did you?" Harvey managed.

"Search the town?" Ben finished for him.

Harvey nodded. "Yes."

Ben hung his head low. "We did, but we didn't find much. Not even that many bodies. A handful at most."

Harvey rubbed his chin. "Yes, that's what I found during my search, too."

"It seems nothing survived the flames," Ben continued his voice breaking. Harvey figured he was thinking of his daughter's fate.

He put a hand on Ben's shoulder. "I'm sorry, Ben. If only I'd been sooner."

Ben shot up and glared at him. "Now don't you go thinking that. If it hadn't been for you going in there like that, my Martha would be a goner, too!" He pointed in her direction. "What happened to Samantha is terrible, yes, but at least you saved one life!"

Harvey flashed him a weak smile, then hung his head low. "Maybe. How many others suffered? I should have come sooner."

Justine clapped him on the back. "Ye can't be thinkin' like that, now," she told him. "Ben's right. There's nothin' ye could have done."

He sighed. "I suppose you're right." Another thought was gnawing at him. The flames were all-encompassing, yes, but there should have been more bodies.

"Don't you think it's odd that we didn't find any more bodies? Not even a skeleton?"

Justine shrugged. "I guess so. Where're ya going with this?"

Harvey shook his head. "I'm not sure, it's just..." He looked at Ben's wife. "Martha! When the fires started, where did they come from?"

Martha looked a little shaken up by the suddenness of his tone. "I...I don't really know," she offered.

"Come on, think!"

"I...Jeffrey came into town along with some strange man and...and things just started lighting on fire all over the place. When I saw the look in their eyes, I turned to Samantha and told her to run and look for Jackson. He'd keep her safe. Only..."

Harvey reached down and squeezed her shoulder. "Jackson's a smart man. He would have known that flames travel up, not down. If I were him and my town was on fire, I'd head to—"

"The mines!" Ben and Justine cried out at once.

He nodded. "Come, we haven't much time."

The four of them raced through the now-empty streets of Chatwick for the entrance to the mine. They had to climb over and around various bits of rubble on the way, but they made good time.

When they reached the mineshaft, Harvey could see a makeshift door of iron covering half of the entryway. It looked like the selfsame door he'd blown off its hinges during his escape.

A big smile swept across his face. "Ho! Jackson!" he called out.

"We're in here, Harvey!" Jackson's melodious voice answered.

He looked at his companions. "Come, help me move this door out of the way!"

The four grabbed the door by its sides and moved it out of the entryway quickly. Several scared but smiling faces greeted them.

Harvey beamed at the townsfolk. "Jackson, you old coot! Come here!" The priest complied.

After a moment, he pushed the priest back off him and looked him in the eye. "How many of the townsfolk were you able to save?"

It was Jackson's turn to grin. "Almost all of them. Even got your father to get out of his favorite chair at Talesin's before the worst of it started."

Harvey grinned from ear to ear. "Dad's safe? That's good to know."

People started to pour out of the opening. Harvey greeted them in turn.

Ben poked his head around. "Did my little girl find you?" he asked. The worry was plain on his face. "Did Samantha make it?"

Jackson smiled at him and nodded. "She stayed right next to me almost the entire time, just like mommy told her." He looked over his shoulder. "Sammy! Come see your daddy!"

"Daddy!" a little girl's voice squealed. She bounded through the mine opening and into her father's arms.

Harvey looked at the two with a tear in his eye. He hadn't been too late, after all. The town may be gone, but the citizens were safe and sound.

That's all that really mattered.

CHAPTER NINE

Sariah tapped her foot on the ground. Her arms were crossed, and she had a bored expression on her face.

"What are we even doing here?" she asked, rolling her eyes.

Will shrugged. "We're watching the enemy."

She sighed and turned to face him. "I know that, but like, why? Why are we watching when we could be—"

"Fighting?"

Sariah nodded. "Yes, exactly. Fighting. What good is all this watching and waiting doing?"

He gave her a stern expression. "Rule forty-three, remember?"

"Ugh." She threw up her hands in disgust and turned away from him.

Of course, she remembered rule forty-three. She remembered all his stupid rules of engagement and all his little sayings. He'd drilled them into her and the other recruits from the first day of training.

"Know your enemy better than you know yourself," Albert answered. He had a smug grin on his face.

Sariah shot him an icy glare and his smile faded. That kid was always looking for ways to score extra points with Will. It was kind of annoying.

"I know that!" she spat back at him. "It's just I'm not one for sitting around and stuff. I need action!"

Will let out a burst of laughter. "We know, Sariah. You've almost gotten yourself killed from rash action on more than one occasion. Or need I remind you?"

She looked from Will to Albert, who was now staring at her wild-eyed. He was shaking his head with his hands out in front of him as if to say, "leave me out of this."

"Humph," she muttered, then she turned away from them again to hide the fact that her cheeks were turning red. "Like I even asked you."

After a moment, she turned back to face them. "Besides," she started, "you still haven't answered my question, Mr. Strategy. What on Irth are we doing here?"

Will's eyes narrowed, and he furrowed his brow. "You really don't know? I explained it all when we got here two days ago. You were staring straight at me."

"We're watching their guard patterns so we can know exactly when and where to strike," she recited, trying to mimic his voice. "Yes, you told me. We got that down on day one. It's been a whole more day since then, and we're still..."

"Standing around, watching?"

"Uh-huh." She nodded and looked up at him. "Yes, exactly. Why the delay?"

"I had to make sure their patterns wouldn't change.

Some stations have rotating guard schedules. If this was one of them and we didn't know that, we'd be toast."

"So, just how much longer do you want to have us wait and watch anyway?"

He shrugged again. "Another day should do it. Then we can plan our offensive."

A groan escaped her lips. "Aww man, another day of sitting around? I could take them all out by myself before then."

Will shook his head. "Do you have any idea how many Dusk Ravens are here in this stronghold?"

Her eyes narrowed for a second while she thought. Eventually, she shrugged. "I don't know, maybe fifty?"

Will nodded. "At least fifty. Maybe sixty by my estimate. You really think you can take on sixty Dusk Ravens by yourself?"

She gave him a wry grin. "We won't know until we try."

"Heh. I admire your spunk." He clapped her on the back. "We both know you're not that good. At least not yet. I can still beat you on a good day."

"Only on a good day," she added, stabbing her finger into his chest.

"Yes, well, you've improved a little."

She shot him a glare.

"Anyway, back to the subject at hand. Let's say you did take out all the Dusk Ravens here. All sixty of them. Then what?"

Sariah cocked her head to the side. "What do you mean? Then we collect our prisoner and leave."

He shook his head again and sighed. "Don't you remember how skittish he was last time we tried to capture him? Once the commotion started, he'd probably just leave. Then we're back at square one." He leveled his gaze at her. "Worse even. Then we won't even know where he is."

She opened her mouth to argue the point further and wagged her finger at him, but the words didn't come. Instead, she lowered her head and took a half step backward.

It hurt to admit it, but he was right. She bit her lip. Stealth really was the name of the game here.

"Well still, time's of the essence. How much longer until the Master attacks again? What if he attacks while we're gone? Is your defense really going to be that we didn't know how in-depth their guard pattern was?"

It was a low blow, but she was right, too.

Will's cheeks reddened, and she could sense him tensing up like he wanted to strike out at her. Then he took a deep breath, and his face slackened. "I suppose you have a point."

"Fine, we attack an hour after dawn, when the guards are tired. Make sure you're ready for it. In the meantime, we'll talk about strategy and get some rest. We're going to need it."

Sariah smiled up at him. "Yes, sir."

Will looked at both his charges with a stern expression. The mission they were about to undertake was dangerous, and he was having second thoughts. He hoped his plan was flawless.

"Now, so long as we stay together, I can keep an invisibility spell around us to hide from the men. If we get separated..."

"Stay low to the ground, and if trouble comes running, don't hesitate, just teleport to safety," Sariah said to him. She was mimicking his voice again. He found it kind of cute. Annoying, but cute.

He nodded. "That's right. Safety is your top priority. We can attempt an assault again later, but we can't bring you back from the dead."

"Don't worry, Captain," Sariah said with a salute. "We've got our marching orders."

Will's mouth suddenly felt dry, so he licked his lips, but it did little to change things. Was he that worried about Sariah and Albert? Who was he kidding, of course, he was. He felt responsible for the lives of all his soldiers. They were like his children.

He looked deep into both of their eyes and saw nothing but readiness and a tinge of excitement reflected back at him.

"All right, let's go. Remember, take out the animals first. They can—"

"See through the spell. Yes, you told us a hundred times," Sariah interrupted.

"Right." He gulped hard. "Let's get going, then."

With that, the three of them left their concealed area in the bushes and started to approach the small fort. It had tall wooden walls that looked freshly built. Will had spotted two guards placed every hundred feet or so on top of the wall, and four guards at the main gate.

None of those would be a major problem. The guard

dogs they had with them, though, those were another story. There was no fooling them.

Will had a plan for the dogs.

He summoned forth an invisibility spell to cloak the three of them, and they started forward, moving slowly to minimize the noise. Soon, they came into view of the main gate.

The two guard dogs stared at them. The one on the right started to snarl.

He summoned a spell to make it look like the guard dogs were standing at attention and to muffle their noise. If it took, the guards standing next to them wouldn't notice a thing.

Will took another couple of steps forward. He inhaled deeply and tensed for the dogs to come running. The one on the right just stood there and snarled, but the left one dashed forward. The two human guards, though, did nothing.

He breathed a small sigh of relief. So far, so good. Now for part two.

Reaching into his pocket, he pulled out a rather large piece of meat. He tossed it in between both dogs. The two animals raced in and started to fight over it while the human guards remained motionless.

A smile crept over Will's face. Success.

He looked behind him at Sariah and Albert and motioned for them to follow. They complied, and the three of them walked by, unnoticed by the warring dogs or the men who were supposed to keep them out.

Several tense moments later, the three passed the guards and were in the structure proper. Will wiped a bead of sweat from his brow and looked at his charges again. They had made it past the first test but now came the hard part. None of them had any idea what the guard situation was like inside, or where the amphorald mage was kept.

They looked around for a doorway into the inner building. If the mage were anywhere, it would likely be deep inside.

A few minutes later, a doorway came into view. It was guarded by two Dusk Ravens, but thankfully no animals. The door looked sturdy and was closed. There'd be no passing by this pair with mere stealth.

He looked over his shoulder and motioned for his two charges to do their thing.

Albert crept forward and eased up next to the guard on the left, then nodded to him. Sariah was nowhere to be seen.

Will turned again and looked at her. She was biting her lip and staring off into space.

He waved a hand in front of her eyes and she snapped out of it. Then she went and took her place by the other guard.

In one swift motion, they slit the throats of the two guards at the same time, so neither could call for help. It was risky to outright kill them, but riskier still to leave them alive and able to call for help.

Besides, he couldn't keep up both illusions for much longer, and the front gate guards would sense a disturbance soon enough.

With the guards dispatched, Will made his way to the door. It was locked. He looked down at the guards. One of them had a keyring on his belt. He motioned to it, and Albert relieved the guard of the ring.

It took three tries, but he found the right one and slid it into the lock. It came free with barely a hint of a click, but even that small noise still sounded incredibly loud in the stillness of the night.

He pushed the door open fast to disorient anyone who might be on the other side, then he pushed his way into the room ahead of Albert and Sariah. Much to his surprise and relief, the room beyond was empty save for a torch burning on the wall.

Will shut the door just as quickly, then let out the huge breath he'd been keeping in for several seconds. He looked at Sariah with a grave expression.

"What was that waiting around for back there?" he demanded.

She gave him a sheepish grin and her face reddened. "Sorry," she replied. "I couldn't help it, I was thinking about Chatwick."

He let out a low growl. "What? Rule one, remember?" He wanted to smack her on the head.

Sariah shot him a defiant glare. "Always keep your mind in the present," she spat back at him. "I'm sorry! I tried. It's just they're my people out there, and they're in trouble. I just know it."

"Harvey's out there, remember? Your town couldn't be in better hands."

She bit her lip and nodded. "I know. It's just I could have sworn I felt something back there. Like something bad was happening. Only what I don't know." She looked at him expectantly. "You haven't felt or heard anything, have you?"

He felt his cheeks start to redden, and he turned away. Do I tell her? Does she have a right to know?

Sariah's eyes went wide, and she shot him an evil look. "You do know something! Out with it!"

Will gave her a sheepish grin and tried to dodge her. He supposed she had a right to know, after all. Even if it would endanger the mission.

"Fine," he said. "The morning we left, someone found a note at the front gate. It said Chatwick was in trouble, and if you didn't show up, everyone's life was forfeit. There, I said it."

Sariah's jaw dropped open, and he heard Albert gasp.

"You were, what? Just not going to tell me?" Sariah demanded.

He shrugged. "What difference would it have made?" He threw his hands up in defeat. "Look, it was a trap. That much was obvious. Harvey had already gone off anyway. We needed you here, not there. If we'd told you..."

"We?" Sariah's eyes were like daggers. "So Ilene knew, too?" She turned and shook her head. "I felt like I could trust you two."

Will reached out and placed a hand on Sariah's shoulder. "Look, once this is over, I'll take you straight there if you want. Promise. It was for the best. You have to believe that."

Sariah looked at him, her eyes still on fire. "I don't have to believe anything," she insisted. "You're right, we need to finish this mission first."

He let out a huge sigh. "Thank the Patriarch. Let's get going."

Before they could do anything else, two Dusk Ravens came crashing into the room. During the earlier argument, Will had let the invisibility spell drop, and they'd been visible for a half-second.

"Invaders!" one of them shouted. It was the last thing he ever did. A second later, a dagger was sticking out of his throat. A similar one was protruding from the throat of his friend.

Albert sat in the corner, looking smug with his arms crossed.

Will blinked a few times. "Did you?"

Albert nodded.

Will walked over and clapped the lad on the back. "Good show, man!" The kid beamed up at him. "Now, let's get going. Our cover's blown. Time is of the essence."

Both Albert and Sariah nodded, and together the three started down the hallway. Fortunately, the building was a small one, and there weren't very many rooms.

The first room they came across looked to be a barracks. Will had Sariah take a quick look inside to see if she could spot the mage they were looking for, but he wasn't there. He shut the door as quietly as he could, and they ran on.

Three rooms later, they came across a strange-looking door. It was made of some type of metal, whereas the rest of the doors were made of wood.

Will motioned for Sariah and Albert to stop. He rummaged around for the keyring. This had to be the right door.

It only took two tries to find the right key, but each second that passed by while he tried them seemed to take an eternity. Somehow, they'd escaped the notice of the rest of the guards so far, even with the earlier outburst, but with four dead bodies in their wake and a whole barracks just a few doors down, it wouldn't be much longer.

The door slid open with a loud creak of metal on metal, and Will forced his way in ahead of his companions. Once they were all inside, he looked around. The room was sparsely populated, with a bed in one corner and a desk covered in parchment and strange whitish gemstones in another.

A lone figure sat at the desk, staring at him.

Sariah pointed her finger at the man. "That's him, all right. That's the guy we're looking for."

The lone figure blinked a few times. "That's a strange way to address oneself when meeting someone new," he said casually, like their breaking in to capture him was the most normal thing in the world.

Will did a double-take. "Beg pardon?"

The mage let out a low chuckle. "Of course, in all fairness, I didn't offer my own name, either." He stood up and stuck out one of his hands. "The name's Scott." He looked first at Will, then at Albert and Sariah. "You three, I imagine, are my new captors."

Will cocked his head to the side. "Captors?"

"Heh." Scott smiled at him. "Well, of course. You didn't think I'd allied myself with the Dusk Ravens willingly, did you? I'd be a fool to throw my lot in with any large political group. Alas, they were of a different opinion. That doesn't really matter now, does it?"

"I guess not," Will offered. This guy was incredibly strange, and unlike anyone he'd ever met before.

How can a guy like this not mind being held captive?

"So, you'll go with us willingly, then?" he said.

Scott smiled. "Of course. Assuming the food is better, of course. I've grown tired of the soldier's gruel."

Will flashed him a big grin. "Well, so long as we don't let Sariah near the fire, the food's decent."

Sariah's eyes went wide, and her cheeks flushed, but she said nothing. The others in the room chuckled at the little joke.

"Besides," Scott continued. "It's not like I have much choice in the matter unless I'm mistaken?" His eyes traveled to the weapons at Will's belt.

"We're not like that. I won't make you come with us and help us if you don't want to. Not even if it loses us the war."

Scott seemed taken aback. "Your mission? That's why you came here, did you not? Will you really throw all of that away for simple honor?"

Will thought for a second, then nodded. "Yes, yes I would. It's up to you, but..." he looked behind him at the iron door. "I think you'd do better with us by your side."

Scott smiled again. "Couldn't agree more." He withdrew his hand, picked up a few random parchments off the desk, then looked at Will. "Now, shall we?"

Will smiled and was about to say something when a chilling scream broke through the morning air. It sounded like a woman being murdered.

"Sariah!" A voice boomed throughout the complex. "I know you're in there. Come out with your hands up!"

Will's blood froze. He'd only heard that voice once, but

he knew it. It was the Master's voice. He looked over at Sariah. She stood frozen.

"Come close, everyone," Will pleaded. "I'm getting us out of here before—"

"I'm sure Mrs. Hensworth wouldn't want to die on your account, Sariah," the Master's voice insisted. "Come on out like a good girl, and she won't be harmed."

Will looked at Sariah. She was still sitting unmoving. He took a step toward her. "It's a trap, Sariah. That's all it is." He stuck out his hand. "Come on, I'll get us out of here."

Sariah just stood there, slowly shaking her head.

"Come on, Sariah. Rule fourteen, remember? Safety first, then attack only when you're safe." He shook her shoulder lightly. "Come on, we've got to go."

"Please, Sariah! Please, don't let me die!" another voice screamed.

All the color drained from Sariah's face. "It's her," she muttered. "It's really her. He has her."

Will waved a hand in front of her face. "Come on, Sariah. It's just a trick. He doesn't have anyone."

She looked at him. "How can you be sure?"

Will threw up his hands. "That's how guys like this operate! All smoke and mirrors. Just come on, already!"

"Please!" Mrs. Hensworth's voice repeated, followed by a strangled cry of pain.

"Look, it's no use," Albert said. "Just grab her, and let's leave, before it's too late."

Will frowned at him. "I'm not going to just grab her like that. She'd fight too much, and then where would we be? Besides, she deserves better than that!"

"Just come on, already. We've almost won the battle. Let's just go!"

"Ahem," Scott said, interrupting both of them. "You might want to stop arguing and go after your little friend before she does anything too stupid." He pointed at the open door behind them and Sariah, who could be seen racing down the hall.

"*Scheisse!*" Will and Albert swore in unison.

Sariah raced through the hallway of the small building, Mrs. Hensworth's screams echoing in her ears as she ran.

When she reached the entry, she almost slipped and fell in a puddle of fresh blood from one of the dead guards but managed to right herself with a burst of magic to heighten her reflexes.

She threw open the door to the building and walked outside. The sun was high overhead, and it blinded her for a few seconds. Blinking, her eyes started to come into focus. There were perhaps a dozen Dusk Ravens standing in the courtyard, all with weapons drawn and facing her.

Her attention was elsewhere. High atop the wall stood a lone figure dressed in dark clothing, cackling and holding a woman hostage. It was the Master, come for her again.

The Master's lips curled upward into a wry smile. "Why Sariah," he shouted down at her. "How nice of you to drop by."

A knot formed in Sariah's gut as she stared up at him. His face looked different from the last time she'd seen him, but there was no mistaking who it was. Memories of their last encounter flooded her brain, but she pushed them away as hard as she could.

Rule twenty, rule twenty, she repeated in her mind as she took a deep breath and tried to calm herself. Rule twenty said to not let the past cloud your judgment. For once, she was glad for Will's crazy-long list of rules.

"You!" Sariah called up to him. "You let Mrs. Hensworth go. She's not a part of this. I am." She stood as firm as she could, but her knees were still shaking.

The Master let out another laugh. "Oh, dear Sariah. Don't you remember? I told you everyone you knew would suffer." He shrugged. "I'm just making good on our deal."

With a massive push, the Master shoved Mrs. Hensworth off the wall. She let out another scream as she fell.

"No!" Sariah shouted. She raced forward as fast as her feet could take her but knew she'd fall short. Mrs. Hensworth fell to the ground with a loud crunch.

Sariah knelt beside her broken body and looked into her lifeless eyes with teary ones of her own. "No!" she repeated. She looked up at the Master. "You monster!"

She summoned forth a blast of magical energy and flung it at him. It hit the wall below where he was standing and took out several logs, but the Master dodged the move in time. He stood on top of another section of wall, looking down at her and laughing.

"You can't run forever!" Sariah called out to him. She lashed out with another blast of energy, but again he dodged out of the way.

"I don't have to, dearie," the Master quipped. "I just have to outlast you."

Sariah heard movement behind her, and she looked to see Will, Albert, and Scott standing in the doorway of the building, watching the scene in front of them. She shot them a quick smile, then stared back at the Master.

"Screw you!" she taunted, then struck again. Once more, he dodged out of the way with seeming impossible grace.

"Sariah!" Will cried. "Stay there, I'll come to get you!"

She smiled at him briefly, then heard the sound of the Master tsking above them.

"I see you brought your friends along. How quaint." The Master spared a glance for the guards in the courtyard. "Guards, kill them," he said with a dismissive wave.

A few of the guards got wicked grins on their faces and grabbed their weapons a little tighter, then rushed her all at once.

Sariah summoned forth a fireball that engulfed one of the closer ones, but she was starting to wear out and knew she couldn't keep it up. She only hoped Will would reach her in time.

Wearily, she grabbed her sword and brought it to bear just as the next guard came close enough to engage. She parried his blow, but there were ten more just like him to fend off, too.

She heard a loud crack as a wall of earth shot up from the ground in between her and the Dusk Ravens, taking the closest one with it.

"Come on!" Will shouted over the roar of the dirt. He held a hand out to her. "That won't keep them out for long."

Sariah took one last look at Mrs. Hensworth's broken body, then took Will's hand. "Let's go."

"With pleasure. Hold on tight."

She closed her eyes and watched as the world around them disappeared into nothing.

CHAPTER TEN

When Sariah opened her eyes, they were several miles away from the Dusk Raven stronghold. Where exactly, she wasn't sure, but it was far away from the Master and his cruelty.

She buried her face in Will's chest and let the tears start flowing. She cried for what felt like hours, though it was probably only a few minutes. All the while, Will held her head gently in one hand and stroked her back with the other.

"It'll be okay," he whispered in her ear. "It'll all be okay."

Sariah pulled back a little and wiped her nose, then looked up at Will. Her eyes were red and swollen, but she didn't care. "How could he be so cruel?" she asked him.

Will shook his head. "I don't know, Sariah, but I wish I did. Maybe then we'd be able to anticipate his next move better."

She pushed Will away hard and shot him an evil glare. "You!" she shouted. "How can you be thinking strategy at a time like this? I just lost one of my childhood friends, and probably several others I don't even know about, and all you care about is the next move?"

He backed away a step and put his hands up.

"Typical male," she spat at him, then turned and crossed her arms.

"Look," Will started. "I'm sure this is very hard for you, but we're not safe out here. Let's at least get back home, and then I promise you can yell at me all you want. Until your throat is raw."

Sariah turned back around a little and side-eyed him. "Really?"

He made the symbol of a cross in front of his chest. "Cross my heart. Whatever it takes to help you get through this. Let's just get home first, okay?"

She took in a deep breath and let her nerves calm down. Once she felt a little more in control of herself, she nodded.

"Okay. Let's go home." She stuck out her hand.

Will smiled at her. "Sounds good. Now hold on tight, everyone."

Several minutes and jumps later, they emerged within the walls of Talon's Reach tired, but overall no worse for wear.

Will let go of Sariah's hand and wiped a bead of sweat from his brow. He looked at her and gently rubbed her cheek where there was still a hint of a tear.

"Hey," he said slowly. "Are we good?"

She smiled up at him, then nudged his hand away. "Oh

yeah," she fired back. "We're just golden." Then she stormed off.

"What did I do this time?" he called after her.

"If you don't know that, you're stupider than I thought!"

Will shook his head and tried to let it drop. She'd cool off eventually.

Scott walked up. "Is she always like this?" he whispered.

He laughed aloud. "Only when I piss her off."

"How often does that happen?"

Will shrugged. "Often enough."

Behind him, he heard Albert snort. He smiled and looked at the fading image of Sariah walking away from him. They'd all lived to see another day. The rest would take care of itself somehow.

When the tattered main gate of Talon's Reach came into view, it brought a smile to Harvey's face. He'd only called the place home for a few weeks, but now that Chatwick was gone, it was all he had left.

He looked back at the throngs of people following him. Almost all of the villagers had survived the fire. Only a handful that the Master had kept with him had perished. He counted himself lucky his people were so resourceful.

"This place is gonna be burstin' at the seams soon," Justine said, poking him in the ribs.

Harvey looked at her and smiled. He was starting to warm to her odd mannerisms after spending so much time with her. "Let's just hope they have enough beds for everyone. These people need rest and shelter."

Justine shrugged. "We'll find a way to fit 'em. Ilene always does." She gave him a wink.

"Ilene's just that magical, is she?"

"Aye, laddie. She's a wonder that one. It's why I follow her still."

Harvey nodded and flashed her a dopey grin. "I can respect that. It's still a lot of new mouths to feed. I'm sure they'll be shocked."

Justine let out a slight chuckle. "Well, she asked for more troops, now, didn't she?" She made a broad-sweeping motion with her hands to encompass the villagers. "Can't say we didn't deliver."

Up ahead, Harvey spotted Lester standing in front of the broken gate. It didn't look any better in spite of the crews trying to repair it. Lester's mouth was open, and his eyes were wide with amazement.

"Ho! Lester! Tell everyone we're home!"

Lester raised a hand shakily to his brow and fumbled a nod, then ran inside.

Harvey chuckled. It was good to be back.

"Ya!" Sariah screamed at the training dummy. She stuck it with her sword blade. Breathing heavily, she wiped a bead of sweat from her brow and then smacked the dummy again for good measure.

Since she'd returned to Talon's Reach, she'd redoubled her training efforts. She intended to be ready the next time the Master came calling. She couldn't afford any more dead bodies in her wake, even if it meant spending more time with Will.

She was still a little pissed at both him and Ilene over their handling of the Chatwick situation. She deserved better than a lie. Lying was what Gabe had done.

Look how that turned out.

"Hey, Sariah!" a voice called out from behind her. It was Harvey.

She spun and let her weapon clang to the floor, then ran over and threw her arms around him. "Harvey!" she exclaimed.

"It's good to see you, too!" Harvey said, placing his arms gently around her and patting her on the back.

Sariah let herself feel lost in his warm embrace and for just a moment, let the Master and the rest of the world lay forgotten. Only for a moment, then she pushed away and looked up into his eyes.

"How is everyone? Did anyone survive? Tell me everything!"

"Easy, easy." Harvey threw his hands up and took a step back. "One question at a time."

Sariah bit her lip. "Sorry. It's just I've been so worried about all of you. I almost went out to find you myself, but every time I searched for you with my magic, I found you safe, so I waited. Come on, spill! What happened?"

Harvey let out a sigh and shook his head. "Well..." He relayed his tale to her, sparing no detail.

"So, the whole town is safe?" she asked him when he'd finished.

He nodded. "Yep. Just about, that is. Even old Mrs.

Hensworth is alive and kicking, though her chickens didn't make it."

Sariah's eyes brightened. "Mrs. Hensworth?" she repeated, barely able to believe what she was hearing.

"Yeah, she's fine." He waved a hand dismissively. "Why, are you eager to steal more eggs?"

Sariah furrowed her brow, ignoring the slight. "Then it really was all a trick. That bastard."

Then who had he killed? Or had he even really killed anyone? She felt more confused than before, but at the same time, incredibly relieved. She felt her muscles relax as the tension faded away.

Harvey cocked his head to the side and frowned. "Beg pardon?"

She shook her head. "Never mind. So what else is new?"

"About that," Harvey started. "I was actually sent out here to call you to a new war council. It seems Sean is back, too, and his news is far grimmer."

"Yeah?"

He lowered his head. "Yeah. It's pretty bad up in Stratton right now, or so I hear. The whole town is crawling with Dusk Ravens, and it's under martial law. You'd barely recognize the place from what I hear."

Sariah bit her lip. Stratton was in such dire straits? That was sad to hear. She'd made several friends there, and now they were suffering.

Did the Master's hate know no bounds?

It wouldn't do worrying about it now. There were plenty of other things to think about, like the next war council. First, though, she wanted to check on her people. She needed to see with her own eyes that they were safe.

"Come on, Harvey. I want to go see my people."

"But, the war council!"

She shrugged. "They can wait a bit longer. The Dusk Ravens aren't going anywhere. Now take me to see our friends from home."

He flashed her a dopey grin. "With pleasure."

The two started walking toward the living quarters. "By the way," Harvey said. "I'm not the only one who's glad to be back here."

Sariah's lips curled into a big smile. "Bear!" she cried.

A barking noise resounded through the air as if in response. Just like that, she was off, arms wide open and ready for a hug.

Scott lowered his head to avoid hitting the ceiling. The forge was in a surprisingly small space and quite hot.

Not shocking considering what went on there, but he felt a bead of sweat form on his forehead almost immediately and quickly brushed it away.

Then the smell hit him, or rather the stench. It smelled like pure sulfur, or maybe something worse.

Just what are they forging in this blasted place anyway?

He shook his head and went through the doorway. A small man, about two thirds the size of an ordinary man, but every bit as broad stared at him with beady eyes. The man gave him a giant grin.

"Ye must be Scott," Padron said. The rearick stuck out his hand. "Nice ta meet ya."

The corners of Scott's lips curled into a grin of their own. "Indeed. I take it you're Padron?"

"Aye." Padron shrugged. "Tha one an' only."

Scott motioned toward the forge with his head. "I see you know your way around a fire."

Padron flashed him another grin. "Aye, lad. An' I hear yer not too shabby with tha magics."

A chuckle escaped Scott's lips. "Heh. You could say that." He shook his head. "To be honest, I'm not good with most spells, but the ones I do know are sure sought after."

The rearick rolled his eyes. "I'm none too sure meself. I've seen a few magitech devices here an' there, but none of it was all that." He lifted the giant hammer in his right hand. "I prefer good, honest steel anyway."

Scott cocked his head to the side. "That so?"

"Aye lad." He patted the hammer a time or two. "A good weapon is all ya need ta take care a yerself."

He smiled at the rearick again. "Well, you might be surprised to see just how good of a weapon I can make, then."

Padron shrugged. "Suit yerself." He pointed to a spot behind him where a couple of weapons lay in a haphazard heap.

Scott wiped more sweat from his brow and made his way over to the pile. On top lay a weapon the likes of which he hadn't seen since his days in Arcadia. It had a small wire running up and down the side, leading up to a jewel setting that held an amphorald.

He took a deep breath. This was why he'd been brought here, but could he even still do it? It had been ages since he'd cast the spell.

There was only one way to find out.

Reaching out with one finger, he gingerly placed it against the gemstone and concentrated. Within seconds, the jewel flared to life, shining for a second, then going dark once more.

A wry grin crossed Scott's face. Guess I'm still good for something after all, he thought.

He hefted the weapon and looked at it. The craftsmanship was good. A little hasty perhaps, but it should hold up nicely. Placing the weapon on his shoulder, he aimed at a lonely chair in the corner and fired.

The amphorald glowed for a brief second, and a wave of blue energy spat out of the weapon. There was a loud crash as the chair splintered to bits.

Padron looked up from his work and blinked. "Blimey! What'ya do that fer?" he demanded.

Scott chuckled. "Just making sure I still knew my stuff."

The rearick looked at him with wide eyes, then at the chair. He shrugged. "Looks like ye know yer stuff all right." He frowned. "Now I need ta go an' ask the ice lady fer a new chair."

"Ice lady?" Scott rubbed his chin. "Oh, you must mean Ilene." He let out another chuckle and patted the weapon. "After she sees what this baby can do, I don't think she'll mind."

Sariah looked out at the crowd of people and frowned. She knew most of them, though there were a few new faces. They were all denizens of Talon's Reach, and there were perhaps twenty in all. She marveled at how big the place was that there were people she hadn't met after weeks of being there.

At her side lay Bear. He looked like he was trying to take a nap. The dog hadn't left her side ever since they'd met back up two days ago. It was like he thought she was going to up and disappear.

Which, if she was honest with herself, was a legitimate concern.

Her stomach started to churn as she looked over the crowd and saw their bored eyes staring back at her. She needed an opener. She cleared her throat loudly.

"Who knows why you're all here?" she asked the crowd. It was a pointless question, of course. Everyone knew why they were there.

A red-headed girl, someone she didn't recognize, raised her hand high.

"You!" Sariah called out. "What's your name?"

"Amelia, my lady," the girl said with a bow.

Sariah scowled and waved her off. "Now, don't go starting with those grand titles. Not with me." She shook her head. "I'm no noble. Just a girl trying to do the right thing. You'd all do well to remember that."

Amelia's cheeks flushed, and she lowered her gaze. "I'm sorry, my la—I mean, Sariah."

Now Sariah felt bad for her. She hadn't meant to be so hard on the girl. Her face softened. "Look, it's okay. No worries, these things happen. Just something to remember for next time, right?" She flashed the girl a toothy grin.

The girl smiled back but said nothing.

Sariah had stalled long enough. She might as well get down to business.

"You're here, of course, to learn about magic," she started, looking at several people in turn like she'd seen Ilene do when she addressed large crowds. She hoped it would keep their attention.

A few of the heads in the crowd nodded, though a couple people near the back looked confused.

"Unless you picked the wrong field, that is," she continued. "Then I guess you're out of luck."

She'd meant the last bit as a joke, but no one laughed. Looking out at the crowd, she still saw mostly blank stares.

Tough crowd. This is going to be harder than I thought.

Sariah bit her lip and looked down at Bear. He was in the middle of a giant yawn.

"Humph," she muttered. "Some help you are."

Bear looked up at her, then went back to acting like she wasn't there.

She had to think fast or she was going to lose them. What she needed was something flashy, a diversion to get them out of their own heads.

Out of the corner of her eye, she spotted a small wooden table on the far side of the courtyard. That would do nicely.

She twirled her finger a few times, and the table lifted up into the air and flew over the heads of the crowd in front of her.

A few audible gasps erupted as everyone's eyes turned to watch the flying table.

Sariah swirled her fingers, and the table turned around several times. Then she grinned at the table and flung a fireball straight at it. The flames quickly engulfed the wood, and the table burst into a thousand tiny, fiery pieces that showered over the assembled group.

Now everyone was looking at her with rapt attention. She cleared her throat. "As I was saying, you're here to learn how to do magic tricks like that. Only, perhaps more useful ones. Tables don't really fight back after all."

This time, she heard a few chuckles, including one from Amelia.

Sariah smiled and winked at her. It seemed she was doing something right after all.

"If you want to learn how to pull off something like that, and I'm sure you all do..." She paused to make sure she still had everyone's attention. It looked like it. "Then you're going to have to start with the basics."

An audible groan escaped the group, and she saw a few people roll their eyes.

Sariah's eyes narrowed and glared at one of them. His name was Hunter. She'd never particularly liked him.

"Hey! Hunter!"

The kid jumped a little and pointed at his chest. "M-me?"

Sariah nodded. "Yes, you! You got a problem with my approach?"

Hunter rolled his eyes again. "Basics are nice and all, but I want to kill some Dusk Ravens!" He looked around at the others. "Heck, we all do. We've got a score to settle with that lot!"

Several cheers came out of the group, and a few people were now looking at Hunter.

Ugh. Sariah rolled her eyes. The kid had a point, of

course, but she was right. Only now she'd have to prove it to get the attention of the group back.

An idea came to her.

"So you think you can just go out and kill some Dusk Ravens. Just like that?" She snapped her fingers for effect.

Hunter grinned at her. "Just like that."

Sariah let out a small chuckle. "Let's see it then. Prove your worth with a small test."

The kid didn't take his eyes away from her. "Bring it."

"Love to." She shrugged and reached into a pocket, producing a small round stone. It had a slight crack on one side but was otherwise smooth.

It was Gabe's old training rock, the one she'd managed to crack while training herself. Why she'd kept it around, she wasn't quite sure.

She walked over to Hunter and placed the stone on the ground in front of him.

"What do you want me to do now? Kick it?" Hunter goaded.

A wry smile crossed Sariah's lips. "Oh no, nothing that hard, I assure you." She patted his cheek gingerly. "At least. Not for someone as versed as you claim to be."

Hunter laughed, but it sounded hollow this time. Sariah wondered if he was starting to second-guess his course of action.

She looked down at the stone. "I want you to lift the stone off the ground using magic."

The kid looked confused. "Is that it?"

Sariah nodded. "That's it. Easy, right?" She backed up a few steps to give him some space and crossed her arms.

Hunter started to wiggle and move at odd angles, but the stone stayed put.

While he worked at the spell, Sariah groaned softly to herself. How long did I tease Gabe about those stupid stones of his? she wondered. Yet here she was, using the same trick to teach her own students.

She chuckled softly and shook her head. In some ways, she was more like him than she was willing to admit.

Meanwhile, Hunter was getting nowhere fast with the stone. He was currently grunting and glaring at the rock and swearing up a storm, but it stayed put.

"Enough!" Sariah shouted over the crowd. Everyone quieted down, even Hunter.

"Not as easy as it looks, is it?"

Hunter lowered his head, and his cheeks reddened. "No, ma'am," he admitted at last.

She shrugged. "It's okay. The first time can be hard. Trust me, I know. I've been there, too." She walked over and patted him on the shoulder. "If you keep at it and are willing to put in the work to learn the basics, you'll get there."

Raising her voice, she added, "You'll all get there. I promise. I'll see to it personally that you all get your chance to even the score. You just need to hang in there and learn."

This time, everyone in the crowd nodded in agreement. Several people shot her smiles, and a few of them even had a gleam in their eyes.

Sariah smiled and looked at each of them in turn. These were her people. She had faith that they would succeed given some time and a lot of effort. She would teach them well. Then they'd crush the Dusk Ravens.

Her fingers trailed down to her side, and she felt the softness of Bear's furry head with her fingertips. He gave an appreciative bark. It seemed she'd even gained his approval.

"Now, who's ready to learn?"

CHAPTER ELEVEN

Sariah slumped onto the couch currently serving as her bed and sighed. Bear leaped up next to her, and she let him lay his head on her lap. Having him there was comforting, and she needed all the comfort she could get at the moment.

"Ugh," she said aloud.

Harvey, who was staying in the same room for the time being, lifted his head up. "Something wrong?" he offered.

She shot him an icy glare and went back to staring at Bear. She was in no mood to talk.

Harvey wouldn't be swayed so easily. He got up from his chair and walked over. "Whatever it is, it's okay. You can tell me."

"It's..." she looked at him for a moment, then lowered her head. "Just forget about it."

He sat down on the other side of the couch and placed a hand gently on her leg. "Is it about Gabe?"

Sariah recoiled from his touch like a snake. Her cheeks started to turn red. "No!" she spat.

It was a lie, of course. She had been thinking about Gabe. She couldn't stop thinking about where he had gone off to and what he was doing. Even after everything they'd been through, a part of her expected him to come back.

A part that deserved to be shot, maybe, but still a part of her.

She wasn't about to admit that to Harvey, especially not after being caught red-handed. She shook her head vigorously. "Heavens no! It's just training, you know? It takes a lot out of a person."

Harvey flashed her one of his signature grins and nodded. "Tell me about it. I must have spent eight hours with my trainees today, teaching them the basics of the sword." He slumped into the seat. "That's some grueling work."

Sariah nodded. "Exactly."

He stretched and then sat up. "It's more than that, isn't it?" He looked at her expectantly. "Come on, it's just us. You can tell me."

She rolled her eyes and sighed again. "Fine. You're right, I was thinking about him. Happy?"

A broad smile crossed his face. "I knew it!" he shouted loud enough to startle Bear, who raised his head and growled at him.

Harvey threw up his hands in mock defense. "Sorry. It's okay, you know. I know you two were close for a while there. It's only natural that it would be hard to let go."

Sariah's cheeks turned a brighter shade of red. "Was I that obvious?"

He let out a slight chuckle. "Let's just say you followed him around like Bear follows you."

She backed away a bit again. "Really? I didn't realize."

"Realize what?" Will's voice boomed out. He materialized in the doorway with Ilene and Albert in tow.

Sariah's cheeks turned an even brighter shade of crimson, and she tried to hide her face. "Nothing," she insisted. "It's nothing."

"Nothing for you to be worried about, at least," Harvey finished in her defense.

Will eyed both of them cautiously like he wanted to press the issue, but he let it drop and took a seat. Ilene and Albert followed suit. Soon, the room was full to bursting.

She straightened up as best she could and gave Bear's head an extra couple of pets. "So," she started. "What brings you here at this late hour of the day?" Her question was pointed at Will, but she spared a glance for Ilene and Albert as well.

The big man shrugged. "Nothing much. It's time for our war council, remember?"

An audible gasp escaped Sariah's lips, and she clapped her hands to her mouth. She had forgotten the war council was tonight. She mentally chided herself for getting so caught up in her own problems she forgot something so important.

"I'm so sorry," she offered. "Training took longer than I expected today, and I guess I...er, we just spaced it." She shot a quick glance at Harvey and grinned at him.

Will shrugged again. "It's no matter. We figured that might be the case. That's why instead of waiting around, we thought we'd come knocking."

He shot both Sariah and Harvey another weird glance.

"Did we come at a bad time? We could come back later if you two were busy with something."

Sariah blushed again. "Oh no, not at all." She shook her head and scooted away from Harvey. "We weren't busy, promise. Just chatting."

"Okay," Will said. There was a hint of mirth in his eyes. "If you say so, I'll believe you."

"It's true," Harvey piped in. "Just talking about how draining the training sessions have been. We haven't had time for much else."

"Oh, I can only imagine." Will nodded and winked at Harvey.

Sariah rolled her eyes. Men could be such pigs.

Ilene cleared her throat. "Anyway, we should get on with the war council." Her chill voice cut through the tension in the room, and everyone shut up and turned to look at her. Sariah admired how she could control a room. It was a skill she hoped to gain someday.

"Since we're on the topic of training, let's start by discussing that." She turned to face Harvey. "Harvey, how is the weapons training faring?"

Harvey sat up and beamed. "It's going great. We got into some intermediate techniques with a few of the villagers today." He paused. "As I told you a few weeks ago, the people of Chatwick are hardy folk. They can rise to meet any challenge. Plus, I think they're a little eager to get back at the Dusk Ravens for burning our home to the ground."

Ilene smiled at him. "Good. I'm glad to hear that, and that's very promising. How long do you think you'll need to turn them into a combat troop?"

Harvey put his hands out. "Now wait just a second.

They're hardy folk, yes, and they're taking to the sword quickly enough, but it'll be a while yet before they can match blades with the Dusk Ravens. That lot has been training for years." He stood up and started pacing. "You can't expect villagers to be ready to face an army after only a week of training, can you?"

Ilene motioned with her hand for Harvey to sit back down, and he complied. "I'm sorry if it came off that way," she said slowly. "I assure you, I don't intend to send them out tomorrow. That would only lead to ruin."

Harvey looked vindicated. "Good."

"I only meant to gauge their overall combat readiness should the worst happen." She was referring to another raid.

A knot formed in Sariah's stomach, and she forced it down. The threat of another Dusk Raven raid hung over all their heads like a death knell. The Master knew where they were. It was only a matter of time until he came after them again.

Unless they found him first, of course. Sariah knew they weren't ready for that yet.

When will we be ready? she pondered. It was the same question that had gnawed at her since her last meeting with the Master. She forced the thought away. It wouldn't do her any good now.

"How about the magic training, Sariah? How does that fare?" Ilene asked, bringing her attention back to the matter at hand.

Sariah forced herself to smile. "Pretty good. Better than I expected, honestly," she admitted. "There's this young girl, Amelia, and a boy named Hunter. They're the heads of the class for sure." She shrugged. "The rest of them are doing pretty good, too, but I don't think they're combat-ready yet, either. Maybe in another couple of weeks."

Ilene simply nodded and smiled at her. "That's good to hear."

The older woman looked at Will. "And you, my dear William? How goes the magitech production and training?"

Will grinned. "I dare say that's the shining star in this whole mess. We've got production ramping up to two weapons a day, and we had a test with our crack troop yesterday. I've got to say, watching those weapons at work makes me wonder why we ever did things the hard way."

"Excellent. So then, what's our next move? When do we plan a counter-offensive?"

Harvey and Will started talking over each other, with Will saying they could march tomorrow if they wanted and Harvey insisting they needed more time for training. It was dizzying trying to pay attention to them both, so Sariah retreated into her mind a bit.

The Master's hardened face waited for her there, as it did most nights. She wondered for perhaps the hundredth time if anything they did would ever be enough to take on the Master. A single touch from his cold, hard hands had been all it had taken to reduce her to a sobbing mess on the ground. How was anyone supposed to fight a power like that?

"What about the Master?" she blurted out suddenly. Then she clapped her hands over her mouth, ashamed she'd actually spoken her worry out loud.

Everyone turned to look at her. There was concern in both Harvey and Will's eyes.

It was Ilene who eventually spoke. "What about him, child? Is there something more we should know?"

Sariah bit her lip. She'd avoided talking about her encounter with him up to this point, but she knew she'd have to go through with it eventually. She let out a deep sigh.

"Look, I'm glad you guys showed up when you did, but you weren't there for all of it. You didn't feel his power. He drained me with nothing but a touch and left me with nothing. Nothing but a world of pain."

"You're not the only one," Harvey admitted. "I felt it, too, in Chatwick. The Master's power is like nothing I've ever seen before." He glanced at Sariah and flashed her a dopey grin. "She's right to be concerned. We need a plan for him specifically, or all else is moot."

Will rubbed his chin. "Well, what, then? What should we do about it?" He looked about the room. "Anyone have a suggestion?"

Sariah lowered her head. "I don't know. I'm sorry." She felt terrible.

Will got up and walked over and placed her head in one of his hands, then lifted her chin until they were looking eye to eye. "What else do you remember about what the Master did? Any detail could make a difference."

Sariah's mind raced. She bit her lip. "I was terrified, okay? I don't remember much. Just staring into his cold, red eyes and thinking all hope was lost."

Albert, who had been quiet this whole time, gasped. Everyone turned to look at him.

"Have something to add, son?" Will asked.

The kid's cheeks burned, and he shrank into his frame a little. "It's nothing, sir."

"It didn't sound like nothing, son. Out with it," Will pressured.

Albert shrugged. "It's just, the red eyes, sir. When I was a kid, I lived near a forest south of here, the Eagle Woods. Some said it was haunted, but I never believed the rumors. One day, I met a child out there while I was playing in the woods. She looked a lot like me, but...her eyes. I'll never forget. Her eyes were a cold red, just like Sariah mentioned."

Sariah perked up a bit as a memory of her own jarred her. "The Eagle Woods? We met someone from the Eagle Wood." She looked over at Harvey. "Both of us did. His name was Vincent. He claimed to be a druid, a master of nature magic."

"You don't suppose—" Will started.

Ilene nodded. "It sounds like it. Perhaps this Master person knows of the nature arts as well. Or, at least some perverted version of them."

Will smiled at her. "We should send a group to check it out. Sariah and I will lead the way, of course." He walked over and clapped Sariah on the back.

She glared at him as if to say, "thanks for volunteering me, jerk," but in truth, she'd be glad for the distraction. She never had been one for staying in one spot.

"I'll come, too," Harvey piped in. "I spent a lot of time with Vincent. He might be more willing to talk to me than either of you."

"Don't forget me!" Albert exclaimed. Everyone looked at him in shock.

Will eyed him quizzically. "Are you sure, lad?"

He nodded. "Positive. Besides, you might need someone who actually knows where these Eagle Woods are."

Sariah had to admit he had a point. "Very well, you can come too," she got out before Will could object.

He turned and glared at her, and she gave him a wry smile. He rolled his eyes and shook his head, then turned back to the others.

"All right, then. We've got our troop assembled. We'll leave in the morning. Anything else to discuss?"

"Wait a second," Ilene chimed in. "If all of you leave, who will be here to train the troops and keep the weapons production going? What if the Master attacks while you're gone?"

Sariah flashed her a weak smile and lowered her head. She hadn't thought of that. She'd been so happy at the thought of getting out of Talon's Reach for a bit she hadn't thought about the consequences.

"Sean can handle the weapons training while we're out," Will blurted. "Josef can handle the magic training. He's the best mage we've got outside of Sariah and I. Scott and Padron are doing their thing just fine. No worries there."

Ilene didn't seem convinced. "What if the Dusk Ravens attack again?"

Will shrugged. "Then, take everyone you can and run away as far as you can." He turned to face her. "Look, I don't like it any more than you do, but Sariah's got a point. If we can't neutralize the Master's spells, then all is lost."

He straightened up and shot a glance at Sariah. His eyes

were bright with an intense fire, the likes of which she hadn't seen since the Battle of Stratton. "We need this," he insisted. "All of us do. It's the best hope we've got."

Ilene looked at each of them in turn. Her gaze was such that Sariah wondered if it was the last time she'd ever see her. Who knew? Maybe it would be. It was a risk worth taking.

At last, she sighed. "Very well. Take your trip, and return as fast as you can. Time is of the essence." She waved at Will dismissively.

Will flashed her a broad smile and bowed deeply. "Of course, your excellence. I wouldn't have it any other way."

CHAPTER TWELVE

Harvey let out an audible groan. His legs were aching something fierce. He didn't mind the occasional march, but Will's pace was practically unbearable—far worse than Gabe's had ever been. Inwardly, he wondered how the others had put up with it for this long.

Leaning in close to Albert, he asked, "Are we there yet?"

Albert shrugged and smiled back at him. "No, but we're getting closer."

Harvey furrowed his brow. "How can you tell?"

The kid shrugged again. "I just know. Grew up in these parts, remember?"

Harvey nodded. "Oh yeah." He flashed the kid a dopey grin. "I didn't even know there was a village out here."

Albert's face became sad and he lowered his gaze. "There's not. Or, at least, not anymore." The kid let out a deep sigh. "There was a thriving town out here for many years, until the Dusk Ravens came. Now it's gone."

"I'm sorry," Harvey offered. He placed a hand on the kid's back. "I had no idea."

The kid looked at him and gave him a weak smile. "It's okay. It was a few years ago. Besides, the same thing happened to your home, too, right?"

Harvey nodded. "Indeed." His thoughts turned inward for a second, and he thought about what he'd like to do to the Master given a chance. Him and Jeffrey, or Humboldt, as the man was apparently named. If it hadn't been for the two of them, Chatwick would still be the same happy place it had always been.

He clapped the kid on the back once more. "Well enough about the past, right? We'll get our payback soon enough."

Albert nodded but said nothing and just kept walking.

The four of them marched for probably another hour in complete silence, no one knowing what to say. Then the air around them started to shift. It felt heavier, and the trees felt a little closer together. Harvey shrugged it off, figuring it was just how things felt in the deep woods, but the others didn't seem so sure.

"We're almost there," Albert said, breaking the silence.

Harvey side-eyed him. "How can you be so sure?"

"The trees," Albert said cryptically. "They start to look different when you get into druid territory."

He cocked his head to the side. "The trees look different?" He looked at the trees, but they didn't look weird to him, just like normal trees. "What, like fewer evergreens or something?" The Alpenwood was made of mostly evergreen trees.

Albert shook his head. "No, like different. It's hard to explain, but you'll see soon enough."

Harvey nodded but was unconvinced.

They took a few more steps, and then the trees started to close in more, blocking out the sunlight from above. It was almost dark enough that Harvey wanted a torch even in the middle of the day, but not quite.

It was then that he saw what Albert meant. The trees surrounding them were still trees, but something about them was off. They were taller, with thicker branches and bigger leaves. Their branches looked almost menacing like the trees were vaguely alive. Alive, and somehow against their being here.

A shiver ran down Harvey's spine. "You know what?" he said to Albert.

The kid looked up at him but remained wordless.

"I think I understand why people say these woods are haunted."

Albert flashed him a smile and shrugged again. "I told you you'd know when we got closer."

Harvey looked around again in wonder then back at the path ahead of them. "Yeah, you weren't kidding."

He walked forward a bit and tapped Will on the shoulder. The big man turned with an annoyed expression. "Let's take it a bit slower from now on, okay?"

Will scowled at him. "Why?"

"Just a hunch," Harvey offered. He flashed the man a dopey grin.

"A hunch?" Will repeated. Harvey nodded. "Better be some hunch."

Harvey just shrugged and flashed him another smile. It seemed to be effective, and Will slowed the pace.

Their pace slowed even further as the path before them disappeared, and they had to start wading through the underbrush. It felt somehow thicker and stronger than normal and seemed to resist their blade strikes.

Harvey poked at one particular bush with the tip of one of his blades, and its vines shot up suddenly, engulfing the blade and wresting it from his grasp.

"Umm, guys..." he started. Everyone turned to face him, but he was too late. Similar vines from the other bushes shot out, entangling their legs and arms, making it impossible to move.

Harvey felt the vines tighten around him. The more he struggled, the tighter they seemed to get, so he just gave in and sat there. Fortunately, the vines didn't seem to have any thorns on them, so while it was tight, it wasn't too dangerous. His head remained uncovered, so he looked around at the others. They all seemed to be in a similar plight.

"Well, that's just great," Will complained. "Looks like we got the right spot, all right. Only they're none too happy to see us."

"I'm sure it's all a misunderstanding," Sariah countered. "Vincent said if we ever needed him, we could come and find him. I'm sure everything will get sorted out soon."

"Yeah?" Will fired back. "Does this look sorted out to you?"

Harvey imagined him making vague motions to encompass his body while he talked, but since all their limbs were covered in vines, it was impossible to know for sure.

Will shot an icy glare at Albert, who shrank away. "This is all your fault!" he shouted. "The last time I ever trust your advice!"

Albert opened his mouth as if to say something but shut it just as quickly.

"Hey!" Harvey chimed in. "He was just doing what he thought was best! Don't be mad at him!"

"Look," Sariah offered. "We just need to figure out who's in charge and have them check with Vincent."

"Who would that be, exactly?" Will spat at her. He struggled against the vines like he wanted to pounce on her, but they kept him in check.

Sariah looked sheepish. "I don't know! Someone?"

Will's eyes took on a fiery haze, and his cheeks burned a bright red like he was about to burst, but before he could yell anything else, a tall, slender gentleman came into the clearing.

"Excuse me," the gentleman said slowly. "Did someone here say the name Vincent?"

Sariah turned to look at him. "I did." She nodded. "He helped me and my friend Harvey out a while back when we were in trouble after we saved him from a wolf attack."

A light of recognition went off in the gentleman's eyes. "Oh, you're that Sariah and Harvey." The man's eyes flashed green for a second, and Harvey felt the vines around him start to loosen.

He looked around and saw a similar thing happening to his friends. Before long, everyone was free to move again. Harvey rubbed his wrists a few times to breathe life back into them and flashed a grin at the slender gentleman.

"My apologies," he said with a grand bow. "My name is Zayne." He offered a hand to Sariah, who shook it. "This was all a big misunderstanding, but we have to be careful these days with the Dusk Ravens out and about. You understand."

Sariah elbowed Will in the ribs. The big man let out a gasp and shot her an icy glare but said nothing. "We understand completely," Sariah replied with a big smile. "Can you take us to see Vincent?"

Zayne bowed again. "Certainly, lady Sariah." He beckoned with his hands. "Come this way. Please, don't poke any more bushes. Some of them aren't as forgiving as these."

Harvey blushed and put his sword away, then followed after the others.

Sariah went after the man known as Zayne through the dark woods, with Bear, Will, Albert, and Harvey in tow. She'd given up tracing their steps a while back. It was a lost cause. Besides, she was certain Zayne had led them in circles a few times on purpose.

I would have done the same thing, she admitted. Hard to storm a place you can't find.

Before long, the canopy gave way and raised several feet into the air. It was still thick, but it felt like they were in a large clearing despite the tree cover overhead.

All around them were people, some with green eyes and some without. Animals followed closely at each of their heels. Almost involuntarily, she reached down to pet Bear's head. The dog accepted her attention happily and gave her a contented woof.

She didn't see anything that looked like a house, but she

knew instinctively this must be what Vincent and the other druids called their home.

"Is this your village?" she asked Zayne.

Zayne nodded. "I know it may not look like much from the outside, but this is where we live, here amongst nature. We wouldn't have it any other way."

Sariah smiled at him. "Looks comfy enough to me." She'd always found the big towns like Stratton to be a bit stuffy and way too crowded. She could completely understand why someone might want to live amongst the trees and nature like this. Especially in this area, where it didn't tend to get too cold in the wintertime.

"So, where do you live, then?"

The druid pointed to a tree a short distance onward. "Over there, with my wife and daughter."

"You have a daughter?" Sariah asked him.

He nodded. "Uh-huh. She's about your age."

Sariah squinted and could barely make out two females standing under the tree. The older one had a big grin on her face and looked very happy to see them. The younger one was indeed about her own age and seemed to be pouting about something.

"They look happy to see you."

Zayne nodded again. "Indeed. My daughter doesn't agree with my role as a scout of the woods, and my wife worries every time I set out, but I always come back home to them. That's what matters." He waved at the two females, and the older one waved back.

She flashed Zayne a half-grin. "Yeah, I hear that." At that moment, she wished her parents could come back, and her expression soured. That was a joy she'd never know again. She let out a small sigh and let the thought drop.

"Listen, Zayne," she started. "I don't mean to keep you from your family any longer than necessary, but you were going to lead us to Vincent." She looked at her companions, and their faces were fraught with worry and concern. "We have an important mission to complete, and time is of the essence."

Zayne gave her another nod. "Right, sorry." He beckoned with his hand. "This way, I'll take you to the Elders' area."

"Elders?" Harvey chimed in. "So is Vincent like a big wig or something?"

Zayne shook his head. "Not exactly. He is one who wanders, so he can never be a chief. He is still well respected in our hierarchy."

Sariah wanted to know more, but Zayne waved off her questions. "Enough chatter. We should be going. I'm still not sure how happy they'll be to see you."

"What does that mean?" Sariah asked, cocking her head.

Zayne's eyes had a distant look to them. "It's nothing," he insisted. "I've said too much as it is. This way, everyone."

Sergeant Ty Genrose looked at the small copse of trees in front of him and sighed. It was a deep sigh full of loneliness and regret.

Why did I accept this assignment? he asked himself for the hundredth time. He knew the answer, of course. It was the same reason he took any assignment from the Master. There wasn't any other choice.

He supposed he could have signed up to help with the Master's experiments instead, but he'd never been much of a researcher. When the Master had told him it was either the forest or research experiments, he'd gone for the forest.

Of course, he was regretting it now. He'd been out here alone for nearly a week with nothing to show for it. How was that going to look to the Master?

Sighing again, he kicked a rock by his foot. It was bigger than it looked, and his foot hurt from the impact. He bit on his cheek to keep from yelping. One must never give their position away for any reason—another command of the Master.

Give it away to whom? There was no one out here in this dander-blasted forest. The trees were too close together, and the vegetation too thick. No one lived all the way out here. So why did the Master care about this stupid forest anyway?

He heard a noise to his left. His blood froze, and he stilled his movements as much as he could and waited. Sure enough, the sound came again. It was a sound he knew all too well as a soldier, the sound of marching boots.

Several minutes later, a rather unassuming group of humans walked by, not a hundred feet off.

Had they seen him? He shook his head. If they had, they would have done something. Instead, they marched past.

He squinted to try and make out their faces through the thick underbrush he was hiding in. The leader was unmistakably female. It took a minute for his eyes to focus on her, but when they did, he caught his breath.

A smile crept across the sergeant's face. Soon, all his waiting and sitting and pissing away the hours would come to fruition. He had something to report to the Master, after all.

If the entrance to the druid's home had been something, the inner sanctum was on another level entirely.

Sariah's jaw dropped as she took in her surroundings. Everything around her had a slight glow to it—even the vegetation, which grew in strange patterns she'd never seen before.

Zayne ushered her and her companions inside the room, and they complied, then he shut some sort of door behind him, and was gone.

Inside the room were three old druids. Two of them Sariah had never seen before, but the third one she would have known anywhere.

"Vincent!" she cried. She threw up her arms and walked over to hug him.

The older druid had a surprised look in his eyes, but he accepted her embrace warmly for a moment, then pulled away. He looked down at her. "So it was you that Zayne found at the edge of the woods," he said. "I'm so glad to hear he wasn't mistaken."

Sariah cocked her head. "What is that supposed to mean?"

Vincent shrugged. "No matter. You're here, and you brought Harvey, I see." He opened his arms wide. "Come here, Harvey."

Harvey seemed a little hesitant, but he walked over and accepted the hug.

The older druid looked at the others in the room. "I see you brought new friends with you. Who are these two?" He stuck out a hand to them.

Sariah made the introductions. "This is Will, my mentor of sorts," she said, pointing at Will. "And this is Albert. He had the directions."

Vincent shook their hands, and they exchanged pleasantries.

"Hey, how's Ferdinand?" Harvey asked him when the pleasantries had ended.

Vincent waved a hand dismissively. "Off somewhere finding new trouble to get into, I presume. I'm sure he'll show up eventually." He looked down at Bear. "I see your familiar is still by your side, Sariah."

Sariah blushed. "My familiar? It's nothing like that. He's just my pet."

The older druid shook his head. "I've seen many whose bond with their familiar is not as strong as the one between you and Bear, Sariah. Don't discount it."

Not knowing what else to say, she nodded. Bear gave an appreciative bark and rubbed her leg with his head.

Sariah indicated the two other druids in the room who, up to this point, had remained still and silent. "Who are your friends, Vincent? You haven't introduced us."

Vincent looked flustered. "My apologies! Where are my manners? This here is Yert," he said, pointing at the oldest one. "He's the chieftain of our clan. This is Erving. He's second in command."

Yert and Erving looked at each of them in turn and nodded once but said nothing.

"They don't talk much," Vincent added in a half-whisper. Sariah nodded and winked at him.

"So," he continued. "What brings you people here? Finally, come to take me up on my offer of help?"

Harvey nodded. "Something like that."

"We've come in hopes of finding something to aid us in our quest to defeat a man known only as the Master," Sariah explained.

Yert let out an audible gasp, and a chill wind blew through the room. "Who is this Master you speak of so flippantly?" he demanded. His voice had an unearthly quality to it.

Sariah knelt in front of him, feeling like it was the right thing to do. "He's a terrible person, Yert," she replied. "He rules an organization known as the Dusk Ravens with an iron fist and will to match. He...he's barely even human."

The old druid nodded once. "Hmm..." He beckoned with one hand. "Come closer, child. I know a little of the mental arts. Let me read your thoughts so I might know him better."

Nodding, she scooted closer. Yert caressed her head with one of his old, withered hands for a moment, and Sariah filled her thoughts with images of the Master. She wasn't sure what she expected, but she felt no pain or discomfort from Yert's mental prodding.

The druid chieftain spoke a few unintelligible words, and his eyes flashed white for a moment, then he recoiled and withdrew his hand. His eyes took on a glassy look, and he retreated back.

"I know this person of who you speak. Only he went by a different name then."

Sariah gasped. "What? What was his name? That might help track him down!"

Yert sighed and shook his head. "I recall it not. Besides, it is of little consequence. Suffice it to say we counted him amongst our number once upon a time, but no more."

"Please, anything you can tell us about him would be of great help," Sariah begged.

Yert shook his head again. "It is forbidden to speak of ones such as him, I'm afraid." He let out a defeated sigh. "Besides, any information I might have would be old. I can't possibly see how it might help you."

Sariah groaned. A thousand questions burned in her head. She was finally in the audience of someone who had known the Master and might know his weaknesses, but he didn't want to talk about it. Would she ever find what she sought?

"Please," she begged. "Anything you might know might help us. We need to know how to neutralize his magic. I'm afraid we're no match for him."

Yert let out what Sariah could only describe as a strangled chuckle. "Of course not, child. None living has ever been a match for his unbridled power. He is only a man. He will pass in time."

Sariah shook her head. "You don't understand! He's out there killing people by the hundreds just for disagreeing with him. You haven't felt his power! It's terrible."

The druid chieftain looked at her with a hint of pity in his eyes. "You have felt his power, haven't you child?" Sariah nodded. "Come, let me feel your memories again."

Having few other options, she complied. She let the chieftain caress her head again as she mentally went back to the time when the Master had assaulted her. The memory felt every bit as real as the actual experience had been. Deep in her bones, she felt the same pain and hopelessness that had filled her just as strongly as she had when it happened.

It lasted for only a moment, then it was over, and Yert's eyes took on that glassy appearance again. "Yes, child, I see now." He raised his head toward the ceiling and paused for a moment before continuing. "'Tis a perversion of nature magic that he is using. A spell that is intended to heal another's wounds, but instead, it drains their power so he can use it for his own twisted ends." He paused again, and a hush fell over the room. "An abomination of nature."

Yert shook his head and let out a deep breath. "The one you call the Master, he sought such power when he was here among us as well. Only, we never believed it was possible. To think he actually succeeded in his demon's errand..." His voice trailed off, and the chieftain closed his eyes.

Sariah's eyes brightened, and she redoubled her efforts. "So you see, you have to help us stop him and put an end to it."

The druid chieftain shook his head again. "I'm sorry, child, but we are not warriors. We know nothing of what it would take to help put an end to this man and his madness. I wish we could help, but there's nothing to be done."

"Please!" Sariah begged again. "There must be something. Anything!"

Yert rubbed his chin thoughtfully. "Well, there is one thing. Only..."

"Yes?" Sariah pressed. "What is it?"

The druid chieftain shrugged and shook his head again. "'Tis only a legend, child, and nothing more. Besides, it's far too dangerous a quest, even for the likes of your group."

Sariah wasn't about to be turned away so easily. "Please! Whatever it is, just tell us. Let us decide if it's worth going after or not."

Yert's eyes looked lost in thought for a moment, then he nodded. "Very well. There is a tale in our village. A legend, really, about a plant that, when inhaled, will paralyze its victim. If you could find a way to make the Master partake of the plant, he'd be powerless to stop you. Only..."

"Only what?" Sariah's eyes brightened. This was her chance. "What's so bad about it?"

Yert put a hand to his lips, and his eyes focused on a distant spot. "The plant. It's in an area plagued by the remnant."

"The what?" She cocked her head to the side.

Yert shook his head. "One as young as you likely wouldn't know of their ilk. The remnant are a lost people. Mindless killers with dark red eyes that roam the Irth looking for their next victim. They are not to be trifled with."

Sariah looked at Will, Harvey, and Albert in turn. Their faces said it all. They'd go through hell with her if that's what it took. She looked back to Yert. "Where can we find this plant?"

The druid chieftain sighed. "Vincent?"

"Yes, sir?"

"This plant we speak of. You claim to have seen it once in your travels?"

Vincent nodded. "Yes, Elder. I have. Or at least, I think I have. Gave Ferdinand an awful fright when he got his snout full of it." Vincent chuckled at the memory.

Yert hesitated for a moment like he didn't want to ask the next question, but eventually did anyway. "Would you take these foolish children to see this plant you speak of, though it may mean your death?"

Vincent bowed his head. "I owe these 'foolish children' my very life. I would gladly give it to their cause." He nodded. "Yes, I'll do as you ask."

The druid chieftain nodded. "Very well. Let it be done." He looked at Sariah and her companions. "You may rest here tonight with Vincent. It's late. On the morrow you must leave. Successful or not in your quest, you must promise never to return. Those are my terms."

His eyes bored through Sariah's very soul. "Do you accept?"

Sariah bit her lip. Here she was, running off on a whim again. Only this time, she was possibly dooming her friends along with her. What choice did she have?

After a few moments, she nodded. "We accept."

CHAPTER THIRTEEN

"So, what does this magic paralysis plant look like?" Sariah asked Vincent. They had been traveling in a southward direction for about three days. He swore they were getting close.

Vincent shrugged. "I only half-remember, to be honest. It was a couple of years ago."

Sariah growled and side-eyed him. "You don't remember? How are we supposed to know if we find it, then?"

The old druid let out a slight chuckle. "Oh, you'll know." His eyes rolled back like he recalled a memory. "Just like Ferdinand did when we found it the first time."

"Yeah?" Sariah pressed. This sounded like a fun story to hear.

Vincent chuckled again. "Yeah. It was pretty funny. He got himself a huge whiff of the plant and just about passed out on the spot." His eyes darted toward a furry form with a red tail not far in front of them. "Didn't you, boy? The poor thing was out for two hours. About the only time I've ever seen him stop moving."

Ferdinand stopped and looked at Vincent. His beady eyes looked like they were glaring at him. Then he lifted his nose, turned back around, and scurried off into the trees.

The druid shook his head. "Poor Ferdinand. He remembers the plant, for sure."

"Well, at least we'll have someone to help show us the way, right?" She winked at him.

"Right." Vincent nodded. "Besides, once we get into the vicinity, it'll be pretty obvious. I do remember a few details. It had white petals shaped like small thorns, and the center was a strange red color. Plus, none of the wildlife would go near it. That's pretty much a dead giveaway right there."

Sariah cocked her head to the side. "You really think it'll have a chance at stopping the Master?"

Vincent shrugged again. "Can't really say for sure. I don't know that it's ever been tested on humans." His eyes dragged toward the ground. "It's worth a shot, though. Something's got to work on him."

She nodded and inhaled a deep breath. This whole quest had seemed like a longshot to begin with, and Vincent's "reassurance" wasn't very reassuring. But something was better than nothing. She only hoped the Eagle's Claw could hold on long enough for them to get back with it.

How long had they been gone now? A week? Then another week to get back? Who knew what the Master could do in that time.

A shudder crossed her shoulders involuntarily, and she brought her jacket in a little closer as if warding off an invisible wind.

The group marched in silence for another hour until the trees started to thin out, signaling that they were nearing the edge of the forest. The mountainous land Vincent had spoken of should be close.

Moments later, the trees gave way completely, and Sariah saw tall mountain peaks stretching out as far as the horizon. Several of the taller ones were capped in white snow that glowed in the sun. The sight was gorgeous.

"Not much farther now," Vincent called out. He turned and looked at the group. "We should be careful from here on. No telling if or when the remnant will show up out here."

There was that word again, the remnant. Sariah had pressed Vincent for details on them earlier, but he'd been tight-lipped, only saying that it would be for the best if they never crossed paths.

Sariah returned her attention to the trail ahead of them. A giant cliff face was rearing its head not far in front of them. What lay behind it was anyone's guess. Could the remnant be hiding out there, waiting to ambush them? If so, then what?

Just then, Vincent stopped and called for everyone else to halt.

"Quiet," he whispered, putting a finger to his lips.

A chill ran down Sariah's spine, and she rubbed her arms for warmth while watching Vincent for a signal. The man was completely still. Even Bear and Ferdinand had stopped in their tracks.

That's when she noticed it was completely quiet. Not even the insects were making any noise.

Vincent crept forward a few steps and put a hand over

his ear. He stayed that way for a few moments, then nodded and looked at the group.

"It's the remnant," he said in a whisper.

Will side-eyed him. "How can you be so sure?"

"Listen," he said. "Do you hear anything?"

Will shook his head. "No, I don't."

"Exactly." Vincent nodded. "That's how I know." He glanced down at Will's side. "Ready your weapons, everyone. They're just around this bend, and they can't be reasoned with. Our only shot is to get the drop on them."

Sariah drew her blade and watched everyone else do the same. Everyone but Vincent that is. He carried a large wooden staff that looked more like an old tree branch than a weapon. Inwardly, she wondered what it could possibly do against a horde of crazed semi-humans. She shook her head. The time for worrying was in the past. Now was time for battle.

The group crept forward slowly, trying not to make any noise. As they came closer to the bend, Sariah could hear the tell-tale sounds of movement and what sounded like some sort of chatter, though it was in a language she didn't recognize.

She could feel her heart beat faster in her chest as the prospect of battle neared. She wondered why she was so nervous. She'd faced many a foe in battle and came out ahead. What made this looming conflict so different?

It was the unknown she decided. She had no idea what kind of enemy she was facing, and that was terrifying.

As one unit, the group rounded the bend and descended upon the remnant encampment. There must have been at least twenty of them, all battle-ready despite how careful her group had been to hide their own movements.

The foul creatures wore mismatched armor and clothing that was half-tattered and looked like it had been scavenged from a hundred different corpses. It probably had.

Their eyes were red and glowing. Those eyes reminded her of the Master and seemed to pierce into her very soul, leaving her feeling cold and afraid.

"Soldiers, advance!" Will cried.

In one swift movement, the group lunged forth, and swords clashed. Sariah could hear Bear growling and saw him disappear into a particularly thick group of the enemy.

She didn't have time to worry about him, though, as there were plenty of attackers for her to fend off on her own.

A high sword stroke came at her, and she dodged back just in time to keep it from doing any damage.

Sariah slashed back with a blow of her own that sent her opponent's blade wide. She followed up with a mid-level swipe that cut through cloth and flesh and left a gaping wound.

Her opponent staggered and disappeared into the crowd as another remnant charged her flank.

This one seemed a little more prepared and held his weapon closer to his body. He made a few furtive swipes toward her middle, which she parried with ease.

She swiped at the thing's legs, but the blow fell short and did nothing.

The remnant hacked at her sword arm, but she parried the strike and turned her blade inward so it could move down his arm and hopefully hack off a couple of fingers.

Fortunately, his blade lacked a guard, and her weapon struck true. The remnant let out an unearthly howl and dropped his sword as it fell from his now mutilated hand.

Not wanting to waste any time, Sariah skewered him and watched him fall to the ground where he lay unnoticed by the rest of the horde.

The sound of a bark and a hiss broke through the crowd. She saw Bear and Ferdinand fighting tooth and claw with a couple of the remaining remnants near the center of the camp.

She swung at another remnant, wondering what was happening with her friends, but she didn't have time to look for them.

A strange noise assaulted her then, and she noticed the sky starting to darken as several clouds moved in quicker than should have been possible. The air around her started to feel electric and crackled in the semi-darkness.

Vincent's staff glowed for a brief second, and a jagged bolt of lightning shot out of the sky, right into the center of the group of remnant. Several of the enemy howled in pain. A few of them fell and stopped moving, wisps of acrid smoke rising from their corpses.

Sariah shot a glance over at Vincent. He nodded and gave her a knowing smile. She didn't have long to be impressed, though, as another remnant took that moment to attack.

Readying her blade, she thrust it in front of her, hoping to end the combat quickly.

Her opponent was too quick for her, and he caught her blade with his own, batting it away.

She twisted the blade mid-parry and brought it back with a quick slice aimed at the creature's neck. This strike found purchase, almost severing the remnant's head in one blow.

The defeated remnant fell to the ground, and she had a moment of respite.

Sariah scanned the area for her friends. Her heart leaped when she saw a remnant creeping up behind Harvey unawares, ready to pounce. She thought about taking it out with a fireball but worried she'd end up sending the remnant plowing into her friend in the process.

Instead, she used her magic to make the ground underneath the remnant explode upward and sent the creature flying in a backward arc. She then sent a fireball on a collision course with her airborne target.

The remnant's body landed a moment later, setting the nearby grass on fire.

Harvey turned and flashed her a dopey grin, and she gave him a thumb's up, then she returned her attention to the remaining foes.

Another remnant was approaching. This one seemed to be one of the last ones standing.

She spun on her heel and made a wild swipe for his sword arm, severing it at the elbow with one blow. The remnant put up little fight as she lunged forward, skewering his heart and ending the battle.

Panting, she looked around. Everyone else seemed similarly winded, but they were still standing. The remnant, not so much. All of them were dead or dying. At the very least, there were no more blades in her face.

Sariah let a broad smile crease her face, and she looked at her friends with a glint in her eye, but it didn't last long.

She heard the sound of clapping break through the sudden stillness in the air. She looked around to see who it was, but it wasn't any of her friends. They all looked as confused as she was.

A dark thought crossed her mind, and a sudden chill ran down her spine.

Could it be him?

Moments later, her thoughts were answered as the form of a lone man materialized. His face looked a little different than it had the last two times, but there was no mistaking how his presence made her feel. A knot formed in her stomach, and she wanted to retch.

Somehow, the Master had come for her yet again.

How did he find us? Her mind raced, but no answers came.

The Master's face erupted into a smile, and his eyes bored into her soul. She felt that same sense of dread she'd felt the first time they'd crossed paths start to consume her.

This time, she was determined to fight it. She made vague motions with her fingers and readied a fireball, but the magic didn't answer her call.

Instead, the Master stuck out his hand, and suddenly she felt stiff as a board. She couldn't move a single muscle.

"Easy now," the Master called out. "We wouldn't want to end this confrontation early, would we?"

Sariah scowled and tried to rush him, but she was rooted in place. She could still turn her head, though, so she spared a glance at her companions. All of them were in a similar state. Even Bear seemed to be glued in place, though he was growling something fierce.

"Thought you could take me out with a simple fireball, did you?" the Master chided her. He shook his head and tsked. "Such foolishness. I know what you're doing even before you do, remember?"

"Just get on with it already." Sariah rolled her eyes. "You talk too much." While she talked, she put all her effort into moving. It was nearly impossible, but she managed to wiggle her fingers just a little despite the Master's pressure.

She grinned at him. Perhaps his magic wasn't as strong as it looked. Either that, or he was over-exerting himself. Either way, it was good news for her.

Her fingers twitched a few more times, and she summoned forth another fireball and sent it hurling in his direction.

The Master held out a hand, and the fire dissipated on some sort of magic shield.

He tsked again. "Foolish little girl. You're going to have to do much better than that, I'm afraid."

"With pleasure," she taunted. She sent another fireball his way, but this one was similarly ineffective. If she could keep it up long enough, he'd start to weaken. Then maybe she could get under his guard.

So long as he didn't get close enough to use his really dangerous power, that is.

The Master cocked his head to the side. "Is that your plan, little girl?" he asked. Shaking his head, he continued. "You still have so much to learn." He took a few steps toward her while she was powerless to stop him.

Sariah's eyes went wide, and she gasped. How did he read my mind? Then she remembered what Harvey had told her about his time in Chatwick and her expression soured.

He gave her a cruel smile and inclined his head. "Indeed, I can. Yours is like an open book." His smile turned into a frown, and he glanced behind her. "Now, about that little lesson I promised you."

The Master's hand shot forth, and a strong gust of wind rushed past her. She heard a grunt from behind her and watched as Will's body was swept up into the air.

"Say goodbye to your friend," the Master taunted her. Then he dropped his hand and Will began to fall, right over the edge of the cliff. He looked helpless as his body fell like a giant stone, unable to fight the magic or help himself.

"No!" Sariah shouted. She fought against her invisible bonds with everything she could and somehow broke free. She heard the Master let out a yelp of surprise but ignored it and broke into a sprint, heading for Will.

As he passed by her, she reached out with both hands, desperately trying to grab onto something and finally found purchase on one of his shirtsleeves. She closed her hand as tight as she could and braced for impact.

"I've got you, Will!" she cried. Her arm nearly tore out of its socket when the impact finally came, but she managed to hold onto him.

All the while, the Master stood by and watched, captivated by her actions. She shot him an icy glare, then returned her attention to Will's helpless form.

Her friend looked at her. "Thank you, Sariah," he said. "You can't hold me up by yourself. Not for long."

"Nonsense," she insisted. Though in reality, she knew he was right. She was already straining to keep him from tumbling the rest of the way. She glanced at his shirt and saw the fabric was starting to unravel at the seam.

"Just grab on with your other hand. I'm not letting you go!" she implored.

Will glanced at her and then back down at his own body and shook his head. "Can't move it, remember? It's no good."

"Come on!" Sariah pleaded. "Fight against it! You can do it!"

Will flashed her a smile as the tear in the fabric of Will's shirt intensified. He eyed the shirt carefully, then returned his attention to her. "It was nice knowing you, Sariah." He gave her a wink and beamed at her once.

All at once, the sleeve of his shirt finished its separation, and Will tumbled into the air, disappearing noiselessly into the mist below him.

"No!" Sariah screamed. Tears formed in her eyes and she closed her fist even tighter, hoping against hope that somehow he had survived the fall. "No!"

Behind her, she heard the Master's cruel laugh. She turned and glared at him. "You'll pay for this!"

The Master tsked again. "I told you, Sariah. I'm going to take everything away from you, one thing at a time. I'm going to show you the meaning of true pain."

With every ounce of strength she could muster, she lashed out at him with her magic. A blue wave of power shot forth from her fingertips, engulfing him. The Master fought against it with his shield, though she could sense it was starting to crack.

Unfortunately, she was running out of power. She dropped the assault and lowered her arms.

The Master dusted himself off and shook his head. "A valiant effort," he taunted. "It came up a little short." He shrugged. "No matter."

He casually walked over to where Vincent and Albert stood, still as statues. "I'm going to take these two with me," he told her like it was a settled matter. As weak as she was, she was powerless to stop him, and he still seemed completely fresh.

"Consider them souvenirs of our time together, if you will." The Master gave her a slight bow, and then he closed one hand around each of their wrists. "Farewell, Sariah."

Sariah's eyes narrowed, and she tried to run forward, but she was out of energy, and instead she tumbled backward, closer to the cliff face.

"No!" she cried. It was too late. The Master had disappeared, along with Vincent and Albert.

Wearily, she tried once again to stand, but failed. Her vision was starting to get blurry. She'd used too much energy in her attack and would need to rest. She stumbled back again just as her consciousness began to slip.

The last thing Sariah felt before everything went black was the sensation of wind beneath her as she went tumbling over the cliff into the oblivion below.

CHAPTER FOURTEEN

Harvey finally felt the bonds that held him in place give way, and he ran to the cliff face that Will and Sariah had gone over.

"Sariah!" he called out. "Will!" He waited several seconds, but there was no answer.

Hanging his head in his hands, he sat down at the edge of the cliff. He couldn't believe it. One moment, they had just fended off a major remnant attack, and the next moment their group was in tatters.

The Master had somehow swooped in and ruined everything. How had he even known about their mission? Something about the whole thing just didn't sit right.

"Sariah!" he called out again. There was no answer. It was useless. His best friend had gone tumbling over a cliff, and he'd been powerless to stop her.

What's the use? he wondered. What good is any of it without Sariah by my side?

He'd never really been sure how she felt about him, though he knew there was something more than just friendship. Now he'd never know what that something was. He'd never get a chance to see if their relationship could work outside of hectic situations.

It was too much for him to handle. A single tear fell out of the corner of his eye and tumbled to the ground as he sat, wallowing in his guilt. If only he'd been stronger, he could have helped her. He just knew it.

The sound of a low whine interrupted his thoughts, and he looked down at his side. Beside him was Bear, nudging his head into his lap. The animal looked almost as distraught as he was.

Mindlessly, Harvey put his hand on Bear's head and rubbed it. His warm fur felt comforting in this dark time.

"It'll be okay, Bear," he told the animal, though he doubted it himself. "It'll all be okay somehow."

Harvey shook his head and sniffed, then brought up his other hand to dry his eyes. He looked back down at Bear, who hadn't moved.

"I don't know how we'll get by without Sariah, either, Bear, but somehow we'll manage."

Bear raised his head, then, and stared up at Harvey. For a second, it looked like the animal was shaking his head from side to side.

Harvey furrowed his brow. That's strange.

"No?" he asked Bear.

The dog barked in response.

"No, what?" He cocked his head to the side.

Bear replied with another two sharp barks, glanced toward the cliff, then looked up at him expectantly again.

Harvey narrowed his eyes. "No, Sariah?"

The dog let out a low growl.

He rubbed his chin again. "No, she's not dead?" He couldn't believe it. Here he was, talking to a dog like it was a person.

Bear gave him another sharp bark, then nodded and laid his head back down in Harvey's lap.

Was it possible? Harvey wondered. He shook his head. It was just the vague hope of an animal. What stock could he possibly put into it?

The dog seemed to have a special connection to Sariah, and to be perfectly honest, he wasn't willing to give up hope, either. Not yet, at least.

He looked down at Bear, who seemed content with his head in his lap, and a broad grin crossed his face.

"Well, if Sariah's alive, then what are we doing moping around here for?" he asked.

Bear shot up and barked at him again.

Harvey nodded. "I agree. Let's get going."

The dog took a few steps along the cliff wall and looked back at Harvey expectantly.

He got onto his feet and dusted himself off, then looked at Bear and grinned again. He beckoned with his hands for the animal to keep moving. "Lead the way."

When Sariah finally opened her eyes, it was several hours later. Her vision was a little blurry, and she had a raging headache.

She blinked a few times to try and regain her focus and groaned. Every fiber of her body hurt like she'd run a marathon, but nothing seemed particularly out of place.

She glanced down at herself. Much to her relief, she didn't find any bones jutting out at odd angles, and there wasn't any blood. At least, not any that she could see.

Which was a miracle in and of itself, given that she'd fallen off a cliff.

Memories of the battle and the Master came rushing back and she shot up, her eyes darting in every direction.

"Easy now," a voice called out from behind her. It was one she recognized.

A warm smile formed on her lips, and she turned to find Will sitting not far from her.

He grinned back at her. "About time you woke up, sleepyhead."

Sariah shook her head, and the motion made her head feel kind of wobbly, so she put a hand up to her head to steady it.

Will got up and walked over to her. There was a concerned expression on his face. "Everything okay? Your entry was a little bumpy, but I thought I blunted most of it."

He placed a hand gently on her shoulder. She looked up at him and gave him a weak smile. With her other hand, she grabbed his hand and squeezed it once. His skin felt warm and oddly comforting.

She cocked her head to the side. "How did you..."

"Survive falling off a cliff?" he finished for her.

Sariah nodded once. "Yeah. That."

Will shrugged. "Not really sure, myself. I thought for sure I was a goner back there when I fell out of your grasp. Turns out, the cliff wasn't as tall as I thought. Maybe only twenty feet to the bottom I'd wager. Since you'd caught me halfway down, the fall wasn't too bad."

"Huh," she replied, not sure what else to say.

Will flashed her a smile. "I guess we should count ourselves lucky that the Master didn't know that either, eh?"

Sariah smiled and nodded again. "Yeah, I guess so."

"Besides," he continued. "It's my fault in the first place."

Her brow furrowed, and she looked at him cross-eyed. "How's that?"

"Rule fifty-two, remember?" he said with a wink and half a grin.

Now she felt even more confused. "Rule fifty-two?" She racked her brain but couldn't remember that one.

"Watch out for cliffs."

"Ah," she said, tilting her head back but still not really remembering. Just how hard had she hit her head anyway? "I know I should remember that one, but I don't. Good rule, though."

"Don't worry about it." He waved at her dismissively. "I just made it up."

She jabbed at his chest. "You tricked me!"

He held up his hands defensively. "Hey, it's all in good fun, right?"

"I suppose so," she admitted. "It's still not fair!" She shoved him.

Will flashed her another smile and started laughing. She joined in, and they both laughed for a solid minute before saying anything else.

After things calmed down, he continued speaking. "Well, I suppose I owe you one." He gave her a nudge on her shoulder.

Sariah cocked her head to the side. It still hurt, but the pain was starting to lessen. "What for?"

"For saving my life," he said with a shrug. "Who knows, I still might not have died right away from the fall over the cliff, but I would have been in much worse shape without your quick action."

She waved a hand dismissively. "You saved my life, too, you know, by breaking my fall. We'll call it even." She flashed him a grin and he nodded.

"Deal," he said after a moment. He let out a deep breath. "How did you manage to fight against the Master's spell like that, anyway? I've never seen anything like it."

Sariah thought about that for a moment but couldn't come up with an answer. Her head started to hurt again, and she squinted against the pain. "I...I don't know," she said after a moment, shaking her head. "To be honest, I'm not sure I did. I think the Master let go of me. Figured my anguish would be all the greater if I could move and still fail to save you."

Will's eyes widened, and he looked at her with an expression that spoke of awe. "You're amazing," he whispered. "I guess I was right about you, after all."

"Yeah?" Sariah asked, not understanding. "How so?"

"I told Ilene after our battle all those weeks ago that you were something special. Something unlike anyone I'd ever seen before. I guess I was right."

Sariah's head started reeling, and not from the pain. Had he really said that about her? She felt her cheeks start to redden, and she lowered her gaze and looked away from him.

"You said that?" she asked hesitantly.

She didn't know what to think. Will had hated her from the first day. He had always been after her, treating her like she was somehow less than the others. While it was true they had grown something of a friendship with each other since she'd still always felt like he was somehow superior to her.

Now she didn't know what to think.

Will nodded and knelt beside her. "It's true," he admitted. He placed a hand on her chin and pulled her face toward his, so they were looking at each other again. "Guess I'm just a big softy, after all."

"Don't say that," Sariah replied. "You'll spoil your image." She flashed him a toothy grin.

Will looked at her intently for a moment, then he let out a slight chuckle. "Well, we can't have that, can we?" He gave her another wink.

"Nope." She shook her head playfully.

Looking deep into his eyes, she found something there that she couldn't quite recognize. She held his gaze for another moment with neither of them saying or doing anything, then his head started to move toward hers.

Heat started to rise as blood rushed to Sariah's cheeks, and she felt her heartbeat intensify as he inched closer.

A second before his lips touched hers, a sense of revulsion washed over her, and she pushed Will's face away with her hands.

Sariah quickly turned away and hid her face. "I'm sorry," she called over her shoulder. She was blushing and felt well and truly embarrassed.

Will backed up and shook his head. "No, it's me that

should be sorry. I shouldn't have taken advantage of you like that."

She turned to face him with a shocked expression. "No, it's not that!" she insisted. "You weren't taking advantage of anything."

He shook his head again. "No, it's not right of me, a man in my position of power over you. I should have just kept those feelings to myself." He got up and started pacing.

She stood up and went after him, placing a hand on his chest. "Hey, it's not like that! It's just..."

Just what? she wondered. She had wanted him at that moment. She didn't know why she had resisted and pushed him away.

Will looked down at her and his expression softened. "Look, I appreciate you trying to soften the blow and all, but I get it. I haven't exactly been the nicest to you. Why would you want a guy like me when you've got Harvey around?"

Sariah started to blush again, and she turned her face to hide it. "Harvey?" She winced. "Is that what you think?" She shook her head. The pain came back again, but she pushed it away. "It's not like that. Harvey and I, we're just...just friends. That's all."

He stared at her intently. "Then what is it?"

She felt his eyes boring into her and couldn't take the intensity, so she turned away again. "I don't know exactly. It's just, I've been down this road before, you know? With Gabe. He was my mentor, too, once, and look how that turned out."

Will grabbed her and pulled her until she was looking

right at him. "Is that what you think? That I'll end up being like Gabe?"

Sariah searched his eyes. She saw a great many feelings there—hurt, longing, and desire. But not betrayal. No, Will wouldn't betray her like Gabe had. She knew that. Still, it didn't feel quite right.

"I'm sorry," she said after a moment. "I just...I can't." She turned away again.

Will nodded and took a few steps away from her. "I understand. I'll respect your decision."

Sariah let out a long sigh. "Besides," she started. "Aren't you with Ilene?"

He balked at her and practically snorted. "Ilene? Heck no! What would give you that impression?"

"Oh, you know." She placed a hand on his chest and moved it up and down seductively. "'My dear William' and all that?" She gave him a suggestive wink.

Will put his hand to stop her and glared down at her. His cheeks were starting to turn beet red. "You heard that bit, did you?"

She nodded and started to grin like an idiot. "Uh-huh. I bet she thinks you're quite the lady's man." As she said the last bit, she playfully jabbed a finger into his chest.

He looked away suddenly. "It's nothing like that!" he blurted out. "It's hard to describe, but you've got the wrong idea."

"Whatever you say, my dear William." She giggled.

"Please don't!" Will begged, turning to face her again. His cheeks were still bright red.

Sariah cocked her head. "Don't what?" She grinned. "Don't call you 'my dear William' in her voice?"

He let out a chuckle and backed up another couple of steps. "Yes," he replied with a nod. "Please don't do that."

"Oh, but it's so fun!" she exclaimed. She took a few steps toward him, and he backed up again.

This time, he ended up tripping over a branch on the ground and fell into a small flower patch.

Sariah burst out laughing.

"Hey!" Will cried. "Not cool."

"Sorry," Sariah said once she was calm enough to keep talking. "It's just, I wasn't expecting you to fall over like that." She stuck out her hand to him. "Come here, I'll help you up. We still have a plant to look for, remember?"

Will looked up at her but didn't budge. "I can't."

She rolled her eyes. "Come on, don't be like that. Be a big man and get moving. We don't have all day."

"No, really," he insisted. "I can't move. It's like before with the Master only, I don't think it's his spell anymore."

Sariah side-eyed him, but he remained steadfast.

She took in her surroundings. They were near the bottom of the cliff, and there was a small stream to their right, and flowers beneath Will, but nothing out of the ordinary.

Then she noticed that there was no wildlife in the vicinity, not even a squirrel or a mosquito. She'd thought it was because of the remnant earlier, but now she wasn't so sure.

"Let me take a better look at those flowers you fell into," Sariah told Will. He just looked at her and did nothing.

She knelt on the ground, getting closer but keeping a safe distance. She put one hand over her mouth to keep from inhaling their pollen. Gingerly, she fingered one of the flowers. It had small white petals, kind of like thorns, and a red center.

A smile crept across her lips. "My dear William, I think you stumbled upon the object of my affection quite unintentionally."

Will's expression soured. "You're not going to let that one drop, are you?"

"Nope." She shook her head and let out another giggle. "Come on, let's get you out of here and gather up some of these flowers, then get back to the group."

It took a mighty shove on her part, but she managed to get Will out of the flower patch and onto stable ground. Within a few minutes, he was starting to wiggle his fingers and toes and had regained feeling in his face.

Sariah grabbed a few of the flowers and placed them gently into some extra fabric, then rolled them up and put them into the bottom of her bag. She sat down next to Will, who was almost in a sitting position by himself. She gave him a light shove.

"That was unexpected," he said at last.

Sariah nodded. "Now at least we know they'll do the trick," she replied. She beamed at him. "And about how long they'll last."

"Indeed. Now we just need to get him to inhale their pollen. Any ideas on that one?"

She shrugged. "No idea. It'll come in time." She patted her bag. "At least now we can fight on equal footing."

"True." Will stretched his arms and got himself into a full sitting position. "Well, I suppose it's about time we get moving."

"No need," Sariah told him.

"Huh?" He looked at her sideways.

Sariah pointed toward the small stream. On the other side was the vague outline of a person and an animal. Their appearance was still a little hazy, but Sariah knew who they were.

"Bear!" Sariah belted out. She heard an appreciative and longing bark in response, then the dog came bounding through the water toward her.

"Hey, I came too!" Harvey cried, running after Bear.

The dog reached her first and practically bowled her over with the force of his body. She sat scratching his head and staring into his eyes.

"I can't help that Bear is faster than you," Sariah called out to Harvey. Moments later, he came into view. He had a harried expression on his face like he'd been through a lot.

She wondered what it had been like for him to watch her fall over the cliff. What would she have done if the positions had been reversed? She pushed the thought from her mind. It was enough that they were back together.

"I'm sorry," she told Harvey.

He cocked his head to the side. "For what?"

"For worrying you over nothing."

"Aww." He waved his hand dismissively. "It's all good now that we're back together."

"Definitely." She embraced him for a moment, then pulled away and patted her bag again. "Plus, we got what we came for."

"Yeah?" Harvey asked.

Sariah nodded. "Yeah."

He furrowed his brow. "And the cost? Vincent is gone, and poor Albert, too."

Will waved a hand dismissively. "Don't count that kid out just yet. Not even the Master could put a scratch on him. We'll get him back in no time."

"Do you really think so?" Sariah asked.

He nodded. "I know so." Will slapped his thighs and shot upright. He held a hand out to Sariah. "Now, let's get going. We've got a war to win, remember?"

The corners of Sariah's lips curled into a broad smile. She accepted his hand. "Yes, sir."

CHAPTER FIFTEEN

Lester walked the walls of Talon's Reach slowly. It seemed pointless to walk along the walls while the front gate lay in tatters—anyone could get inside the gates now if they wanted to—but he did it anyway. Such was his job, and at his age, it was all he could do to help ensure the safety of his fellow townsfolk.

Not that much of anything happened as a rule. No one had come to the gates since Will and Sariah had returned to town two days ago, and before that, there'd been nothing for weeks.

He scanned the horizon, determined to do his job to the best of his abilities. The sun was high overhead, but the air was still a little bit chilly. It was autumn and would be winter before long. He hated winters, but he'd survived many of them anyway.

It appeared today would be no different than most. Nothing was out there.

Lester propped himself up against one of the

supporting walls and wiped his brow. Marching in full gear was exhausting work. He took out his canteen and took several deep, steadying breaths, then took a long drink of water.

Just when he was about to give up for the day, he saw it. It was still quite far away, but there was no mistaking it. A lone figure—a man—was walking straight for Talon's Reach. He was carrying something in his hands.

What is that? Lester pondered. He put a hand over his eyes to block out the sun and squinted as hard as he could. It was hard to make out from this distance, but he was pretty sure he knew what it was. Though why he couldn't begin to fathom.

In the distance walked a lone man in a Dusk Raven uniform. He looked to be completely unarmed. In his hands, he waved a bright white flag.

A chill ran down Lester's spine. The man by himself obviously posed no threat, but that's what made the whole scene odd.

What the heck is going on? he wondered. Is it the Master come to taunt us again? He shook his head. That seemed unlikely.

He shrugged his old, tired shoulders and pulled his coat a little tighter around his slim frame. He supposed he'd find out soon enough.

Sergeant Ty Genrose swallowed hard. He looked at the people assembled. Some of them he recognized. Sariah and

Harvey, he'd seen several times back in Stratton. They were easy to pick out. The rest of them he'd never seen before.

"Who are you? Why did you come here?" one of them asked. His name was Will.

The sergeant took a deep breath and released it slowly. "I told you, I'm a sergeant in the employ of the Dusk Ravens, and I'm here to deliver a message to your leader."

Will eyed him cautiously and started pacing, turning around him in a wide arc, though his eyes never broke contact. Ty figured it was some kind of intimidation tactic. If it was, it was working great. He squirmed a little and fought against his bonds to no avail.

A bead of sweat formed on his forehead and started trailing down his nose, itching all the way. He desperately wished he could do something to disperse the sweat or scratch the itch, but bound as he was, that was impossible. Instead, the slow-moving liquid only made his sense of fear all the more intense.

His eyes darted around the room and met Sariah's. She was looking at him with a look of awe mixed with confusion. He supposed he deserved it, after all he'd done.

"Look," Ty started. "If you'll just take me to your leader, we—"

"Why should we do that?" Will shouted from behind his shoulder. The sound made him wince.

Ty rolled his eyes. "I don't like this any more than you do, I promise." He raised his hands up a little and shook the shackles that bound them. "Are these really necessary?"

Will darted in front of him again. "They are until we

know your true purpose. You're an enemy combatant. You're lucky we didn't kill you on sight."

"The white flag—"

"Who cares about your supposed truce? Was the Master so kind the last time one of you darkened our doors? I don't think so. How do we know this isn't some kind of trick?"

Another of them, Ilene by name, put a hand on Will's shoulder and pulled him back. "At ease, soldier," she said in an icy tone.

The big man looked back at her and scowled, then he backed off. "But—" he whined.

"But nothing," Ilene replied, glaring at him. "We must honor the truce until we have reason to believe otherwise."

Will threw up his hands and stalked off to a corner of the room.

Sergeant Ty took in a deep breath and tried to calm his nerves. It was easier without that big brute breathing down on him.

Ilene cocked her head to the side and approached him. She reached out with one hand and gently touched his cheek. Her hand was icy cold to the touch, much like her voice.

"There now," Ilene said. "Let's talk like civilized people, shall we? Why did you come here?"

"I told you earlier, lady. I have a message from the Master for your leader."

She nodded. "That would be me. I am the leader of Talon's Reach."

Ty's eyes went wide. "You are? You're the leader?" Was

she telling the truth? She looked so tiny and frail. Yet, there was no hint of mirth or malice in her eyes.

Ilene nodded again. "Indeed, I am. Now about this message?"

"Right." He nodded and cleared his throat, then inhaled deeply. "I am to tell you that the Master has taken hostage the one named Albert and is holding him at his base near Stratton. He said he would hold the boy for one week after this message was delivered. If you want to see him alive, you should come unarmed and unaided to the Master's base and bring Sariah to trade for him."

His message finally delivered, his features slumped and he lowered his gaze.

Ilene blinked a few times. "That's it?"

He nodded once. "Yes, my lady. That's it." He jangled his chains again. "Now, can I go please?"

The icy woman looked into his eyes and gently caressed his cheek again. "If what you say is true, then we will let you go. Until we know for sure..." her voice trailed off.

Sergeant Ty Genrose let out a deep sigh. "I understand. Take me to my cell."

"Can we trust him?" Will asked Ilene later. They were alone at last. Sariah and Harvey had both argued with them almost all day about how they had to go after Albert right away. It's what the kid would have done for any of them.

They weren't wrong. That's precisely the kind of thing Albert would have done. Will let out a low sigh. He hoped the kid was safe.

Ilene shook her head. "I'm not sure," she admitted. "It's pretty obviously a trap."

Will nodded. "Of course it's a trap!" He rubbed his chin. "To send one of his lackeys to do his bidding rather than come himself? The nerve of that guy."

"Yes, indeed," Ilene replied. "Can't imagine why he wouldn't come himself." She rolled her eyes at him.

"Come now, Ilene," he said. "Don't go giving that madman any credit. You've seen how he operates."

She nodded. "That I have. Which is why I find his little message dubious at best."

"Agreed. Besides, the army's not ready yet. They still need training, and we only have twenty or so magitech weapons built up. Hardly enough to arm them." He stared at the rug in the middle of the small room. "We need more time."

Ilene walked over to him and put a hand on his shoulder. Like always, her touch felt cool against his rough skin, but this time there was a certain warmth to it that was ordinarily absent. Her eyes searched for his and finally found them.

"Poor little Albert," she said. "He must be so scared, alone like that." Ilene gently traced a hand over his cheek, then dropped her hand and turned to face the small fire they had built earlier.

Will looked at her as they stood side by side, staring into the fire. The small woman looked so striking in the firelight. He could see a slight glint of the fire reflecting off her eyes, which felt distant. Yet, there was a hint of determination mixed in there, and also a deep sadness. Or loneliness, perhaps. It was hard to tell which.

"Yes, poor Albert," Will repeated. "Poor Vincent, too. You didn't know him, but he sacrificed for us as well." He hung his head. How could he honestly be thinking about throwing their lives away so callously? He didn't see an alternative and let out a tired sigh. They simply weren't ready.

"And yet," Ilene said in a voice almost that of a whisper. She was still staring into the fire, barely moving.

Will looked at her anew. There was something different about her, he decided. Something new. Or perhaps something old. The sadness had left her eyes, leaving only the grim determination he'd sensed a moment prior.

All at once, he understood her true motives. He gasped. "You want to go after him, don't you?" His eyes searched hers for a glimmer of an answer.

Ilene flashed him the tiniest hint of a grin. "Maybe," she admitted with a shrug.

His lips curled upward into a giant smile. "That's my girl!" He patted her on the shoulder, then an odd thought came to him. "Wait, you're not actually planning on going out there alone, are you?"

She side-eyed him and jabbed a finger into his chest. "Of course not! I'm not suicidal."

"Thank the Patriarch!" Will breathed a sigh of relief. He took a few steps then turned to face her again. "So when do we tell the troops?"

The Master took a hesitant step out of his stronghold. An aide was waiting for him. The aide scraped and bowed once he caught sight of him. The Master scowled and kicked him for being so weak.

"So sorry, Master," the aide quibbled, quickly getting back to his feet and bowing again.

"What's this problem you summoned me for?" the Master fired back. "I thought I told everyone not to disturb me during my research!"

The aide bowed again and whimpered under his breath. "Of course, Master. I'm so sorry, I—"

He served the pathetic man a swift punch to the gut, and the aide doubled over in pain, writhing on the ground.

The Master shook his head and tsked. "Good help can be so hard to find." He scanned his surroundings and spotted another man cowering in a corner.

"You there!" the Master said, pointing toward the shaking individual. "What's your name, Sergeant?"

"M-me?" the man replied like it was the first time he'd ever opened his mouth.

"Yes, you," The Master nodded. "Get over here! What's your name, Sergeant? Don't make me ask again."

The scared man bowed and scraped his way over to his side. "I'm no sergeant, Master, just a lowly servant."

He took hold of the man by the nape of his neck and lifted. "Stand tall, man. Stop bowing and scraping so much! Do you want to live your whole life on the floor?"

The scared man yelped. His eyes darted in every direction like he wanted nothing more than to run away. Then he stood his ground.

"Humph," the Master muttered. He supposed he could respect the man a little. "That's better. Now, what's your name? Don't keep me waiting."

"Yes, Master," the man said with another bow. "It's Ben, sir."

"Sergeant Ben, give me a report. What's going on around here?"

Ben shook his head. "I told you, Master, I ain't no—"

"Do you want the promotion or not?" The Master was starting to lose his patience with this one as well, and he raised a fist as if to strike him.

"Yes, Master! Of course, Master!" Ben replied, raising a hand to protect his face and cowering only slightly less than before.

The Master lowered his hand and looked at Ben again. He was filthy and dressed in rags, but at least he had a strong survival instinct. It was more than he could say for some of his underlings. He supposed it would have to do.

He dusted off Ben's clothing a little and then instantly regretted it as his hand felt like it had just been through a trash heap. The Master wrinkled his nose and moved his face away from the sniveling excuse for a sergeant.

"Now tell me, Ben. What's going on around here that's so important it needed to interrupt my research?"

Ben gave him a slight bow. "Of course, Master. It's the Eagle's Claw, sir. They're...well you see, they're on the move and..."

The Master raised an eyebrow and scowled. "And? Don't make me beat it out of you." He raised his hand menacingly again.

Much to the Master's surprise, this time Ben didn't flinch.

"Their army, Master," Ben explained with another slight bow. "It's here. All of it."

The Master blinked a few times, and he looked at Ben incredulously. "They came?" he repeated. His expression turned to one of disgust, and he huffed. "How did they get past my spies?"

Ben bowed and lowered his head. "I don't know, Master, I—"

He shoved Ben out of the way. The newly promoted sergeant muttered something under his breath, but the Master wasn't listening. He was too shocked by this new development to pay any more attention to the man.

The Master walked out, leaving the entryway behind. He looked over at the mangled remains of a building to his left. Giant heaps of stone, twisted metal, and glass hung suspended in some odd formation he couldn't place. It was one of several such structures in the area.

He liked it here, with all the death and decay from days long past. It was welcoming for a guy like him. It's why he'd made his base here all those years ago.

It didn't take him long to come across the enemy's encampment. Their hasty arrangement of tents and wagons stood out like a sore thumb amongst the foliage and wrecked buildings. A sea of white tents, all flying the Eagle's Claw flag, stretched out in a little clearing, not a thousand feet from his doorstep.

He looked around for that new sergeant—Ben was it?—again. It didn't take long to find him.

"You!" he shouted.

Ben stood tall, though his legs were shaking a little. "Y-yes, Master?"

"Where's my shipment! The one from Zachariah. Where is it?"

The newly promoted sergeant looked confused for a moment, then a wave of recognition washed over his face, and he nodded. "It's over this way, Master." He pointed toward a couple of nearby barrels that had a ship insignia emblazoned on them.

"Ah," the Master said. He rushed over to the barrels and ripped the lid off the nearest one with a quick tug from one hand. Inside, he saw thousands and thousands of tiny black granules. "My secret weapon," he continued with a grin. "It's come just in time."

He dipped his hand into the barrel's contents and lifted up a small portion of the bounty. Several black granules ran through the gaps in his fingers. The black sand felt off somehow like it was heavier than it should be, and it smelled terrible. He'd seen it working on a small scale once before, and it had been quite the sight to behold. Almost as destructive as fire magic, but without the tiring side effects.

"It may not be magitech weaponry," he mused, "but it sure packs a hell of a punch." He nodded and closed the barrel back up.

"Sergeant Ben! See that this is taken to the officer's tent."

Ben gave a slight bow. "At once, Master."

The Master watched him summon a few troops to get the barrels to their destination, then he walked back to the top of the hill where he could see the enemy camp. He spent a good several minutes staring at their tents and the soldiers milling about. They had no idea what they were walking into. The corners of the Master's lips curled into an evil smile as he took it all in. Eagle's Claw had come for him at last. He hadn't been certain his threat was going to work, but it had. They had come.

Sariah had come.

At long last, things were falling into place. It was finally time to kill them all.

CHAPTER SIXTEEN

Sariah inhaled sharply. She looked down at her side where her sword still hung at her waist. Beneath her clothing lay two other important objects—Lucien's dagger, which she still carried with her as a weapon of last resort, and a small leather pouch.

The pouch contained the powdered remains of the paralysis plant. It was her only hope to stop the Master in his tracks so she could put an end to him. Mindlessly, she patted the location of the pouch to make sure it was still there and secure.

Of course, she had no idea how she was going to get the Master to actually inhale its contents, but there was time for that. They had to get through his army first.

She sighed and looked out over the field in front of them. It was dotted with old, decrepit buildings the likes of which she had only seen once before, during her battle with Lucien all those months ago.

Back then, she hadn't given them much thought. Much like that time, she couldn't guess their contents. Each of those buildings could easily be hiding a dozen of the enemy's troops, and she'd have no way to know for sure.

"It's a little different when you're the one doing the invading, huh?" Will asked from beside her.

She gulped down hard and nodded. "Yeah. Just a bit."

Will shoved her gently. "Don't worry about it. This is no different than the Stratton operation. There's just a few more of them this time. And now there's more of us, too." He flashed her a grin.

"I'm not worried," Harvey chimed in. He was standing on her other side.

Sariah snorted. "Then you're the real moron."

Harvey looked at her and shrugged his broad shoulders. "We took them out pretty easily back in Talon's Reach. We'll do it again."

She shook her head and surveyed the field again. There were easily three hundred Dusk Raven troops on the ground in between her and the supposed entrance to their stronghold where the Master lay. That was just the troops they could see. Who knew how many were still hidden?

A chill wind blew through the trees, making her shiver. "Let's just get this over with quickly, shall we? Albert and Vincent are still in there somewhere. I'm worried about them."

Will nodded. "Me too, sister." He patted her on the back. "Don't worry—that kid's resourceful. I'm sure he's still alive somewhere in there. We'll meet up soon enough."

She reached out with her magic to try and sense their presence for the hundredth time, but it was no use. There were far too many bodies here for it to be of any use. She let out a sigh and tried to push it from her mind. She still had to get past the enemy forces.

"Ready to crack some Dusk Raven skulls?"

Sariah smiled up at him. "Hell yeah, I am." She cocked her head to the side. "What's the plan again?"

Will roared and rolled his eyes. "Don't tell me you forgot already!"

She burst out laughing. "Don't worry, I remember. My memory's not that bad."

Harvey joined in on the laughter, and soon, Will did, too. It helped ease her tension a little, but there was one thought still nagging at her in the back of her mind.

Where was the blasted signal?

Albert looked at Vincent. The old druid had his eyes closed like he was napping, but he knew better. The man hated looking at the cell.

He supposed he could understand. Vincent was a man used to nature. Their hastily constructed cell, in the back of one of the old dead buildings that dotted the landscape, held nothing of the sort. The walls were some kind of sleek stone, and the bars that kept them in place were a cold, hard iron. No grace, no elegance.

He, for one, had had enough. "I'm getting out of here," he said aloud.

Vincent, for his part, just looked at him and shook his head. "How do you plan on doing that, exactly?"

Albert shrugged. "I'm not sure yet. I'll figure it out. Will always said we could do anything with magic if we tried hard enough. Why not this?"

"There are hundreds of them out there, kid. Even if we get out of this cell, then what?"

"I don't know, but something will come to me."

The old druid sighed and shook his head again. "Well, wake me if you're successful, I guess." Then he closed his eyes and went back to napping or whatever it was that he was doing.

Albert tsked and sat up. *Does he think so little of me, too?*

Even the Dusk Ravens seemed to think he wasn't a threat, seeing as they hadn't shackled him. Of course, they hadn't chained Vincent, either, come to think of it.

Idiots. Just wait until I get out of here, then you'll see just how much of a pain I can really be.

He looked around the little cell. There wasn't really anything to work with. Even the food they got—what little of it there was—came without any sort of tray or wrapping that could be used to help them.

He'd have to get through the bars. If only he could push them just a little further apart, he could squeeze through.

Wait a second, he thought. *He could move them out of the way. He'd seen Sariah move heavy objects with magic. This was the same thing.*

He shook out his hands and started concentrating. As he worked, he pushed his hands outwards. At first, nothing happened. Then, little by little, he watched the iron bars give way as he pushed with his hands again until finally, there was enough room for a human to squeeze through.

Sweating, he looked back at Vincent, who was staring at him in amazement. He grinned at the old druid. "Coming?"

Vincent got up and dusted himself off, then made a shooing motion with one of his hands and nodded. "Lead the way, young master."

Sean gritted his teeth and looked over the field below him. He and his crack troops were high up in one of the buildings behind the main Dusk Raven force.

Not too far ahead of them, partially hidden by the trees, was a large tent. A few Dusk Ravens could be seen running to and from the tent every few minutes. That tent was their target—the officer's den.

The plan was simple. Take out the officers and the troops would be confused and lack direction. Basic strategy, really. They hadn't counted on the tent being so heavily guarded.

He wiped a bead of sweat from his brow before it could fall into his eye and cloud his vision. Standing guard at the tent were a dozen battle-ready soldiers. All of them were mages from the look of it. They had a few dogs with them, too, meaning invisibility and stealth were out of the question, and that was just the defenses he could see. Undoubtedly more troops were waiting within the tent.

A chill ran down Sean's spine. He looked over his own troops again. Five brave souls—all of them his friends—had volunteered to go with him on this crazy mission.

He mindlessly chewed on his cheek, wondering if they'd be enough.

Shaking his head, he turned his attention back to the opposing force. There was no sense worrying about it now. Reinforcements wouldn't be coming for some time, and they were too deep in the enemy camp to sneak back out.

One of his troops nudged his shoulder, and he turned to look at him. The young woman had a hesitant look in her eyes like she knew just as surely as he did that this was a suicide mission. They'd all signed up for it willingly, though.

Sean patted the barrel of his magitech weapon and gave the young soldier a nod and a wink. That was the signal they'd agreed upon to say they were moving out. She nodded and winked back at him, then grabbed her own weapon tightly.

His shoulders tensed, and he readied his legs to pounce down from their cover onto the troops below. Before he could do anything, he heard an explosion come from nearby that caught him off guard. He turned to look. A plume of smoke was rising in the distance.

Sean's mind raced. Had someone come to help them?

He didn't have long to ponder this development. There was movement in the camp below. Around half the guard had gotten up and started running toward the smoke. He couldn't believe the luck. Their odds of survival were improving dramatically.

Sean looked at his troops once more, a big grin on his face. Then, with as much force as he could muster, he let out a war cry and dropped down on his foes.

Harvey covered his ears to block out the noise from the explosion. That had been a lot closer than he'd expected. He blinked and watched as the massive plume of smoke rose from the center of the Dusk Raven's forces.

"Is that the signal?" he asked Will hesitantly. They'd gone over the plan several times the night before, but he hadn't remembered a giant explosion being part of it.

Will looked at him and shrugged. "It is now."

Harvey grinned from ear to ear. He grabbed one of his two swords and looked at the enemy forces. They were standing, looking just as confused as he was.

Poor guys. They'll never know what hit them.

Vincent crept along the side of the building, following closely behind Albert. The two of them had escaped their cell, but there was a sea of Dusk Ravens all around them still, and they had nothing for backup.

If only Ferdinand were here, he thought. That old fox would know how to get us out.

He looked over his surroundings. There was precious little vegetation around here, and he was without his staff, a grim outlook for a druid like himself. Albert was with him, and the little guy had proven plenty resourceful.

A contingent of Dusk Ravens passed by ahead of them. He pulled on Albert to keep the kid from walking into their path. He was powerful, but a little oblivious.

The kid looked at him and gave him a half-smile.

Vincent supposed he should be happy. Without the

kid's help, he'd still be in that blasted cell, facing who knew what fate. But there was still plenty of danger all around.

His eyes darted toward the distance, and he saw it. It was barely there at first, but as it came closer, there was no mistaking that hint of red.

Ferdinand! he thought. His beloved fox had come for him at last!

The small animal came up to him and licked his palm a few times. He gave the fox a few light pets. "Ferdinand, you old rascal," he whispered. "I'm so glad to see you."

Ferdinand nipped at his heels a few times, then darted off. Vincent cocked his head. The blasted beast was headed right into the middle of camp!

He shook his head. "No, Ferdinand! Let's get out of here."

The fox seemed persistent, so he relented. He beckoned for Albert to follow, and the young mage did as he was told. Together, they crept forward perhaps twenty feet to where Ferdinand stood, pawing at a few strange barrels.

"What is it, boy?" Vincent asked. He crept forward as slowly as he could to not make any noise and inspected the barrels. They were full of a dark, sand-like substance that smelled like sulfur. He was confused at first, then recognition finally crossed his face. He knew what Ferdinand wanted them to do.

Vincent looked at Albert. "All right, boy, listen carefully. I want you to send a fireball into those barrels over here. Then run like hell."

Albert eyed him cautiously. "Won't that give off our position?"

He let out a slight chuckle. "If I'm right about this, they'll be too preoccupied to worry about it."

The boy shrugged. "Okay, if you say so." He moved his hands to ready the spell.

"Actually, wait just a second. Let's back up a bit first. Just in case."

The boy nodded. "Whatever you say."

Sean pulled the trigger on his magitech weapon. Blue fire shot forth from the barrel and blasted into the chest of the nearest mage. The enemy let out a yelp and fell to the ground.

All around him was similar carnage as the troops with him fired their own weapons on the unsuspecting Dusk Ravens.

"Die, scum!" he howled at them.

More Dusk Ravens came pouring out of the tent at the sound of the commotion. These ones had their swords drawn. He fired his weapon at them again and again, and they fell like flies. Even so, there were far more of them than there were of his crew.

Three more Dusk Ravens came out of the tent. He pulled the trigger on his weapon, but this time nothing happened. He smacked the side of it a few times and looked at the amphorald, but it was no longer glowing.

"Stupid thing," he muttered. He threw the weapon to the ground and readied a fireball. He had more than one trick up his sleeve.

The fireball took out two of the Dusk Ravens before they could close the gap, but the last one came in fast.

Sean ducked to avoid the man's sword blow just in time. He pulled out a dagger that he had at his waist and slammed it upward as hard as he could, hoping to find purchase.

The blade sunk into his opponent's sword arm, and the man dropped his weapon, screaming and falling to the ground. Another fireball took him out and kept him from getting back up.

He scanned the area around him. Three of his friends were still standing, as were a dozen or so Dusk Ravens. The girl that had looked so hesitantly at him moments earlier lay lifeless and broken, not five feet to his left. Sean bowed his head for a brief second, but that was all he could spare. The remaining enemy combatants were approaching quickly.

"Retreat!" he called out. "Fall back!" His troops backed up slowly, firing their weapons to keep the Dusk Ravens at bay and managing to take out another few before their own weapons were similarly spent.

One of the remaining Dusk Raven officers flashed him a toothy grin. He dropped his sword and started moving his arms in wild directions.

Sean knew what was coming. The man was readying a spell to take them all down.

His back bumped into something hard, then, and he realized he'd backed his fellow soldiers straight into a wall. He let out a short sigh. There would be no retreat. This was it.

The young boy stood tall and started readying a spell of

his own. Maybe if he was lucky, he'd take the officer out at the same time.

Padron raced through the trees, hefting his mighty axe. He swung it in broad, wild arcs, separating the heads and limbs of the enemy troops from their bodies as he went and leaving a bloody wake behind him.

A Dusk Raven mage stood in front of him. The man had a fireball in his hands and was pointing it right at him.

The rearick howled and threw a dagger at the mage before he could react. Seconds later, the mage fell to the ground, gurgling blood from a gaping wound in his neck, the fireball dying with him.

Padron smiled. He'd almost forgotten what real combat was like. This was what he lived for. Mining was fine and all, but the battlefield was where his real strength lay.

Off to his side, Harvey charged into a particularly thick group of Dusk Ravens. He had one sword in his hands and another flying beside him like some sort of magic soldier. The boy had grown into something special.

Another enemy troop came at him then, and he hacked at them with his axe, leaving a large bloody gash across his chest.

The rearick's thoughts flitted to Sariah for just a moment. She was out there somewhere, but where he didn't know, and he couldn't very well look around while there were heads to separate from bodies. She couldn't be far behind Harvey and Will. She had never been one to back down from a fight.

Just then, a blazing fireball raced past his head. He felt the heat of the flames and smelled the stench of burning hair—his own hair.

He looked in the direction the fireball had come from to see another mage gunning for him. The woman already had another fireball at the ready.

Padron reached for another throwing dagger but came up empty. He shrugged. It looked like his luck had finally run out.

He flashed a grin at the enemy mage and readied his axe to throw at her. It wouldn't stop the fireball, but at least he'd take her out, too.

Moments later, the mage screamed and fell to the ground. Padron blinked and saw a fresh blade sticking out of her back.

From behind the mage, Sariah looked at him and flashed him a toothy grin. He gave her a wink. Then she was gone, and more Dusk Ravens had taken her place.

With a loud howl, he rushed forward, determined to pay Sariah back with more dead bodies.

Sariah's eyes darted all around. She'd lost track of both Harvey and Will in the fighting several minutes ago. At least Bear was still with her. One hand traveled down to his head, and she patted it appreciatively.

The beast had more than proved his worth already today, saving her hide more than once, and still he fought onward.

She saw a few Dusk Ravens up ahead and sent a fireball

in their direction. They all succumbed to the flames quickly.

Looking around again, she realized she was nowhere near the front lines where she was supposed to stay. Somehow, she'd gotten into the thick of the enemy camp.

Up ahead, she saw the remains of one of the giant dead buildings. This one had smoke rising up in front of it from the remains of a massive explosion. She supposed this was where their earlier help had come from.

There was no sign of anyone in the vicinity.

Where had they gone, and who was our mysterious helper? She also wondered where Albert and Vincent were.

That was her real concern. She'd told Will she would behave and stay with the group, but she had to find them. They were held prisoner because of her, and she needed to make sure they were safe personally.

She scanned the horizon, but there was nothing but brown uniforms, blood, and broken buildings in every direction.

Moments later, she saw another giant explosion. The force of this one was so strong it knocked her to the ground. Hastily, she got up and dusted herself off.

Just what was going on?

The explosion had been massive. Vincent had tried to warn him, but it had been far more impressive than Albert would have thought possible.

Now he and Vincent were running after that little fox of his, headed even deeper into the enemy camp. Vincent had assured him the fox knew what he was doing, but he wasn't so sure.

All the Dusk Ravens had run like crazy after the first explosion. The ones who had survived that is. Some of them hadn't been so lucky. It had been the perfect opportunity for them to escape unscathed. He didn't know why they were running deeper into the camp.

The fox had gotten them past more than one sticky situation already, and the Dusk Ravens were all running in the other direction now, so he supposed he might as well stick it out.

What a great opportunity this was to really get back at them. He hadn't forgotten their losses earlier. If he managed to take out a few of them in return, he wouldn't argue.

They pushed through another copse of trees, and a giant tent loomed in front of them. Albert let out a slight gasp. Surprisingly, the tent was mostly empty. What few Dusk Ravens around it were on the other side, contending with some sort of disturbance.

In the middle of the tent stood another couple of barrels that looked suspiciously like the ones he'd blown up earlier.

Just what kind of destructive technology were the Dusk Ravens hoarding up here? He shrugged. It didn't matter. He knew what to do.

Albert made sure Vincent and Ferdinand were well behind him, and he readied another fireball.

Sean grunted as his back hit the wall hard enough to knock most of the wind out of him. He scrambled back to his feet and surveyed the situation.

Another large explosion had rocked the land. This one had been much closer than the earlier one. He could feel the heat of the flames when it had knocked him to the ground.

The officer that had been ready to kill him and his fellow troops hadn't been so lucky. His back was covered in black scorch marks, and he was face down in the dirt. Sean slid his dagger through the man's chest anyway just to be safe.

He looked behind him to see his other remaining troops also appeared to be safe. Apparently, they'd been just far enough away from the blast to escape harm. He thanked the Patriarch for this miracle and thought about what to do next.

Their weapons were spent, and his energy was nearing its low point, but at least they'd carried out their mission. Now all they had to do was get out.

Just then, two hazy figures emerged from the wall of smoke that used to be the officer's tent. He couldn't make them out at first, but once the smoke cleared a little, he smiled.

"Albert?" he said hesitantly. He blinked, unable to believe his eyes.

The boy raced forward to embrace him. "Sean!" Albert cried. "You're safe!"

Sean embraced Albert warmly, then pushed him away. "I'm safe? I was the one who came to save you!"

Albert smiled at him and shrugged. "Well, what did you do that for, you big lout?"

"Oh, Albert. You always know just what to say." Sean patted him on the back and ruffled his hair.

Albert cocked his head to the side. "What about the others? Did anyone else come with you?"

"Only the whole dang army, you silly kid!" Sean beamed at him and threw an arm around his shoulder.

Albert chuckled and shrugged. "I guess that explains why all the Dusk Ravens were running the other way..." The young boy started forward, back toward the messy remains of the tent. "Well, come on, then. We can't keep the army waiting."

Sean grinned at Albert and started after him. "No, I guess we can't."

Harvey grunted and lunged low, slicing into his opponent's middle with practiced ease. The Dusk Raven soldier fell to the ground clutching his stomach so fast it was all he could do to keep a hold of his sword.

The young man looked at his other sword hovering in the air. Fresh blood coated it along the length of the blade. "You have it so easy, you know," he told the piece of steel.

Another Dusk Raven howled and raced toward him. He sent his floating sword flying toward the woman's body, and it practically beheaded her in one swift motion.

He liked having two weapons, he decided. Even if making the other one fly did slowly drain his magic reserves, it sure came in handy.

A low whistle came from his left, and he looked to see Will, appreciating his handiwork.

"Nice job, kid," the big man said, clapping him on the shoulder.

Harvey groaned. "Shouldn't you be killing some more soldiers of your own?"

Will shrugged. "You see any more of them around here to kill?"

He looked around. There were plenty of bodies of the dead and dying. Most of them were Dusk Ravens, though several belonging to the Eagle's Claw were mixed in among them, too.

Will was right. No one seemed to be left standing, at least not that he could see.

"Did we do it, then? Were we successful?"

Will let out a slight laugh. "Don't get ahead of yourself, kid. We got through the front lines easy enough. The Master is still out there somewhere. We're nowhere near done yet."

Harvey frowned. "Oh yeah. I almost forgot about that part amongst all the carnage."

"Where's Sariah?" Will asked with a frown. "Weren't you supposed to watch over her?"

His blood froze. He hadn't noticed until now, but he hadn't seen her in a while.

Will's eyes went wild. "How did you lose track of her! I gave you one mission last night! Keep. Her. Safe!"

Harvey gulped down a knot of fear that formed in his stomach and looked around wild-eyed. "I...I don't know. She was right there a moment ago, I swear!"

The older man rolled his eyes. "I can't believe this! This whole thing is for naught if she doesn't make it!"

"Miss me?" a voice called out a short distance in front of them.

Harvey's face relaxed, and the tension left his body. "Sariah!" he cried. He ran toward her. "You're safe!"

" I brought friends," she continued with a wink. She pointed behind her to where Vincent, Albert, and Sean all stood. They looked a little worse for wear, but they were all alive.

"Vincent! Albert! Sean! You're all safe!" He went over to the younger two and embraced them.

"Albert was the real hero," Sean explained, winking at the lad.

"That so?" Harvey asked.

Albert gave him a nod in return and beamed up at him. He smiled at the young boy and ruffled his hair.

Turning his attention back to Sariah, he shot her a level gaze. "How did you...?"

Sariah shrugged. "You gonna stand there wondering all day, or you gonna hug me, too?"

"What am I thinking?" He shook his head and embraced her as well. She felt warm and inviting in all the right ways. "I'm so glad you're okay."

"Yeah, well, we're not done yet," she said softly in his ear. She pushed away from him and looked over at Will and blushed.

Harvey looked from Will to Sariah and back again. Both of them had odd expressions on their faces. He wanted to pry further, but it could wait. There were more important matters to tend to.

"So, where do we go next?" He asked the group.

"Into the lion's den, of course," Will replied.

"Anyone know where that is?"

No one had an answer. None of them had been inside the Dusk Raven stronghold before. The entrance couldn't be that well-hidden, could it?

"Over here!" a voice called out from off in the distance. "The entrance is this way!"

A chill ran down Harvey's spine. He could have recognized that voice beckoning them onward toward the Master anywhere, and he was none too happy about it.

His face hardened, and his eyes narrowed as he let the realization wash over him.

"Gabriel?" Sariah said, breaking the silence.

CHAPTER SEVENTEEN

Sariah raced toward the sound of Gabriel's eerie voice.

Her mind raced. Had Gabe really come back for her? If so, was it as a friend or a foe? Which did she even want? It was too much to think about, so she shoved it out of her mind.

"Wait!" a voice called from behind her. It was Harvey.

Sariah turned to face him. "You heard him, Harvey," she said. "He said the Master is this way."

Harvey glared at her. "You're just going to run after him and believe him after all he's done?"

"What other choice do I have?" She threw her hands up. "It's not like we have any other leads to go on!"

Harvey reached out and grabbed her to stop her. "What if it's a trap? He works for him, remember?"

She shrugged him off her and scowled. "So what if it is? That's why we're here in the first place, remember?" She wagged a finger in his face while she spoke, then backed off a bit. "What else would you have us do? What's your 'grand master plan,' huh?"

He shot her a pleading look, his eyes full of concern, then his eyes darted all around, scanning the others' faces. Sariah looked at them, too, but all she got were blank stares and a shrug from Will.

"Fine," Harvey relented with a long sigh. "We do it your way."

A smile crept up Sariah's lips. "I thought you'd see it my way." She looked at the rest of her friends. "Now, who's with me?"

Will came forward, as did Harvey and Vincent, with Ferdinand in tow. Bear let out a sharp bark and went back to his place at her feet. Albert gave her a sheepish look, and then he looked back toward Sean and started nervously shuffling his feet.

She walked over to the two of them and placed a hand gingerly on Albert's shoulder. "It's okay," she told him. "I understand. Your friend is already tired and gave his all. Why don't you get him to safety? We can handle it from here."

Albert nodded at her once, and the two of them went off in the direction of Ilene and the remainder of the troops. A short distance down the field, she saw Padron, who waved at her and joined Albert and Sean, helping the young man keep his friend standing as they walked away. After all the recent bloodshed, it was a welcome sight.

Sariah turned her attention back to the rest of her crew. These were the people who had stood by her side through thick and thin, and always had her back. She looked into each of their eyes in turn and saw nothing but grit and resolve.

Her mouth opened almost on its own, and she felt like

she should be giving them a speech. Some sort of pep talk about how this was the end, and they were going to prevail, but nothing came out.

After a few awkward moments, she finally blurted out the first thing that came to mind. "Well, what are we waiting for, then, ya bunch of ingrates? Let's get going!"

Sariah's friends beamed at her, and a cheer erupted from the group. With a broad sweep of her hand, she beckoned them to follow her into the unknown.

It didn't take long before the group came across an old wooden door stuck into a wall. The door itself was ordinary enough. In fact, the only odd thing about it was the fact that this building actually had a door, whereas so many of the older structures around them did not.

Will walked up to it first, brushing Sariah to the side.

"Hey!" she cried, but he ignored her pleas.

"Let me go in first," he insisted. "If it is a trap, I should be the one to trigger it."

Sariah glared at him and put her hands on her hips. "Why is that, exactly? What gives you the right to throw your life away like that?"

Will took in a deep breath. "I've lived a good life. Besides, you're the lynchpin of this whole operation."

Just then, Harvey stepped forward. "Let me do it. Whatever's waiting on the other side, I can handle it. I promise."

Will looked at the young boy and shook his head. At the same time, Sariah smacked Harvey hard in his chest.

"No way!" she shouted. "I'm not having you throw yourself in front of a trap meant for me again!"

"Again?" Will asked.

"It's a long story," Harvey replied with a sigh and a roll of his eyes.

"No matter, I should be the one to open the door. You're young, like Sariah. You deserve to live more than I do."

Sariah stepped in between him and Harvey and put a hand on both of their chests. "Neither of you is doing anything of the sort. If anyone is springing the trap this time, it's me."

Harvey opened his mouth to argue, and Will's cheeks started to burn a bright red.

"Uh, guys," Vincent called from behind them. "Nothing happened. Let's get going."

All of them turned then to face Vincent, who stood in the entrance with the door hanging open in front of him. A dark, dimly lit maw greeted them, but there didn't appear to be any traps or imminent danger.

Will let out a sigh to calm his nerves. "Well, fine, we'll do it your way."

Harvey walked down the hallway slowly. He had managed to take the lead somehow, though he wasn't really sure how that had worked out.

So far, nothing had happened. They'd entered the complex with no resistance—not a single soul had stopped them. It was enough to keep him on edge. Surely the Master had some nasty surprises in store for them down here. It was only a matter of time before they stumbled into something.

The group came across another crossroads in the tunnel up ahead, and Harvey pointed his torch down both pathways. He frowned. He thought he recognized the tunnels but couldn't be entirely sure.

"It's no use," Will called out from behind him. "We're going around in circles in this maze."

Harvey growled and turned to face him. "I suppose you want to go back to taking the lead, then?"

The big man took the torch from his outstretched hand forcefully. "With pleasure." Then he walked ahead of Harvey and started looking down both tunnels and scratching his head.

"It's the left one," Will said, nodding his head.

Harvey frowned. "How can you be so sure?"

Will looked at him for a moment. "I don't know either, okay! Let's just pick one!"

Sariah walked up to both of them and put a hand on Will's shoulder. "Hey, keep calm. This is part of his plan, right? Wear us down and get us ragged, then he can swoop in and catch us off guard."

The big man's face softened, and he nodded at her. "You're right." He pulled on his face and took a deep breath. "Which tunnel do you think we should go down, then?"

Sariah closed her eyes for a moment, then pointed down the left tunnel. "That way. I can sense life down that way."

"Of course!" Will exclaimed. "I should have thought of using magic. Left it is."

Harvey rolled his eyes and took the torch back from Will, then started down the left tunnel. Before long, the hallway began to widen. A small light appeared in the distance. It was dim, like a torch, but it was there.

They slowed their approach a little as they came to an open doorway. The light was coming from just beyond it.

Harvey strengthened the grip on his weapon and readied his other one with his magic, then he burst through the door.

Before he could do anything else, he heard the door whoosh shut behind him like some magical force had sealed it. Despair started to sink in as he realized he was now separated from the rest of the group, and from Sariah.

The sound of chilling laughter roused him from his thoughts and caused him to turn his attention to the other figure in the room.

Harvey's hair stood on end as he locked eyes with his enemy, and his fingers clenched around his sword blade. He knew this man all too well.

"You!" Harvey shouted.

Jeffrey Humboldt nodded and took a step forward, brandishing his own blade in front of him. "Welcome back, Harvey." The mine foreman's lips curled into a wicked smile. "Miss me?"

Sariah pounded on the door a few times to no avail. "Harvey!" she cried. There was no response.

The door was sealed shut, and no amount of magic power had unsealed it. She'd even tried to pound it with a fireball, but the thing was made of a stout metal and it had no effect. Harvey was as good as gone.

Will put his hand on her shoulder and turned her to face him. "Hey," he said quietly. "It's not your fault."

"Not my fault?" Sariah balked. She reared on her heels and turned the rest of the way. "This whole thing is my fault! Harvey's in trouble in there, and I can't do anything to save him!"

The big man backed off a step and put his hands up in a defensive position. Vincent, for his part, leaned against a wall and remained silent.

"I'm sorry," Will said after a moment. He hung his head low. "I shouldn't have—"

"No," Sariah cut him off. "No, you're right." She let out a breath and leaned against the door. "We all knew there would be untold dangers down here. Even Harvey. It's just...I wanted to face them together."

Will nodded and patted her on the arm. "I know."

He opened his mouth to say something further, but never got the chance. The sound of wild howls broke through the silence of the hallway, from the direction they'd just come from.

Sariah's blood chilled, and she crouched down to the ground instinctively. Next to her, Bear let out a low whine and settled into an attack stance. She put a hand on Bear's head and leaned in close to him.

"What is it, boy?"

The animal pointed his nose in the direction of the

howls and bared his teeth, then started pawing the ground anxiously.

"I understand, Bear," Sariah said in a hushed tone, nodding. "Trouble."

The howling noise grew louder, and the three remaining members of the group each drew their weapons and waited for whatever was making the noise to appear. It didn't take long.

A massive black wolf came dashing around the corner. The creature was at least as big as the wolf she'd fought back in the Alpenwood all those months ago, and from the looks of things, twice as cruel.

Behind it, Sariah could make out the outline of a few Dusk Raven soldiers, one of which was holding a massive leash tied to the creature's snout.

Will took one look at the wolf, then looked back at Sariah. "Go!" he commanded.

Sariah furrowed her brow. "What?"

"Go!" he repeated. "Find the Master! Finish the quest! We'll hold off the...backup."

She looked at Will first, then Vincent. The old druid nodded once and motioned toward the hallway.

"But!" Sariah squealed.

Will shook his head. "No time to argue, just do it!"

"He's right, you know," Vincent added with a shrug. "We'll make it out okay." He put his hands on her shoulders and looked her in the eyes. "Finish the mission."

Sariah gave them both another glance, then returned her attention to the wolf. The giant beast gnashed its sharp fangs at her and glared with its dark red eyes. Something about the animal's stare seemed unnatural, and it caused a shudder to go up her spine. She stood mesmerized by the thing, unable to move a muscle.

Vincent screamed at her again, but the sound barely reached her ears, and she couldn't make out the words. All she could do was stare at the massive wolf as it let out a low growl and lowered its head.

The druid gave her a hard push toward the open corridor, but she remained rooted in place, unable to fight against the beast's control.

In front of her eyes, several things happened at once. First, the wolf pounced at her. Then, Will moved in front of it just in time to take the brunt of the beast's blow. The two collided in a ball of fur, claws, and steel and tumbled to the ground.

At the same time, the small form of Ferdinand leaped into the fray, and Vincent started chanting some sort of spell.

Will spared her a glance. "Go! Get out of here already!" he cried. "While you still can!" Then he pushed out with both hands and managed to fling the beast off of him so he could regain his footing.

Sariah looked about as if in a daze. Will's words had broken her out of the semi-trance from the wolf, and she was able to move again.

Instinctively, her hand went to the sword at her hip, but she didn't draw it. Looking over the wolf, Will, and Ferdinand fighting together, she hesitated.

How could they possibly conquer it without my help? She bit her lip and shook her head. Will was right. Worse, she knew he was right. There only one thing left to do.

"I'm sorry!" she yelled at her friends. Then she turned and ran as fast as she could.

The hallways continued their twisting and turning for several minutes as Sariah ran down them blindly, trying to distance herself from the sounds and screams of the battle. Screams that were likely coming from her friends.

She leaned against one of the walls and took a deep breath. She felt her stomach lurch, but she fought against it. There weren't really any other options.

A few minutes later, she realized she was well and truly alone, except for Bear. The big dog hadn't left her side once the whole time. Sariah gave him an appreciative scratch behind the ears and tried not to let depression sink in.

The sound of boots scuffling against the ground assaulted her ears from off to the left. Her blood froze, and she inched in that direction as quietly as she could.

Several Dusk Ravens came bursting into the hallway, then, weapons raised at the ready.

With a slight yelp, Sariah sent a fireball pelting into the first one. He fell to the ground, but there were at least a dozen more after him.

There was only one thing left to do—she bolted, running down the hall as fast as she could, Bear at her heels.

One of the Dusk Ravens flung a dagger at her, and she used her magic to force it out of the way. Sweat was dripping down her brow, and she was beginning to tire. She needed to do something to slow them.

Sariah turned to face the Dusk Ravens. She pelted another couple of fireballs at them, and it slowed them down. Then she lifted her hands, and the ground rose with it, filling the hallway with dirt and debris until it was closed off completely.

The immediate threat neutralized, she let herself lean against the wall again to catch her breath.

She looked down at Bear. "Where is the Master hiding, anyway?" she asked.

As if in response, Bear let out a sharp bark and took a few steps to her left.

"Bear?" she asked, doing a double-take. She hadn't actually expected an answer. "What is it? What did you find?"

The animal barked again and started panting at something. There was nothing around her but more empty hallways.

Sariah wiped some sweat from her brow and shook her head. The darkness and isolation were messing with her mind. She took a few deep breaths to calm her nerves.

Then she heard it—the distinct sound of someone else breathing near her.

Was it the Master? Her blood froze, and she tried to stand as still as possible to avoid detection. She waited for a few moments, but nothing happened.

All at once, it hit her—Bear's behavior and the strange breathing noise. It wasn't the Master. It was..."Gabe?"

The air started to shimmer, and the figure of a man materialized in front of her. Gabriel looked down at her with a grin on his face and gave her a mock bow.

"I thought you'd never ask."

The Master tapped his foot impatiently. He looked at the empty doorway in front of him—the door he'd intentionally left wide open for Sariah—then back at his assistant Daniel.

He was starting to run low on assistants after the events of today. How was he supposed to know that the stupid bitch's forces had found out about his secret weapon?

Not only found out but used it against him in spectacular fashion, turning the tides of the war. It was enough to put anyone in a sour mood.

"It's no use, Daniel," he said almost mindlessly. "She should be here by now. What's taking so long?"

His assistant bowed deeply. "I do not know, Master," he offered.

The Master scoffed. Daniel was loyal and powerful in his own right, but he wasn't the brightest. Yet he'd stood by him longer than anyone else. That deserved some respect.

Just then, he heard a scuffling noise outside his laboratory. His ears perked up. It seemed his guest of honor would be here soon after all.

He took one more long, wistful look at his assistant's face. There were lines there he hadn't recognized before. Or maybe he'd just never paid attention. How long had Daniel served him, now? Ten years? Twenty? He'd lost count ages ago.

The Master shook his head to clear his thoughts and let out a long sigh. Such wistful thoughts wouldn't help him now. Only power would. And he knew where to get it.

"Looks like I'll need your services one last time, my dear Daniel." He placed a hand gingerly on the man's shoulder.

Daniel simply nodded once and said nothing. If he knew what was coming next, his eyes did not betray it.

The Master gave him a wry grin and patted him on the back. Loyal to the last, he thought. Under different circumstances, maybe...but alas, it was not to be—such a shame.

He let his fingers gently caress Daniel's hairy scalp. The man's hair felt oily like it hadn't been washed in days. It imparted a bit of a sickly feeling on his fingers, which he found wholly appropriate.

Then he started channeling his spell.

Harvey looked at Jeffrey and snarled. Thoughts of Chatwick, burned and gone beyond recognition, filled his head. It was all Jeffrey's fault, and now the former mine foreman was going to pay for it with his life.

"What's wrong?" Jeffrey asked. "Come at me, already!"

Harvey let out a slight chuckle. "With pleasure." Like a bolt of lightning, he advanced. He rushed for Jeffrey, sword out.

At the last moment, he turned to the side and let go of his sword, letting it fly forward on its own toward his opponent's head.

The mine foreman hastily backed up and shuffled to avoid the blow. The blade slid past his cheek, leaving a tiny mark.

Jeffrey reached up and brushed his cheek. Noticing the blood, he growled at Harvey and flashed his teeth at the man in a wicked grimace.

"Nice trick," he said in a smooth voice. "Now, you're weaponless."

Harvey smiled back and flicked his wrist, and the weapon came flying back into his palm. He brought his spare sword to the ready as well, letting it float next to him.

"Think again." He turned his blade in his palm, keeping it pointed at his foe and at the ready.

Jeffrey shook his head. "You've got balls, kid, I'll give you that." He shrugged. "But will it be enough?" His eyes went about the room. "No backup to help you out this time."

"Didn't need it last time, did I?" Harvey bared his teeth. "Or did you forget that ass whooping already?"

The old foreman's eyes flashed black, and he moved forward with a speed that should have been impossible given his size.

Harvey was almost caught off guard by the sudden attack, and he brought up his blade to block Jeffrey's just in time. The blow was aimed at his head, but he pushed it back.

That was followed with a quick succession of attacks, each one pushing him back a little further as he fought to stay standing. A thrusting blow came at his middle, then a vertical swipe came for his sword arm and another for his free arm, each with more force than the last.

Harvey's breath quickened, and he readied himself for another assault as a quick lunge came at him to his hind leg. He fended this off as well, but a searing pain shot up his leg, letting him know he hadn't been quite quick enough.

The young man bit through the pain and worked to maintain his footing as another barrage came his way.

Sweat began pouring down his forehead as he defended himself. He searched in vain for an opening that wasn't coming, even using his second sword a few times to try and force his opponent back to no avail.

A droplet of sweat fell into his eye, and it stung. Harvey blinked involuntarily. At that moment, Jeffrey made a lunge at him that he wasn't prepared for. The young man threw himself toward the floor to get out of the way, dodging the blow just in time.

He hit the ground with a loud thud. As he did so, he heard Jeffrey chuckle. The foreman had the advantage, and he appeared to be the better swordsman overall.

Shaking his head to clear the pain, he worked to get back to his feet. Harvey knew he had to do something and fast.

He switched tactics and reached out with his magic, summoning a giant blast of energy.

Jeffrey's helpless body flew through the air and crunched into the wall. The mine foreman looked down at his body with a stunned expression.

Harvey used the break in the action to wipe the sweat from his brow and ready himself for the next round.

"Ugh," the mine foreman managed, spitting out a bit of blood in the process. "Well done, kid," he said with a half-smile. He got up and dusted off his tunic. "It won't be enough, though."

Sariah reared back a half step and rolled her eyes. "Gabe?" On the one hand, she couldn't believe it was really him. On the other, she was relieved. "What are you doing down here?" She gave him a particularly hard shove in the chest.

He raised his hands in a defensive position. "Saving you, of course!"

"You?" She blinked a few times and looked away. "Saving me?" She pointed at her chest and guffawed, then crossed her arms. "I don't need saving."

Inside, her head was spinning. She didn't know if he was there to help her or take her to his Master. She shook her head, unsure of which she wanted more.

"Come now, you didn't really think I'd let you face the Master alone now, did you?" Gabe asked her with a wry grin. He placed a hand gently on her shoulder, which she quickly brushed off.

She shot him an icy glare. "That's why I came here with my friends! My real friends! Which is more than I can say for you!" She spat at his feet.

Gabe frowned at her and whined. He looked around the small corridor. "Where are these 'friends' of yours now, then?"

Sariah wagged a finger at him and opened her mouth to argue, but nothing came out. Her friends were gone, likely dead. At least part of that was probably Gabe's fault, though mostly hers. She'd dragged them all into this.

At the very least, he could have come out of hiding and helped earlier.

She had to admit the prospect of help was nice. The last thing she wanted was to be alone in front of the Master again. Even if said help was from an unlikely source.

She just didn't know if she could trust him.

Bear looked at her expectantly and gave her a sharp bark. She eyed the beast curiously. Did he know her deepest thoughts?

Ludicrous! she thought. And yet...She had to admit, Bear hadn't been angry at Gabe like he had been the last time. Was it a sign she could trust the man, after all?

Sariah bit her lip and looked up at Gabe. He didn't look anywhere near as threatening as he had the last time.

Her mind made up, she threw up her hands in defeat, then nodded. "Fine. Lead the way."

Will lashed out against the massive wolf again, slicing down its front paw. The beast yelped, but it looked otherwise unfazed.

"Little help here?" he called over his shoulder.

Vincent shrugged. "I'm trying, but there's not much a druid can do surrounded by brick and stone." He shook his head. "This beast doesn't want to relent."

Will scowled and raised his blade to fend off another attack. As he did so, he saw a small flash of red run between his legs to strike out at the beast.

It was Ferdinand, come to defend them both. The small beast made a big show of gnashing its teeth and claiming dominance, but it did little to slow the wolf.

Ferdinand did manage to get a few bites in at the creature's face, but his offense was short-lived. The wolf batted at him with one of its massive paws, and the fox went flying into a nearby wall where it lay unmoving.

It gave Will an opening, and he used it to make a mad lunge forward with his blade, aiming for the creature's head. The tip of the sword sliced through one of the foul beast's eyes, and it howled, rearing back in pain.

"Come on, git!" Will heard one of the Dusk Ravens call out from behind the beast. The wolf snarled and started advancing again, looking like it was ready to end the conflict with one giant pounce.

Will tightened his grip on his sword and readied a fireball to back it up, waiting for the wolf to be in the middle of his pouncing arc to release it for maximum effect.

Just then, the wolf stopped. Its shoulders started to slacken and it laid down on the ground, motionless.

"I said git!" the Dusk Raven yelled at it. He brought out a rather cruel-looking whip and cracked it at the wolf. The wolf did nothing.

Will spared a moment to glance back at Vincent to check if he saw the same miracle. The druid's eyes were glowing a deep green color, and he seemed lost in thought.

Suddenly it struck him—Vincent was using his magic to control the beast!

"That's the ticket!" he shouted at the druid, a broad grin overtaking his face. "Make it attack its masters!" Still, the wolf lay motionless, and the smile started to drain from Will's face.

Whether Vincent hadn't heard him or couldn't muster that level of control, he didn't know. Either way, he'd have to handle the Dusk Ravens himself.

He turned his attention back to the wolf's masters and lashed out with the fireball he'd prepped for the wolf. It hit one of them straight in the chest, and the man flew backward, awash in flames and acrid smoke.

The other Dusk Raven, the one with the whip, spared his companion a brief glance then got ready to strike. He summoned his own fireball, which he sent barreling toward Will.

Will dodged the mass of flames with practiced ease and started closing the gap, throwing another fireball for good measure. This one didn't have the intended effect.

The Dusk Raven guard cracked his whip, and the tip grazed across Will's face, leaving behind a searing pain and a shower of blood from the bridge of his nose.

Will brushed off some of the blood and kept heading forward, sword in front. Once he was close enough, he made a lunge for the enemy's head, which the man batted away with his own blade.

Grimacing, Will braced for a real battle. He wove his sword with alarming speed, up and down, back and forth. The Dusk Raven parried his strikes, but it was apparent the man was tiring quickly.

An opening in the Dusk Raven's defenses came a moment later, and Will took advantage, plunging his blade into the man's chest. He fell with a loud thud and stopped moving.

Will took a few breaths to steady himself and looked at the dead bodies.

"Yeah!" he exclaimed. "That'll teach you to mess with the Eagle's Claw!" he added, pumping his fist.

"I wouldn't be so quick to party," Vincent muttered from somewhere behind him.

He turned to face the druid. The old man was leaning next

to his pet Ferdinand, eyes still burning bright green. "Eh?" He cocked his head to the side. "We beat them back, didn't we?"

The druid shrugged. "We beat the humans, yes. Their pet?" He pointed a long, bony finger at the wolf that still lay motionless on the floor. "I won't be able to hold him back much longer."

Will took another look at the massive beast. He could see now that the creature was straining against something like it wanted to pounce and devour him but couldn't.

"So, what do you suggest we do?"

Vincent shrugged again and gave him a broad grin. "Run, of course."

Will looked down at the massive beast. It would be so easy to end its life with a well-placed sword strike right now. But miss, and the beast might come to life again. He pondered his options, then nodded.

He tipped his sword at the beast and went over to where Vincent was standing. "Pleasure doing battle with you, sir," he told the wolf. Then he turned, and they ran in the other direction.

A few moments later, they heard a loud howl as the beast regained consciousness, but nothing came running after them. Will quickened his pace anyway. He had to catch up to Sariah. At least, that's what he told himself.

Sariah rounded another corner in the wild maze. She was having a little trouble keeping up with Gabe, who kept shouting over his shoulder, "It's just ahead."

"It's just ahead," she muttered mockingly under her breath. It did nothing to calm her nerves.

Not much later, the hallways around them started to shift and change. It was gradual at first but appeared to be deliberate. The stones in this new area were more refined and in better shape like they'd been installed later. Sariah figured they were finally getting somewhere.

An odd smell assaulted her nostrils. It smelled of urine and stale blood. The stench made her wrinkle her nose and almost cough.

Gabe, Sariah, and Bear rounded another corner, and Sariah spotted a door left eerily open in the middle of the hallway. The door looked to be made of a different material than all the others in this area.

She felt a chill run up her spine and a knot formed in her gut. They were here. She didn't know exactly how she knew, but the Master waited for them just beyond the doorway.

Gabe looked at her expectantly and nodded at the door. "He's just up ahead," he told her.

Sariah nodded back. "I figured as much." She beckoned with her hands. "Well, go on ahead then."

He shook his head. "Uh-uh. We go together." Gabe was holding out a hand to her.

She looked at the hand like it was death. The thought of touching him again made her feel a little sick to her stomach and somehow elated her at the same time.

She stood and considered him. She made the choice when she accepted his help in the first place.

Slowly, Sariah reached out and took Gabe's hand. His

skin felt smooth and surprisingly warm. A shiver ran up her arm, but she ignored it.

Hand in hand, the two of them walked through the doorway, with Bear close behind. Somehow it felt right like it had always been fated to happen this way.

A grim sight greeted the three of them in the room beyond the door. The Master was standing hunched over the mangled body of some poor victim. His eyes were glowing a sickly red color, and he had a slick, evil grin on his face.

"Sariah," the Master let out slowly. He looked over at her companion. "Gabe." There was a hint of surprise in his voice. "How kind of you two to come at last." He gave them both a slight bow.

"Pleasure's all mine," Sariah replied as defiantly as possible. Then, without warning, she lashed out with her magic, sending a blue wave of energy at him.

The Master laughed and held up his hand. The magic energy dissipated against his shield before it hit him.

"Tsk, tsk," the Master said, shaking his head. "You still haven't learned your lesson." He flicked his wrist, and a massive fireball erupted from his hands, heading straight for her and Gabe.

Gabe moved quicker than she would have thought possible and blocked the flames with a shield of his own, though Sariah could see the action taxed him.

Sariah looked at Gabe for a second, then back at the Master. "You're going to have to do better than that." She flexed her arms and readied another spell.

The Master flashed her a toothy grin. "Oh, my dear, I've only just gotten started."

Harvey grunted and forced Jeffrey's blade back. The big man finally seemed like he was getting winded. Of course, so was he.

Jeffrey struck out again, aiming low. Harvey jumped to avoid it and sent his free sword flying forward at the same time.

The blade impacted Jeffrey's non-sword arm, leaving a nasty gash before it fell to the ground.

"You'll pay for that, whelp!" the mine foreman shouted. He glanced at his injury then back at Harvey. There was an intense fire in his eyes. Once again, Jeffrey pressed the attack like the injury hadn't even happened.

Harvey brought up his weapon to parry Jeffrey's strikes. One of the blows ended up nicking him on the shoulder, sending a wave of pain down his arm.

Wincing from multiple small injuries, he focused his efforts on holding his blade aloft and looking for an opening that didn't seem like it would ever come.

But come it did. Jeffrey made a low lunge for his hind leg again. This time Harvey was expecting it, and he danced to dodge it, leaving Jeffrey over-extended.

Harvey brought his blade forward quickly, striking at the outstretched arm and almost severing it in the process.

Jeffrey hissed and let the sword drop. "I'll see you in hell, Harvey!" he spat, backing up a step and nursing his wound.

A dopey grin crossed Harvey's lips. "Good thing you'll get there first, then." He raised his blade again, aiming to sever the man's head and end the combat quickly.

Before he could act, he saw a glint of metal in the low light as a dagger materialized in Jeffrey's hand. The snake of a man hurled it at him with one last thrust.

The small blade moved quickly and impaled Harvey in the shoulder. The young man let out a scream and staggered, clutching the fresh wound.

Almost without thought, he sent a fireball barreling toward the mine foreman, which hit the man dead in the chest, sending him flying into the wall once more.

With one hand on his shoulder, he crept forward. The mine foreman lay on the ground, barely moving. He had a wry grin on his face.

"Good one," the mine foreman let out through painful breaths. "Too bad you hadn't done it earlier." He let out a cold chuckle. "The blade's poisoned, you know. It'll get you in time."

Harvey looked at his shoulder, and his eyes went wide. Then he took another step forward and lashed out with his sword, severing Jeffrey's neck. The mine foreman's head fell to the side, still holding that wicked grin.

Harvey took a few deep breaths to calm himself. "Yeah?" he said to Jeffrey's dead body. "Well, I got you first."

Looking at his shoulder, he wondered if he should remove the dagger. He had already lost a decent amount of blood, and he didn't want to lose more. He'd have to find something to stem the injury with and hope the blade wasn't really poisoned.

And that he could find Vincent in time.

Both of those options would have to wait a bit longer. A shrill cry broke through the stillness of the hallways, belonging to his friend.

"Sariah!" he called out. "I'm coming for you!"

Sariah clenched her teeth and sent another fireball careening toward the Master. Not that it did her any good. He either dodged them with seeming ease, or they dissipated on his shield. It felt like the Master could hold out forever.

She could already feel her strength slipping. She needed a miracle and fast.

Bear rushed forward, then, fangs and claws at the ready. He pounced for the Master's middle. The old man seemed ill-prepared for the assault, and Bear managed to force him back a little before the Master flung the animal away with another spell.

The poor dog crashed into a nearby wall with a loud, sickening crunch and lay still. She waited a moment, but he didn't get back up.

Sariah let out a terrible scream. "Bear!" she cried. "No!"

Rushing forward, she called on what little reserves she had to summon another wave of energy and send it crashing into the Master.

Gabe joined in at the same time, sending his own wave of energy hurtling forward.

The two spells crashed into the Master's body, and Sariah watched as his pale magic shield finally crumbled under their combined efforts.

Howling with rage, the Master fired back, sending out a massive shockwave that sent the earth beneath them flying everywhere and forced them both onto their backs.

Sariah scrambled to her feet and raised her hand, readying another spell, but found that she could no longer move.

The Master gave her a wry smile. "That's right," he said slowly, each word seeming to cause him pain. "Did you forget so easily? You're...you're mine to control!"

Sariah fought against the paralysis, but it was no use. She was too exhausted to do anything. Frantically, she looked down where her own paralysis powder lay in a pouch at her waist, as useless right now as she was.

"What's the matter?" the Master asked, cocking his head to the side. "Giving up already? Tsk-tsk."

She looked up at him with a hate-fueled glare and spat at his feet. "Go to hell."

"Oh, my dear Sariah. I'm already there." He flashed her another wicked grin and raised his hands to summon forth a spell that would kill her.

Just then, Will came rushing into the room, Vincent close behind him. "Keep your hands off her!" he shouted. The big man sent forth a few fireballs. The Master managed to dodge out of the way, but only barely.

"She's not your plaything!" another voice uttered. Harvey came staggering into the room a second later, brandishing three swords, two of which he sent flying in the Master's direction. She looked longingly at Harvey for a moment. He was hurt, but at least he was still alive.

The Master howled and ducked behind a large table to take cover. He summoned forth new spells of his own to combat the foes. A flurry of fireballs and energy bolts filled the room, flying in every direction.

It was all her companions could do to take cover before they were consumed by the onslaught.

"Fools! All of you!" the Master shouted. He was holding his hands up, and his eyes were glowing that cold, red color. "You are all my playthings now!"

Sariah looked around her. All her friends were now paralyzed, just like her. She fought against her invisible bonds again, but it was no use. The Master was too strong.

Her foe stepped forward, grinning from ear to ear. Sariah could see a few fresh scratches on his face, but he had survived all their attacks and still seemed to be at full strength.

"I told you, Sariah. I told you I would take everything from you." He moved closer to Harvey, who was the closest person to him. "Now I shall finally make good on that promise."

The Master produced a dagger from within his robes and held the small, twisted blade aloft. "Let's see what your friend here thinks about a knife to the heart, shall we?"

Sariah's eyes narrowed as she watched the Master raise the dagger that would end Harvey's life. She knew she needed to act now if she were to save him.

"No!" she cried. She strained against her invisible bonds with all her might, but nothing happened. Her mind raced, trying to come up with a way out, a way to save Harvey.

Then it hit her. Most of the Master's tricks were mental —the different appearances, the illusion with Mrs. Hensworth, all mental magic.

Maybe the paralysis is a mental trick, too?

It was worth a shot. If it was mental, then all she had to do was believe strongly enough, and she could fight it. She focused on the invisible bonds that held her, telling herself they were fake, even though every ounce of her body protested otherwise.

She pushed forward with one arm, and very slowly, it budged. Then it moved again. Each movement felt sluggish like she was carrying hundred-pound weights on each limb, but it worked. She managed to get to her feet.

Finally upright, she scowled at the Master, a defiant glare in her eyes, which now glowed a red color similar to his.

"Stop!" she commanded. In one swift motion, she plucked the bag of paralysis powder from her waist and threw it in the Master's face. At the same time, she sent a small fireball hurtling toward it. The resulting explosion, though small, was spectacular to look at as the paralysis powder went flying everywhere, coating both the Master and Harvey in the process.

The Master took a step away from Harvey in shock, then he stopped moving altogether. The veins in his forehead looked like they were about to burst, but the man was helpless to stop it.

Sariah took a small step. It no longer felt difficult, like it had before. The Master's spell was no longer in effect.

"Not so fun when you're the one paralyzed, is it?" Sariah taunted, giving him a wry grin.

"H-how? H-how did y-you?" the Master asked. There was the tiniest hint of fear in his eyes as he watched Sariah move closer. It was a first for him.

She shook her head. "You'll never know, will you?" She shrugged. "It doesn't matter. You'll die knowing that you were finally bested at your own game."

Reaching into her shirt, she pulled out Lucien's dagger and stared at the cold metal. "How fitting," she said, "that the weapon that started it all will be the one to end it, too."

"Y-you...y-you'll n-never...w-win."

Sariah flashed the Master another smile. "Won't I?" She let out a slight chuckle. "Who's going to stop me this time?" She didn't wait for an answer. Holding the dagger aloft, she plunged it into his heart.

The Master's body writhed, and blood began pouring from both his mouth and the wound. Then he fell to the ground, dead.

Sariah watched with a look of half awe, half relief as the Master's face and body twisted and turned until it reverted to its original form. She looked down at the strange face that stared back up at her with glassy eyes, and for a moment, she thought she recognized him.

Then exhaustion from the intense battle started to settle in and everything went black.

CHAPTER EIGHTEEN

When Sariah awoke, it was somewhere else. She was in a bed again, though this time she recognized it. It was the bed she'd used so often at Talon's Reach.

She sat up with a start, and her eyes darted around.

"Easy now," a soft, warm voice cautioned. "You've been asleep for days."

"Harvey?" she said slowly.

"Yes," he said with a nod and a dopey grin. "Will and Ilene are here, too." He waved toward figures standing in the corner of the room, murmuring. Their frames started to come into focus.

Sariah smiled back at him. "Oh, I'm so happy you're okay!" she exclaimed. She reached forward and embraced him. His body felt warm and inviting, though she didn't linger long in the embrace. They had company, after all.

Harvey ruffled her hair. "Of course I'm okay," he quipped. "You saved me, remember?"

Memories of the battle with the Master came flooding back, and a sinking feeling overtook her gut.

"Bear?" she asked hesitantly. "Where's Bear?" She started to get up, but Harvey forced her back down.

"In the infirmary with Ferdinand," Harvey replied. "Don't worry. They're both a little worse for wear, but I hear Vincent is taking great care of them."

Sariah smiled again. "Vincent's okay, too?"

Harvey nodded. "Yep." He looked lost in thought for a second. "It's a good thing, too, or else..."

"Or else what?" Sariah waved a hand in front of Harvey's eyes.

The young man shook his head. "Nothing. It's nothing. Suffice it to say, we all survived the battle, and it's all thanks to you. You're the real hero, you know?"

She felt her cheeks begin to grow hot, and she buried her face in his chest. "Don't say that. Don't say I'm a hero."

"Why not?" Harvey replied with a chuckle. "You are, you know. I'm surprised Will and Ilene have been able to hold off throwing a parade for you as long as they have." He looked in their direction and winked, then turned his attention back to her. "You're gonna be a big deal around here from now on. Even bigger than before."

Sariah waved a hand at him dismissively. "Don't say stuff like that. It makes me uncomfortable." Her cheeks felt even hotter.

He flashed her another dopey grin and lifted her chin with one of his hands until they were looking at each other. "Hey," he said. "Don't worry. I'll be right here with you the whole time. I won't let it get to your head."

She gave him a hard shove, and he reared back. "Don't tease me like that! Not when I just got up!"

Their little quarrel seemed to rouse Will and Ilene from

their own conversation, and they both started making their way in her direction.

Sariah squirmed a bit and looked at Harvey. She bit her lip and lowered her voice to a whisper. One question was still burning in her mind, and she wanted it answered before the others could hear. "What about..." she hesitated still. "What about...you know..."

Harvey's eyes dimmed, and he nodded once. "Gabe, you mean?" he answered a little too loudly.

She winced and inclined her head.

Her friend shrugged. "He disappeared right after the final battle. No one knows where he's gone off to."

"Well, he isn't here, that much is certain," Will boomed in a voice loud enough to make Sariah's ears ring.

She winced again and looked away from him.

"It's a good thing, too," Will added with a nod and a smug grin.

Sariah cocked her head to the side. "Why is that? He helped as much as anyone."

Will gave her a stern look and sighed. "One good deed doesn't absolve him of his multitude of crimes. He still has plenty to answer for."

She wanted to argue with him, but she knew it wouldn't do any good.

Ilene's eyes went to Will and then to her. She cleared her throat. "Enough about that. How are you feeling, dearie? Better, I hope?"

"Uh-huh," she nodded again. "Much better." Just then, her stomach gave off a loud growl. "Apparently quite hungry."

The older woman gave her a broad smile. "Of course,

dearie. You've been asleep for a few days. It's only natural."
She gave her a pat on one of her legs and held out her
hand. "Come. Let's get you some food."

Sariah eyed the hand cautiously, and her gaze
narrowed. "What, no parade first? No speech to the public?
No grand banquets?"

"Oh, we thought we'd let you eat first, then we'd get to
all that." Ilene's expression was deadpan.

Sariah's eyes widened, and her hair stood on edge. She
backed away slowly and looked at everyone in turn. After a
few moments of blank stares, Harvey flashed her a grin
and busted out laughing. Everyone else joined in, and soon
enough, Sariah did too.

"You really had me going there for a minute," she told
Ilene.

The older woman smiled at her. It looked strangely out
of place on her face. "We talked about it, really we did.
Because you deserve it, of course, after that performance."
Her eyes went to Harvey. "Harvey made us promise not to
do anything fancy, so we honored his wishes."

Sariah looked over at her friend and smiled. He gave
her a slight bow in return. "Thank you, you old goofball."

Without further ado, she accepted Ilene's outstretched
hand and let the woman guide her toward the mess hall.
Harvey and Will followed behind them. Soon, amazing
smells filled her nostrils, of bacon, sausage, and of course,
eggs. Her stomach growled again as she thought about how
eager she was to stuff her face.

Right before turning into the mess hall, she paused.
Ilene and the others gave her a worried look, but she
waved them off. Another thought was gnawing at her, and

it wouldn't let go, and she wanted very much to attack her breakfast with a clear head.

"There's one more thing that's been bugging me about the final battle. About...the Master," she told them.

Ilene tilted her head to the side. "Yes, dearie? What is it?"

Sariah bit her lip. "Well, the thing is, in the end, after he was dead and all, he looked kind of...familiar."

Harvey gasped. Ilene and Will lowered their heads.

"That's because he is. Or, rather, he was," Will blurted out. "Familiar, that is. To everyone most likely." He let out a deep sigh and shook his head. "Once he was dead and could no longer hide his face, the truth came together rather quickly, how he had amassed so much power and his hatred for Ilene. All of it. You see, his real name was Alaric."

Sariah and Harvey both gasped, and her heart almost leaped out of her chest. "You don't mean...?"

Will nodded. "The one and only. The crown prince of the realm. Ilene confirmed it just yesterday."

As Will was speaking, Ilene produced a shiny object from within a pouch at her waist. Sariah recognized it instantly, and her eyes grew wide.

"Is that what I think it is?"

The older woman nodded. "Yes, this is the amulet you found way back when. It served as proof of Alaric's birthright." She let out a slight laugh. "Probably why he wanted it back so badly in the first place, and why he was willing to kill to keep it secret."

Sariah nodded. "I suppose that makes sense." Her chest felt lighter at that revelation like she finally had some modicum of closure. She hadn't realized until then that she'd even been holding onto anything.

"Plus," Ilene muttered. The older woman lowered her gaze and shuffled her feet. "He is kind of my brother."

Sariah's eyes widened to the size of saucers, and she let out another gasp. "You don't mean? Then you're a...a..."

Ilene waved dismissively. "Was, rather. I gave up my rights to the throne years ago for personal reasons I'd rather not go into here." She put a hand on Will's shoulder. "Will was my attaché back then. He came with me to act as my personal bodyguard."

Sariah's head was spinning from all the new information. To think that the one who'd been trying to kill her was the crown prince. And now the leader of the resistance was a princess? It was too much to handle on an empty stomach. She leaned against a wall and put a hand over her head.

Just then, Lester, the gate guard, came running toward them. He had a concerned expression, and his face was red like he'd been running. "Sariah! Ilene! Will!" he shouted, breathing heavily in between each name.

Will went over and put a hand on his shoulder. "Yes, Lester? What is it? What's wrong?"

Lester doubled over and took in several labored breaths. "It's...It's...the Dusk Ravens, sir. They're here again. Under a white flag."

The big man side-eyed Lester. "The Dusk Ravens? We wiped them out."

Lester shook his head and tried to stand upright somewhat unsuccessfully. "They're here, sir. A whole contingent of them from down south. A big man is leading them by the name of Zachariah."

Will grabbed the hilt of his sword, as did Harvey. He looked at Sariah. "Stay here, I'll go round up the troops."

The gate guard put out a hand to stop him. "Hold up," he said. "They're not armed or here for battle."

Everyone looked at Lester like he'd grown another head. Sariah's head was swimming. If they were unarmed, then why were they here? Surely it was too early for them to have heard about the Master's demise.

"Sariah," Lester continued. "Zachariah said he'd...he'd only talk to Sariah." The gate guard took in another couple of breaths. "He's here under a white flag. I think it's safe."

Her friends turned to look at her, and she gave them all blank stares and a sheepish grin.

"What does a leader of the Dusk Ravens from the south want with you?" Will asked in a heated tone.

She looked at everyone in turn before finally answering. "How the hell should I know?"

Sariah stood at the edge of the platform containing Ilene's throne in the grand courtyard. She watched as the man known as Zachariah strolled into the room, flanked by a few people in the brown Dusk Raven uniform she'd grown to hate so much.

Part of her wanted to kill them all where they stood. Another part of her wanted to run, but she stood firm. Behind her, Will, Ilene, and Harvey all stood tall.

"Greetings," she said in a low tone. She looked back

over her shoulder at Ilene, who gave her a smile. "Why have you come here?"

"Your excellency," Zachariah said with a grand bow. "We came as soon as we heard the news that the Master was dead at your hands."

Sariah eyed him cautiously. How could he know that already? It only happened a few days ago. She supposed she'd hear them out.

"And?"

Zachariah had a confused look on his face. He said nothing for some time. "Your excellency," he repeated. "I assure you, we mean you no harm if that's what you're worried about."

She shot him an icy glare and thought again about frying them all where they stood but did nothing. "Continue," she offered, slighting bowing her head.

"We have come to offer you our services. That is if you would have them."

Sariah almost fell over from the shock. Heat rose to her face, and her blood started pumping faster. She took in a deep breath to calm her nerves. "What game are you playing?"

"I'm sorry?" Zachariah replied with the same confused look.

Her cheeks grew flush with anger. "How dare you!" she spat at him. "You chase me to the ends of Irth, burn down my village, destroy my family, and now you, what? Want me to help you?"

Zachariah stood up straight. His full height made her back up involuntarily. Will and Harvey were tall, but this guy was massive.

"Your excellency, we have the best of intentions, I assure you." His gaze trailed downward until he was looking into her eyes. Much to her surprise, she saw a certain warmth reflected back in them that only managed to set her even more on edge.

"We didn't like the Master's rule any more than you did," he continued. "We had little choice. He was the only game in town, as it were."

She thought about that for a moment and figured there was some truth to it, but she still didn't quite buy it. "So what? I should just forgive you, is that it?"

Zachariah nodded once. "What we offer you, we do in full earnest. You have bested our leader in combat, and it is our thought that in so doing, you should become our leader in his stead." He bent his knee and stooped his shoulders to bring his face closer to hers. "Besides, you couldn't do any worse than he did."

Sariah's mind raced, and she started pacing. What was she supposed to do with a bunch of criminals and villains?

"I don't know," she said slowly.

"Please, your excellency."

"Stop calling me that!" she hissed. She paced some more and wiped a little sweat from her brow. Her stomach growled again, and she was really regretting her choice to do this before eating breakfast.

Zachariah bowed deeply. "My apologies, Sariah. I was only trying to give you the honor you deserve." He straightened back to his full height. "Think about my proposal. A full army at your disposal. The very backbone of the nation's trade routes at your beck and call. Such power could be quite...intoxicating."

Sariah paced some more until she'd done a full circle around the giant man. She looked up at Ilene, Will, and Harvey, who seemed to be every bit as dumbfounded as she was. Harvey threw up his hands and shot her a dopey grin. Will and Ilene both shrugged.

"Well, you're no help," she scoffed and shook her head to clear it.

She looked up at Zachariah again. Something told her his intentions were pure. Just to be safe, she used her magic to scan his thoughts. There was a lot there to decipher—more than she'd been prepared for—but his words were indeed true. The offer was genuine.

What would Gabe have done? He would know what to do here.

She paused, wondering where he was. She spared another glance at Zachariah. She supposed with the power of the Dusk Ravens and their spy network behind her, she'd have the resources to find out the answer to that question.

Then what? She bit her lip hard and winced at the pain. What did she want? She didn't know if she even wanted to find Gabe, and if she did, she wasn't sure if he'd be a friend or a foe.

Her head spun, and for a moment she thought she'd fall over, but she managed to stay upright. Of the many thoughts that went through her head, there was one she kept coming back to.

The Dusk Ravens had to be stopped. All of them. If even a shred of their criminal enterprise remained standing, there was a chance another Master might come and threaten her friends' peace and freedom once more.

She had managed to best the last one, but who knew what would happen in the future? She knew all too well, the best way to unravel any organization was from within.

A wry grin spread across Sariah's face, and she looked into Zachariah's stoic eyes. "Very well, sir," she said slowly. "I accept."

THE END

AUTHOR NOTES - PETER GLENN
AUGUST 13, 2020

First of all, thank you so much for reading through this entire book, and for now reading these author notes! It means the world to me to be able to share these characters and this journey with you! If it weren't for you fans, I would never have become an author.

And there we have it. The fourth Sariah novel, and the conclusion of her epic quest to take down The Master. I, for one, really loved that ending. I thought it was fitting how she dispatched him with the dagger that Lucien had originally used to try and kill her. Kind of brought the whole thing full circle, don't you think?

This book might have been the easiest of the four to write, even if the plot did change about four times while I was sitting down writing it. I did tell you all I was some-what of a reformed pantser (person who writes without an outline), didn't I? Well that couldn't have been more true than when I was writing out the outline for this book.

For starters, The Master didn't originally invade Talon's

Reach until about halfway through the book, and Ilene never went on her rant about isolation. Personally, I think the story reads much better this way, but it would have been interesting to see how the other storyline would have played out.

Next up, there wasn't a search for a paralysis plant at all, and Vincent and his fellow druids played even less of a role than they ended up playing in the overall scheme of things. And let's not even get started with Albert and Sean. They didn't even get a mention in the original outline. And I really enjoyed how they both played a part in the whole thing, too.

So yeah, lots of changes to how everything shook out, but I'd like to think they were all for the better. I know I sure enjoyed how things turned out this time around. All the way down until the last page of the final scene.

Anyway, what's next for Sariah and friends? Well, I'm really not sure yet. I have a few ideas for some storylines that I could bring forward. Her little love affair with Gabe still needs some resolution one way or the other, and she's now gotten herself embroiled in the Dusk Raven ranks, and a tricky plot from the royalty of the region. And then there's Zachariah's region, filled with spies and pirates galore (and maybe even a new race of amphibious people to contend with).

That's a lot of potential for new adventures I could take Sariah, Harvey, and Bear on. Not to mention the other members of our supporting cast.

What do you think? If you could pick one of the above stories for the next Sariah novel, which would it be? Drop me a line at peter@peterjglenn.com and, if it's popular enough, I'll make it into reality and give you credit!

Anyway, if you liked this book, *please* leave a review. It really does mean the world to me. Just ask my wife, my kids, or any of my friends. I rave about every single one. They're each like a little present. A gift of gratitude for me to cherish.

Plus, a bunch of good reviews *might* just help that next book come out that much faster. (Maybe. It certainly wouldn't hurt anything lol.)

Loved the book a lot? Give me a follow on social media, too at: www.facebook.com/authorpeterglenn OR join my mailing list: www.peterjglenn.com/email. Better yet, do both! The more the merrier! I also have giveaways (like signed copies of my books) and exclusive behind the scenes info for my mailing list subscribers, so join up!

I'd love to get a shout out from you in either spot and hear about what you'd like to see in an upcoming Sariah Chronicles adventure, or any of my other upcoming series, like *The Guardians of Kallor* saga (my first Epic Fantasy trilogy, and my first love, completely re-written with tons of gritty action scenes), or *The Immortality Curse*, a brand new Urban Fantasy adventure following an unlikely 300 year old hero who's tired of life but can't seem to die no matter what crazy job he takes on. You can find out more about both those new series on my website. The first *Guardians of Kallor* book will launch in September of 2020!

Who knows? Maybe I'll even name a future character after you (if you want. I'd never do it without permission). I know as an avid reader and fan, I would be over the moon if one of my favorite authors did that. Well, it could happen to you. Just ask!

Thank you again for joining me on this journey and sticking with it until the very end, and I do hope you'll join with me again in future books.

Auf Wiedersehen.

AUTHOR NOTES - MICHAEL ANDERLE
AUGUST 15, 2020

First I need to get out "Thank you for reading our stories!" If I don't, I'm going to rant at how horrible I suck at Blue Bell Ice Cream for typing it Bluebell in the last books' *Author Notes*.

Or wait, maybe the editors changed it? Maybe, oh MAYBE, I had it right, and someone else messed it up? *No?*

<<Sigh>>

While I wouldn't mind blaming Peter for my problem (however intoxicating a thought that would be—I love playing with my collaborators in the author notes), it just wouldn't be right.

OR, I could make up a (fairly accurate) story of how I've been away from Texas so long that one of the foundational cornerstones of my summers has become foggy in my memory.

Well, ok, the *spelling* is a bit foggy, but the taste of a homemade Vanilla with Big Red (another Texas favorite) as a float is amazing.

I think it is summertime for me all wrapped up in a memory that must be tasted to be understood.

Root beer floats and Coke floats are a fairly close second and third place. By the way, I've tried using Natural Bean Vanilla ice cream, and it is NOT the same as Blue Bell Homemade Vanilla.

Thank you so much to Peter for pulling together Sariah and enhancing the *Kurtherian Gambit* series with his energy, creativity, and many (many...many) rewrites. He's done a fantastic job, and if you get a chance, check out his other work to see if any of his stories entice you.

Then, when you are done with those stories, come back and grab another Kurtherian Gambit Universe book.

I sincerely hope you don't just read one (series) ;-)

ONE HUNDRED AND THIRTEEN!

Consider this the epilogue. I just looked at the temperature outside here in Henderson, and it's @#@#%!#%!#~#TY!! Hot.

I'm not sure I wasn't hallucinating from the heat, but I just noticed two red guys in bodysuits saying they are going to stay out of my backyard because, and I quote, "It's hotter than hell here. Let's go back downstairs!"

(*Editor's note: Must be friends of Pandora's.*)

Damn folks, I don't care who you are, that's hot.

Ad Aeternitatem,

Michael Anderle

OTHER BOOKS FROM PETER GLENN

The Sariah Chronicles

OTHER BOOKS FROM LMBPN PUBLISHING

For a complete list of books from LMBPN Publishing please click the link below:

https://lmbpn.com/books-by-lmbpn-publishing/

CONNECT WITH THE AUTHORS

Peter Glenn Social

Website: www.peterjglenn.com

Email list: www.peterjglenn.com/email

Facebook:
www.facebook.com/authorpeterglenn

Michael Anderle Social

Website: http://lmbpn.com

Email List: http://lmbpn.com/email/

Facebook:
https://www.facebook.com/LMBPNPublishing